A TIME TO WEEP

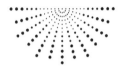

TRACY HIGLEY

FREE SAMPLE

Hello Friend!

I hope you'll enjoy *A Time to Weep*, and when you're done, you'll be eager to continue Sahara's adventure in *A Time to Love*.

I also wanted to give you a big, juicy excerpt of another book I think you might like—*Nightfall in the Garden of Deep Time*.

However...

One thing that always frustrates me when reading books: I'm looking at the pages of the book that are left to read, thinking there are many more chapters to come, and then the book suddenly ends and everything left is actually a big sample of another book.

Do you find that annoying, too?

So to avoid frustrating you, I'm instead giving you a LINK to the first seven chapters of my newest book. I'm hoping it'll be the next book you dive into, after you finish Sahara's adventures!

Grab it here: https://dl.bookfunnel.com/33onz156mq

Previously, in *A Time to Seek*...

Sahara Aldridge, a young Egyptologist in 1922, is working in Egypt alongside Howard Carter, searching for the tomb of Pharaoh Tutankhamun. Sahara's parents, also Egyptologist, were lost at sea near Venice when she was fifteen years old, but she has been provided with an education and opportunities by Lord Carnarvon, who also provides the funds for the dig.

When Lord Carnarvon visits the digsite with Evelyin, his daughter and Sahara's friend, Evelyn brings a torn page from Sahara's mother's journal, recently found. The page shocks Sahara, hinting at the possibility of time travel, which would explain a freak incident Sahara had years earlier. Against her good judgment and logic, she attempts time travel again, but fails.

She returns to England for the summer, but finds letters between her parents, which again make her suspect she can travel in time, if attempted correctly. She must get back to the Valley of the Kings and try again.

That autumn, after four seasons of fruitless digging in the Valley of the Kings, a small step is found at the digsite, indicating the likely presence of a tomb.

As the team begins a frantic pace of digging, an American reporter, Jack Moretti, shows up with an interest in the digsite, but more especially, in Sahara. But when Jack mentions the name of his aunt, Giada Moretti, memories come racing back to Sahara.

She has met Jack's aunt, when she was fifteen, after her parents left for their fateful trip to Venice. She's always wondered Giada was responsible for her parents' death, and carried guilt for giving Giada information about her parents' location.

Obviously, Jack cannot be trusted, despite her attraction to him.

Determined to avoid him, she finally attempts time travel again, this time succeeding.

Jack will not be put off, however, and she agrees to spend time with him, to ask more questions about his aunt. Her suspicions have increased. What happened to her parents?

In a quick flashback to Sahara's parents, Renae and Alexander, they are on a trip back in time, while Sahara is fifteen. While there, they run into another time traveler who recognizes them as college friends of her employer, Giada Moretti. Renae and Alex are clearly terrified she will report their whereabouts back to Giada, who will kill them. Renae also reveals to Alex that she is expecting their second child.

Sahara continues to suspect Jack is connected to the deaths of her parents. But can she prevent their deaths? She determines to practice time traveling, and decides to visit Tutankhamun's time.

She arrives in 1325 BC and learns the pharaoh has just died, perhaps been murdered, and the palace is a dangerous place. When she discovers Jack has followed her there, proving he can also travel in time, questions multiply.

As Sahara and Jack attempt to help the widow of Tutankhamun escape political turmoil, Jack explains some rules of time travel, still trying to convince Sahara his aunt did not send him to Egypt with any ulterior motive.

Another surprise awaits Sahara, as she discovers her parents *were* here in 1325 BC, along with another daughter, but have recently left. Sahara is thrilled that her parents must be alive, but also devastated, as she understands her parents have abandoned her, to travel through time with her younger sister.

In another flashback to Renae and Alexander, we see them on their fateful trip to Venice, leaving Sahara at fifteen, in the year 1905, and traveling back in time to 1814 to meet "The Great Belzoni," the man whom they know will eventually discover the tomb of Seti I in Egypt. They attempt to divert him from his work, but before they can, Giada Moretti shows up. They run, and in the excitement, Renae goes into labor early, and in desperation the two jump back in time again to 1720, where their second daughter is born.

In ancient Egypt, Jack begins to explain some of the rules of time travel to Sahara, which are governed by a secret society called Tempus Vigilia. Trips to the past must be at least eighty years apart. It is impossible to travel to the future. Time travelers are not allowed to marry and have children, because those children might be dangerously "amplified" in their abilities.

Jack and Sahara grow much closer during their time in ancient Egypt, helping the pharaoh's widow, but Sahara is again devastated to learn another rule of time travel—when she leaves this time, she will return to a fraction of time *before* she left, thereby erasing her time in the past. None of what she has accomplished in the past will remain. She can, however, die in the past.

In another flashback, Renae and Alexander are preparing to leave their time spent with Tutankhamun. They must return to the year 1737, because their daughter Persia's birth in 1720 means she can never travel with them forward in time. They must remain stranded in the past, to stay with Persia. But they have a plan to be reunited with Sahara, and have come to 1325 BC to place something in the tomb of Tutankhamun before it is sealed.

Sahara and Jack escape back to 1922, but as she returns, Sahara wishes she could retain her actions in the past. She arrives in 1922, expecting Jack to follow her within the hour, but he does not arrive. The next morning, she discovers that she's been missing for days.

Jack explains yet another facet of time travel. While most time travelers can only observe the past, and their time there is erased when they return, there are a few people—Revisionists— who are able to return *after* and not erase their actions. Sahara is apparently a Revisionist, no doubt because she is the daughter of two time travelers.

As the digsite team prepares to open the tomb of Tutankhamun, Sahara determines to continue time traveling, in an attempt to intersect with her parents and sister somewhere in time.

And despite her continued suspicion, it's clear Jack Moretti has no plans to leave Egypt.

PROLOGUE

July 2021

*I*n one sense, each of us is a time traveler.

Most of us never realize ourselves to be such, since we perceive our travel as having only one direction, a one-way journey, as it were, and always forward. But we are traveling through time all the same. Every morning we awake in yesterday's future.

Or at least, that is the way those who cannot travel backward *ought* to think of it, to catch a glimpse of the wonder of it all. To see this thing we call Time as a road under our feet, and we the never-failing traveler across Time, slipping along toward the future, albeit unable to break through the forest on either side, nor escape the gravity which keeps our feet trodding the path.

And yet, that is not how I see Time. Not any longer.

Oh, perhaps in those early days of traveling to the ancient past, I believed I'd merely been pulled backward along that path, to an earlier milestone on the Road of Time.

Now I know better. Now, after all these years, I know a different truth.

There is no road.

The road is an illusion, given to us at the beginning, to help us make sense of the world as we open our eyes.

But we can be weaned from our dependence on this linear falsity.

And then... And then it is as though a hawk swoops down from heaven, catches us in gentle talons, carries us away. We are lifted above the path and the bordering forest—those illusions we believed to be everything. Lifted higher, until we see the whole countryside. And then the whole country. The continent, the sea. The seven continents and seven seas. The ball of Earth, the wheeling stars and planets.

The road has disappeared, and it has taken all of Time with it.

There is only the Eternal Now, with its tranquil stillness. Its childlike trust. Its holy knowing.

I have sought, all my life since learning I could be lifted outside the Road of Time, to bring a taste of this stillness back from my travels, even as I walk the path with you. And perhaps, at times, I have even been successful.

But it was not a lesson I learned all at once. Nor a truth easily accepted.

I began with a time of seeking. Seeking with all my heart.

And at first, my feet still walked the illusory road. I needed to accept a critical truth: that what we call *the past,* and even *history,* cannot define who we are. We must leave all those mis-remembered and misinterpreted fragments behind, to find our future.

But I was yet to learn that even *the future* has a falseness about it. That we can spend ourselves building palaces in the air, never knowing who we truly are, nor who we could become.

The search was necessary. It is always necessary.

And so I journal the seeking.

But in any search, before truth can be grasped, there also must be a time to let go.

And while there must be a time to seek, there must also be a time to weep.

CHAPTER ONE

November 26, 1922
Valley of the Kings, Egypt

*I*n a narrow, bleached-out desert trench, where I'd been shoved to the back of a small crowd, I bounced on my toes to see above heads and fumed at my ridiculous position.

This moment would change the course of my life. It would change the future of Egyptology, even the profession of archaeology itself.

And three Egyptian workmen blocked my view.

I jostled past the men, deeper into the trench that led to the second sealed door of Tut-ankh-amun's tomb. I ignored the tense mutterings at my intrusion, stationed myself as near as possible, and braced sweaty palms against my trousers, the powdered ash of desert sand coating my hands.

Ahead of me, my childhood friend Lady Evelyn Herbert, in a downy blue jacket and skirt as pale as the sky, clutched her father's pinstriped arm as though she feared ancient ghosts might escape the tomb. Behind, the desolation of the desert pressed against us all.

The crown of Lord Carnarvon's balding head seared under

the unforgiving sun, his spicy-scented pomade gleaming like hot tar. The Earl rapped his silver-tipped cane against the trench wall. "Well, old boy? Are we going to have at it, or not?"

Howard Carter glared over his shoulder at his patron. "Whatever's beyond this door has waited three thousand years. I think it can wait a few more minutes while we do this right!" He shoved his Homburg hat backward and returned his attention to the plastered doorway and the tiny chisel.

Howard once told me, in a rare moment of vulnerability, that the chisel was a gift from his grandmother on his seventeenth birthday. I blinked away a swell of pride for my mentor, despite his coldness toward me the past few days. He'd waited decades for this moment.

Beside Howard, Arthur Callender braced a hand against the door, still covered with the ovals and lines, jackals and men, of the Necropolis Seal, as though he could push it inward. "Pecky" Callender, as he was nicknamed, the large-built Brit whose engineering prowess with Egypt's National Railway had earned him awards and respect, had been brought in, to organize the project that hopefully lay beyond this door.

Eve's eyes sought my own and she reached her free hand to grasp mine. "Aren't you so excited, Sahara?"

I returned the grip and stepped out of the shadows. "So excited."

Yes, I was thrilled. But I was also privy to knowledge that no one else in this trench could know, about what lay beyond.

Howard and Porchy dared only to believe we'd found an intact royal cache. Perhaps a stash of mummies or embalming goods.

But their fondest hope, to discover a royal tomb, was more than optimism for me. I'd stood beside this doorway only days after the ancient Egyptians sealed their young pharaoh's body inside, piled with everything he would need in the afterlife.

The past thirty-six hours had seen a flurry of activity, as the first door Howard and I found a few weeks ago at the bottom of the sixteen steps was carefully dismantled, then a nine-meter descending passageway cleared of rubble, before this second sealed door came to light.

"Shouldn't it be easier, Howard, darling?" Eve mopped a dainty handkerchief against her forehead and peered around Carter's shoulder. "Since it's been opened before?"

Being significantly taller than Eve, I could see over Howard's shoulder to his slow progress.

Howard grunted. "Been centuries, though. Maybe millennia." He tapped the doorway's upper corner beneath his chisel. "See the size of this replastering? A small-built man could barely squeeze through here."

"Yes, yes, we know." Lord Carnarvon smoothed his mustache, a nervous habit. "Perhaps a few items have been plundered through there, but nothing large. Nothing significant. It's all still beyond, waiting for us. If you ever manage to break through!"

I pulled a brush and pick from the pocket of my cracked-leather jerkin and tried to breach the father-daughter barrier. "Do you want help?"

Howard ignored my offer.

The short-lived warm feelings between us, surrounding the discovery of the steps and first doorway, and the arrival of the esteemed Porchy Herbert, Earl of Carnarvon, and his daughter Lady Evelyn, had given way over the past few days to annoyance at my odd disappearance into the second millennia BC, and suspicion over my friendship with the American reporter Jack Moretti.

I couldn't blame Howard for either sentiment. I'd given him no explanation for the days I'd been missing. And try as I might to trust Jack, I had my own suspicions about him.

I replaced my tools and clenched my fists, fingernails denting my palms with small crescents. How was I to make my mark on archaeology if I weren't allowed to be part of it?

Howard leaned away from the small hole he'd opened in the doorway. "There—that's through, then." He pointed to an iron testing rod leaning against the hard-packed trench wall. "Hand me the rod."

Eve grabbed it up before I had a chance, and thrust it into Howard's hand.

Despite my certainty about what we'd find, the breath caught in my chest and a current swept me. The hair-tingling prickle of anticipation.

Howard nudged the rod into the hole.

We all seemed to suspend breath as one.

The rod disappeared inward, inch-by-inch, until Howard's fingertips grazed the door.

He turned and exhaled. "Empty."

A hallowed beat of silence, and then a *whoop* behind us, from the three workmen.

No more rubble to clear. No false door against a wall. The space beyond the door was a chamber, waiting to be entered.

Howard yanked out the rod and chiseled the hole larger, with renewed fervor.

It felt like a decade later before he had it large enough for a decent look.

Someone behind me struck a match and a candle was passed forward.

Howard held the candle to the hole. It flickered in the escaping air and he took a step back. "Foul gases, perhaps."

Three-thousand-year-old air. What a thought.

I forced myself to stop biting my lower lip. My tension could not speed the process. Did Tut-ankh-amun's sarcophagus lay on the other side of this door?

The candle flame steadied, a finger of light too tiny to do much, but Howard pushed it through the opening, and peered in.

Lord Carnarvon and Eve, Callender and I, leaned forward, though we could only see the back of Howard's head.

We waited. An eternity.

"Well?" Lord Carnarvon's single word punched a hole in the silence. "Can you see anything?"

"Yes…" Howard's voice, hushed into sacred awe, enveloped us. "Wonderful things."

No celebration from the workmen at this utterance, only reverent silence.

I glanced back and found all three with their *tarbushes* pulled from their heads.

Moments later, Howard had the hole wider, an electric torch inserted, and Lord Carnarvon joined him at the opening to peer inside.

Eve's fingertips brushed her lips. "What do you see, Father? We're absolutely *dying* out here! Tell us something!"

"It's… it's nearly too much to describe."

I rubbed a hand against my jaw, tried to force the tension from my neck.

Eve plucked at her father's jacket. "Oh, do let us *see!*"

The two men stepped back and Howard handed me the torch, albeit with a grudging scowl.

Eve and I put our heads together at the hole, cheeks scratching fragmented stone, and I swept the beam of light into the chamber.

I sucked in a ragged-edged breath at the unimagined wealth piled inside. The glint of gold winked at us from every corner. Gilt-edged chariots, thrones and beds inlaid with ivory and precious stones, life-size golden statues of men and animals, alabaster jars, tools for farming and hunting and warfare. The endless jumble overwhelmed the senses.

"Enough, then."

I released the electric torch to Howard's waiting hand. "How will we ever accomplish it?"

Lord Carnarvon tapped his cane once more. "We're going to need help, here, Carter. And lots of it."

"And security." Howard ran a hand through his thick hair. "Once the press gets ahold of this news—" At this, he flicked a distrusting glance at me. "We're going to have everyone from government officials to foreign royalty clamoring for a tour."

I licked dry lips, tasting dust and salt. "Or trying to pilfer something for their collections."

Neither of the men, who sometimes participated in such collections, replied.

Howard glared up at the sun. "It's getting late. Too late to dismantle the door. We'll seal the hole, close Callender's wooden grille at the bottom of the steps, and post a guard. Get started first thing tomorrow."

But in the morning, I was relegated to a lesser role than the day before. Howard and Arthur Callender supervised the few workmen allowed beyond the wooden gate, along with the Egyptian Antiquities Inspector Ibrahim.

Lord Carnarvon, Eve, and I waited in the shade of a nearby canopy. Eve and her father lounged with drinks-in-hand.

I perched on the edge of a camp chair, shifting every few minutes in a useless effort to get comfortable, and drumming my fingers on my legs.

"Sahara, will you stop that fidgeting!"

I glared, Eve's petulant tone grating on me. "I should be down there."

"Well, complaining won't make it happen."

True enough.

A movement in the sky to my left caught my attention. A flash of blue and yellow, like sky and sun, with a trail of cloud-white behind.

Two figures ran along the hill of sand, the shorter of them with arm upraised. A man and a boy, flying a kite.

Eve shaded her eyes with a hand. "Isn't that your... friend?" She leaned on the last word with obvious intent.

I shrugged, too aggravated to answer.

Jack ran alongside our young digsite laborer, Nadeem, who wrangled the kite expertly, his head thrown back to watch it dance and soar across the cloudless sky.

As if aware of our attention, the two slowed and dropped to the slope, facing us. Nadeem kept the kite afloat, but fell backward into the sand as though exhausted.

Jack braced his forearms across his knees and leaned his head back to catch the hot breeze.

The pair had become fast friends these past two weeks, as Jack waited for the story we both knew was about to break. In fact, he'd spent more time with Nadeem, whom he called "a good egg," than he had with me. But that was my own fault.

I had work to do. And the revelation that I could travel through time, like my rogue parents before me, changing history for better or worse as I did, had me more than a little terrified. I didn't ask for this ability, was fairly certain I didn't want it, despite Jack's appealing suggestion that some Higher Power had a cosmic purpose for my life.

Although I had to admit, the revelations of the past few weeks had lifted me from a dark place I hadn't known I occupied. It turns out that recollections of the past, and even interpretations of our history may, or may not, reflect reality. I no longer needed to see myself as abandoned, rejected. Unworthy of love. It was time to build a new identity for myself, a new place of value.

And that new identity began here, in that trench, focusing on the work I was meant to do.

"That's him, isn't it, Sahara?"

Jack lifted his head and waved at us.

I'd spent the past two weeks avoiding Jack and all the distraction he represented. The additional suspicion that Jack's aunt, Giada Moretti, was involved with my parents' disappearance helped me keep the man at arm's length, despite our shared experience helping the widow of Pharaoh Tut-ankh-amun three thousand years in the past.

Yes, questions about time travel plagued me, but I shoved them down, unanswered, slamming a lid on that boiling pot.

I returned Jack's wave. "Yes, that's Nadeem."

"Ha!" She grinned. "You can't fool me, Sahara Aldridge. I was talking about Jack Moretti, and you know it."

I leaned back in the dusty chair and looked away from the kite fliers.

She eyed me closely. "Well, I will just say that he looks like good father-material to me."

I ignored her smirking.

"Tell her, Pugs," Eve leaned toward her father, "she shouldn't be turning up her nose at suitors."

Lord Carnarvon ignored his daughter's injunction.

A hoot from the direction of the tomb entrance brought him to his feet, still leaning on his cane. The man seemed more frail this season than ever. Was he ill again?

"Ready, at last?" Carnarvon's bony shoulders hunched toward the tomb.

Howard's hat, then head, appeared on the stone steps. "We're ready."

Eve and I jumped to our feet.

Howard held up a hand, fingers splayed like a barrier. "Just you, Porchy. We can't have everyone traipsing in there before we know what's what."

Lord Carnarvon took a step forward, but then reached back and grabbed Eve's hand with a warm smile. "Evelyn's coming, too. She's waited her whole life for this."

As the two joined Howard at the steps, I swallowed against the hot tightness in my throat. I had also waited my whole life. But I had no affectionate father here to advocate for me. Instead, my father was somewhere floating through history with my mother and sister.

A *Revisionist*, Jack had called me. Someone who could travel in time and change the past. But it was my future that would define me.

A future, it would seem, which I had no ability to affect.

CHAPTER TWO

November 27, 1922
Valley of the Kings, Egypt

The shoreek dough refused to cooperate.

I slapped it against the tabletop, then flipped it twice to beat it into submission, but it struck the surface like a sack of barley.

I used a flour-dusted forearm to swipe errant hair from my eyes and took a step back from the table.

No one loitered in the American House's kitchen at this time of evening, after dinner was cleared and Panya, the house cook, finished preparations for tomorrow. I was free to pound out my frustrations on the shoreek and put together the sizzling speech I planned to blast Howard with tomorrow.

"Hey, there." A voice from the dim hall beyond the kitchen startled me. "What did that dough ever do to you?"

I wrinkled my nose in the general direction of Jack Moretti. "It's overworked."

"Hmm." Jack leaned a shoulder against the doorframe. "Sounds like it's not the bread dough you're fighting."

I pushed away the lump and shrugged. "It's all ridiculous. I know more about what's in that tomb than any of them, and yet they spend the day taking down the door, rigging up lights, starting to catalogue, all without me. How am I supposed to build a career if they're going to push me out?"

"And is building your career so important?" Jack crossed to my table and snatched a butter cookie from the night's first attempt at reducing anxiety in a frenzy of baking.

I swatted his hand away before he could grab another cookie. "How can you even say that? You know what it means—"

"I just thought by now you would have started looking for your parents again."

"I told you, Jack. I'm done with all that. At least for now."

Again, I pushed down the overwhelming urge to ask him every question about traveling through time that had accumulated in my brain in the past two weeks.

"You can't live in fear forever. Denying who you are."

"I'm an Egyptologist! That's who I am!"

"And you're a Revisionist. Arguably a more important fact."

"Well, I didn't ask for that. I didn't ask to have parents who abandoned me at fifteen to go touring through history, leaving me an orphan who never even got to meet my sister."

"So, go find them."

"Just start randomly jumping through time, from one tomb to another across this Valley? Taking a chance on missing them again? Maybe they're not at any of those times or places. Maybe they never even left Venice after she was born."

"So, start with Venice."

"I'm not like you, Jack. Heading out on every lark that strikes my fancy."

Jack chewed his cookie in silence.

I crossed my arms and looked away. The idea *had* played at the edges of my thoughts for the past two weeks. If my parents traveled backward to meet Giovanni Belzoni in Venice before he reached Egypt, as my mother's newly-found journal page indicated, it was likely they were in Venice somewhere around 1815. Could I find them there, in that tiny city? Or even travel to

Venice now, and search out records of the family of three who may have lived there more than a hundred years ago?

"If that's where they've been, why couldn't they leave me some sort of word? Why didn't they pass a message down through the years somehow?" I cringed after I said it, hearing Eve in my head—pouting over not getting my way.

Jack's hand shot to the butter cookies and he had one bite out of a second before I could stop him.

"It doesn't matter. There's no way I can travel to Venice and back now, right when we're about to start clearing the Antechamber. I have to be here, if only to document the process from the outside."

"Sahara, I know how you feel about creating reform in the archaeological process. And this tomb is the perfect chance for you to make a difference. But perhaps you're meant to make a difference in some other way—"

"I don't want to talk about it, Jack. I hate the idea of changing history, of being some kind of freak. I don't want any part of it."

"You can't just ignore your abilities."

"Watch me."

"Sahara—"

"I'm serious, Jack. You can tell your secret society I won't be breaking any rules."

Tempus Vigilia, the "Society" governing the far-flung assortment of time travelers, had its Codex we must all abide by, Jack had told me. Not to mention its Knowledge Base of everything known about time travel.

You can't go to the future. You can't go back to a time closer than eighty years. Never within eighty years of where you've been. You must be touching an object from the past. Be standing where you will appear in the past. When you return, you erase any changes you've made. You can die in the past. On and on and on, with rules and principles and policies. It felt as though I'd been sent once again to a strict boarding school I had no wish to attend.

How could I get him to leave? This conversation was the very reason I'd avoided him for weeks. I didn't want to argue about my abilities, or even think about my parents leaving me behind.

Jack sighed and dropped into a chair, stretching long legs and crossing his ankles. "Tempus Vigilia is just as committed to preserving history as you are. But I think it's hasty, to dismiss your ability. You're not a freak. You were given something special. *You* are special."

I poked a shallow dent in the shoreek dough, fighting the warmth behind his words. Did I even believe it? Was there a Higher Power behind all of this, someone who was pulling the puppet strings to make me dance? To what end?

"And how about you?" I tossed the ball of shoreek into the nearby trash bin. "You have gifts. Talents. And you keep them tied up in a leather portfolio where no one can see them."

"No one wants to see my photographs, Sahara."

"I do."

We locked eyes for a moment, but I broke the contact quickly. Why couldn't I simply question him about his past, about his Aunt Giada and her interest in my parents? Every time I tried to go deeper, tight feelings of suspicion shut me down, and I forced Jack to back away.

A rustle at the doorway drew our attention.

"A bit late for a gentleman caller, don't you think?"

Helen Winlock, one of the Met archaeologist's wives, pursed her disapproving lips in our direction.

Jack pulled himself from the chair. "I was just leaving." He bowed in Helen's direction. "You're looking lovely this evening, Mrs. Winlock."

Her lips twitched and she straightened. "Yes, well. Good to see you, Mr. Moretti."

Jack nodded at me, grabbed one more cookie, and scooted from the kitchen with a grin.

"Be careful with that one, Sahara." Helen watched Jack's retreating figure. "Reporters come sniffing around, making you believe they're interested in you, when all they really want—"

"Thank you, Helen. I appreciate the concern. I'll be careful."

Helen shrugged a petite shoulder and disappeared.

Only a minute later I heard footsteps in the hall again.

"Jack, it really is getting late—"

But it was Eve who breezed into the kitchen, breathless and bright-eyed.

"Oh, outstanding!" She pulled white gloves from her delicate hands. "I've found you immediately."

"What's happened, Eve?"

Her smile lit up the room. "We've seen it, Sahara. I just had to come and tell you, though Howard would kill me if he knew—"

"Seen what?"

"The burial chamber!"

I growled under my breath, but then circled the table, grabbed her hands, and pulled her to sit across from me.

"Tell me everything."

Eve glanced at my cookies. "Are those ghorayebah cookies?"

I pushed the plate toward her. "Tell me!"

She nibbled on a cookie. "Well, you know we've been wandering around that Antechamber all day, just looking at everything, taking it all in. There's so much in there, you simply would not believe. And even another room—Howard's calling it the Annex—off to the side, stuffed with hundreds of jars. No idea what's in them."

She glanced around the kitchen. "Do you have anything to drink in here? I'm absolutely parched from all that tomb-dust."

I retrieved a glass, and pitcher of lemonade from the ice box, urging her with my eyes to continue.

"But those two huge statues—you remember, we saw them when we first looked in?"

Two identical life-size statues of a beady-eyed pharaoh, in black resin and gold, framed either side of the north wall of the Antechamber, as though standing guard to something even more valued behind.

"The burial chamber is behind them?"

Eve sipped her lemonade. "Now, don't rush my story. But, yes. Howard suspected there was something behind the wall, and if it were a tomb, well, then obviously the sarcophagus would be there. So the four of us—Howard, Pugs, Pecky, and myself—we all snuck back there tonight, after everyone else had left."

"But shouldn't he have waited for Lacau? Or at least Chief Inspector Engelback or Ibrahim?"

"Howard said that if we waited for the Department of Antiquities to open the wall officially and find the sarcophagus, it would only cause more furor over everything. He wants to systematically catalogue and empty the Antechamber first. But that could take months, and of course we could not *possibly* wait that long to satisfy our curiosity."

Eve's "we" implied she was part of the dig team, as if I were only an interested outsider. It was not her fault, so I held my frustration in check.

"So you broke in?"

She grinned, checked over her shoulder to be sure we were alone, and nodded. "Just a small hole, at the base of the wall, big enough to let the three of us crawl through. Pecky was too large, of course. And it was likely already broken through at that spot by the same ones who broke through the doors."

"And?"

"Gold, Sahara! So much gold—a huge gold box shrine, with glyphs everywhere. Open doors, where we could see into another golden shrine within the first, this one with alabaster vessels and a linen pall drooping above, all spangled with gold stars." Her words were coming in a rush now. "And then—would you believe—a *third* golden shrine inside the second, with protective goddesses and more glyphs everywhere, that Howard says is sure to contain the sarcophagus and the mummy. Oh, Sahara, I wish you could have been there!"

"So do I." I sat back in my chair, a coldness stealing over me.

But Eve gushed on. "We three were simply in a daze when we left, I tell you. Just wandered out of that tomb as though we'd been blinded and stupefied by all that gold."

"I'm happy for you, Eve. Glad you got a chance to see something so important."

She sighed contentedly and traced a line of condensation down her half-full lemonade glass. "I'm sure it was just *the moment* of my entire life. I shall never forget it."

I reached for a ghorayebah. Perhaps if I filled my mouth with sugar it would stop me from saying something I'd regret. But the cookie tasted like ashes.

"Oh!" Eve reached for her handbag, settled at her hip in the chair. "I almost forgot. I brought you something from the tomb."

"Eve! You shouldn't have taken—"

"Oh, pish-posh. There are simply a million things in there and no one will miss one small item." She pulled an item from her handbag, a large brass coin, aged to a green patina.

I frowned. "You didn't find this in the tomb, Eve."

She sniffed. "I just said I did, didn't I?"

I reached for the coin. "But that's not possible."

"I told you, no one will miss it. And I remembered how your dear father collected all those old coins. This one seemed like something he would've had in his collection."

The coin was in my hand now and I was turning, turning it, unable to believe what I was seeing.

"Where did you find this, Eve? Tell me *exactly*."

"Well, I don't understand why you're getting so huffy. I thought you'd appreciate a little token, since you weren't able to be there…"

"*Where*, Eve?"

"There was this magnificent little chest, there by the north wall. All painted with red and green and yellow. Hunting scenes, I think. We didn't open it yet, of course. But this coin was sitting on top, holding down a crumbly piece of papyrus covered in hieroglyphs, as though someone had left a note." She giggled. "What a place to leave a love letter, eh?"

The coldness I'd felt earlier fled. In its place, my fingers burned as though the coin in my hand were on fire.

It was no Egyptian coin. For one, the Egyptians of the Late Kingdom, when the tomb had been sealed, had no coinage.

But even more importantly, this was a Roman sestertius. The

profiled head of Nero and the words **NERO CLAVD CAESAR** in relief around the perimeter were unmistakable. Minted sometime during Nero's reign, from 54 to 68 AD. And identical to a coin I well-remembered from my father's collection.

"The letter—can you describe it?"

"Oh, you know I've never learned all those hieroglyphs like you and Howard."

"Do you remember anything?"

"Let's see. There was one string of symbols at the very top. As though it were someone's name or a title, perhaps. A sun. A small little bug, maybe an ant. I can't remember—Sahara, whatever is wrong?"

She took my hands in hers and pulled me to her.

"Shall I fetch a physician? You look positively overcome!"

Overcome. Yes.

S for sun. S for Sahara.

A small bug. A for ant. A for the second letter of my name.

Somehow, in some millennia past, my father had left me his Roman Nero coin, perched atop papyrus written in our secret father-daughter code.

A message for me, from my lost family.

Two items that if found, would confuse everything we would learn about Tut-ankh-amun's burial site and even Egyptian history.

Waiting in a tomb I was not allowed to enter.

CHAPTER THREE

November 28, 1922
Valley of the Kings, Egypt

I spent a restless night, waiting for the arrival of morning and what I must do.

My insistence to Jack that my work here was all that mattered had fled with Eve's news. If there was a chance to reconnect with my family, I could not ignore it. While my future legacy still loomed as critical to my value to the world, it was also true that the past must be fixed before I could move into the future. Including any future with Jack.

At first light, I was in the kitchen, gulping down hot coffee. It was too early for breakfast, and the thought of eating nauseated me anyway.

I went to the verandah and scanned the lightening horizon and the empty gravel drive in front of the American House. No carriages, donkeys, or cars loitered, hoping for passengers to the digsite.

Should I wait?

The papyrus in that tomb drove me down the steps, across the drive, and into the road to the Valley of the Kings.

A crescent moon still hung in the pale eggshell of a sky. The wide dome stretched, blank and impenetrable, over the empty desert and my lonely walk. But I was nearly blind to the vastness. A piece of papyrus I had never seen filled my vision.

Papyrus I needed to find before Howard Carter or anyone else did.

What would happen, if the message from my father made its way into the hands of a professional?

Our simple substitution cypher, if anyone thought to approach the decipherment that way, would quickly reveal a message written in English, perhaps addressed to me. The very presence of such a cypher, not to mention my name, and whatever message it held, would throw the discovery of the tomb into a completely new light. Perhaps even reveal the secret of time travel to the world.

What was my father thinking, leaving such a thing, in such a place? How could he possibly know I would find it, before anyone else, and understand what it meant? Further still, how did he manage to bring a coin from the first century back more than a thousand years? I'd tried to take possessions back in time with me and failed. Was there a trick to it, one Jack hadn't yet taught me?

I took deep breaths of the desert dust. The morning was cool, but the sun would soon reach the lip of the desert and even now threw my long shadow behind me as I trudged alone across the valley. A few brownish-green weeds struggled for life at the sides of the road, poking up to reach thirsty fingers for any moisture they could find.

I slid a hand into the pocket of my trousers as I walked. The brass coin met my fingers, cool and solid, still there. Not an illusion. I rubbed it between thumb and forefinger as though it were a genie's lamp that could magically summon my parents.

This one is from Rome, Sahara. When Nero was emperor and building great things...

I sank into the memory of time spent with my father,

moments spent touching each of the coins in his collection in turn, listening to his explanation.

How would my life have been different, if I had been able to join him in his work fifteen years ago, instead of being sent off alone to school and then trying to make my way into a career alone?

Already my limbs felt weighted as I trudged the road, the product of my sleepless night, and the strange turmoil of emotions since Eve brought the coin.

The upper swell of the sun cleared the edge of the desert, and I blinked and squinted at the piercing light, like a finger of God stretching out to strike my cheek.

Was I stepping into the next phase of some great plan? Were all my steps pre-determined? If past and present and future were all the same, then did any of us even have free will over the choices we made, the actions we took?

I reached out, through the sunlit air, with a wisp of what could be called a prayer, but felt more like the casting of a thin line and hook into the boundless ocean of the sky.

If you do exist, God, I need a bit more.

As if an answer, the roar of an engine crescendoed behind me. I turned to the blooming dust cloud, the sun at my back.

A motorbike crested a small hill, careening toward me.

I waited and clutched the coin inside my pocket.

The motorbike drew near and slowed.

"Sahara? What are you doing walking this early?"

Herbert Winlock, head of the Met's work at Hatshepsut's Temple, squinted at me from under the leather cap he strapped over his egg-like head.

The motorbike's fumes mingled with the dusty air, and I ran a hand through my hair in frustration. Winlock hardly seemed like the answer to a prayer. My early start was meant to beat everyone else to the tomb, but with Winlock on a motorbike and Howard likely already there, how could I hope to find my father's message before anyone else saw it?

"Headed for the tomb. Couldn't sleep, and wanted to get an early start."

He grinned. "Same." He inclined his head toward the back of his bike. "Want a ride?"

The familiarity of mounting his motorbike behind him prickled my skin, but I couldn't afford delay.

"Sure. Thanks."

I positioned myself on the back, and the bike shot forward. Despite my reticence, I grabbed Winlock's brown and green tweed jacket between my fingertips, the fabric scratchy but at least secure, giving me a chance to keep my seat.

"Big day! For all of us!" Winlock's staccato shouts over the roar of the engine barely reached my ears. "Helen and the girls are so eager to see it all."

I nodded, even though he couldn't see my response. Winlock's tenderness toward his two young daughters always left me turning away, a bit teary-eyed.

We reached the Valley of the Kings in a few minutes. The sharp points of canvas tent poles, like miniature white pyramids, rose to greet us.

I escaped from the motorbike as soon as it stopped and slapped the desert dust from my trousers.

Winlock was still rolling his bike to the side of the tent when I reached the wooden grille at the bottom of the sixteen steps. It was ajar. No need for the key that kept it locked overnight.

I rubbed a palm against my chest, trying to push away the weight.

Howard must already be inside.

Again the daydream of a different life intruded. It could've been my father and me who found this tomb. Working alongside each other for the future of Egyptology. Instead, I had to scramble for every advancement I made, with Howard's variable moods and grudging half-respect dogging me at every step.

I grabbed the rough spindles of the wooden gate and pushed it open. Then breathed in a moment of grateful appreciation that I was here at all. Arguably the most important discovery in the history of Egyptian archaeology, and I was among the first to see it. A smile found its way to my lips. My father would be proud.

I ducked under the lintel and stepped across the threshold.

The cool silence of the tomb reached out for me. The electric bulbs strung along its upper walls smelled of burning dust and seemed misplaced in the stale air. But it was the jumble of shapes and colors that assaulted my senses.

Hundreds of items had been stashed in the tomb. The back wall was dominated by three elongated beds, carved to resemble a lion, a cow, and a hippo, and painted in gold and black. Leopard-painted stools, a small ebony throne, piles of white food vessels. Another gold throne, inlaid with glass and precious stones. And to my right, two life-size statues of the pharaoh, striding leg forward, faced each other as guards of the burial chamber beyond.

I wanted to handle everything at once, yet preserve everything from the touch of human hands. To take it all into myself, and yet to give it as a gift to the world at the same time.

"What are you doing here?" Howard appeared from behind a dismantled chariot, his hair gel smooth and his shirt, tie, and jacket impeccable. Had he slept at all?

"You need my help, and I deserve to be here." A much-abbreviated version of my prepared speech. My diatribe fled the moment I stepped into the miraculous tomb.

Howard's fists went to his hips and he surveyed the tomb's contents. "We can't have everyone in here."

A sour taste surged in my throat. My hasty morning coffee on an empty stomach.

"I'm not everyone. And you can't take this from me."

He huffed. "Well, don't touch anything."

I cringed at the sharpness of his voice, echoing off the fragile artifacts, as though they would tumble at the sound of it.

Howard moved away, toward the south wall of the tomb.

But then I exhaled, relief loosening the tight muscles in my neck. He couldn't have found the papyrus yet, and must not have seen the coin. He wouldn't be taking such a wide-ranging inspection of the tomb, if something so shattering had been discovered.

Don't touch anything.

But I was going to do more than touch. I was going to take something from this tomb, an act that was ethically blurry at best, and an action I would normally condemn.

Winlock entered behind me, and the two began talking about the order in which to catalogue, and when to have Harry Burton begin his photographic chronicle.

I slid to the wall at my right. The two sentinels on either side of the wall loomed above me, eyes piercing as though they too condemned the actions I intended.

Eve said the painted chest was in front of this wall. I scanned the floor, saw the barely-concealed hole where the three intruders piled baskets and propped some reeds last night, after their secret entrance into the burial chamber.

There, near the opening. A chest with a curved lid, about the size of a carpetbag, with scenes in blacks and browns, reds and yellows, covering every inch of it.

And balanced on top, one small piece of papyrus, no bigger than my hand.

"We've barely begun to even understand what's in here, let alone start opening things." Howard was at my shoulder, looking at the same small chest that drew me.

How could I grab up the papyrus and stash it in my vest with Howard looking on?

In what state would I find the papyrus? Would it be fresh and new, like the piece I'd translated in the villa of the foreigners quarters in The House of Rejoicing, where my parents had stayed with my sister? Or three thousand years old, which would make more sense?

"Is this the only room? Do you think there's more?" I jutted my chin toward what Eve had described as "the Annex."

Howard followed my look. "There's another room over there. It's as full as this one." He eyed the two guarding statues and glanced at me. "And perhaps another chamber behind this wall, eh?"

"Maybe a burial chamber." I couldn't resist.

His eyes narrowed. My friendship with Eve was no secret, and even Lord Carnarvon had been known to share details with me.

"Howard, have you seen this?" Winlock's voice sounded far away, as if he had disappeared into the Annex.

Howard waited a beat, his eyes still suspicious on me, then turned and followed Winlock's voice.

It was now or never. I stepped to the painted chest. The papyrus was there, edges curling and crumbling to dust as I feared.

And my suspicions bore out. The six small symbols at the top spelled *Sahara*. I could not translate the entire message by sight, but knew my name at once.

Howard called from the other chamber. "Sahara, come make a list for me."

I heard the invitation for what it was—a way to keep an eye on me, not a way to share.

Heart pounding, I reached for the papyrus, snatched it, and felt it crack and begin to disintegrate in my hand. My stomach roiled at the unprofessional and horrifying way I was treating this ancient artifact.

I should have been wearing gloves. Preservation techniques should have been followed. The piece should be placed between glass as soon as possible, not pushed into the inner pocket of my leather jerkin as though it were nothing more than a market list.

What damage had I already done? What further damage as it rubbed between my vest and my shirt, perhaps absorbing the clammy sweat that had broken out across my body?

I spent another hour in the tomb, the papyrus burning against my chest. But I would not give Howard the satisfaction of this first day without me, and my professional curiosity over each artifact nearly outpaced my personal curiosity about the message inside my vest.

By the time the sun had fully risen and new team members were assembling, I retreated to the back of the small crowd that gathered to hear Howard's explanation of what would happen in the next few days.

So many had come, from Luxor and from the American House. They clustered under the canopy tent, with a line of idling motorcars, and horses pawing the sand in front of their carriages.

I found a driver with a broken-down Ford and convinced him he could make additional money by taking me back to the American House, and returning for a new fare before anyone else was ready to leave.

With a last glance at the crowd, reassuring myself Howard hadn't noticed my departure, I climbed into the Ford and escaped.

I kept the papyrus in my vest for the entire jolting ride, fingers spread obediently on my thighs, pressed into my skin in an effort to slow my pounding pulse.

Alone in my room at last, I pulled the papyrus from my vest with shaky fingertips and laid it on my desk.

My eyes blurred with unexpected tears.

It had been months since Eve brought my mother's lost journal page, found in a desk drawer at Highclere. Her handwriting, and the tangible piece of her voice, had been like a balm and a hot poker at once.

Today, standing over the message from my father—a message for *me* and not simply a lost scrap of his writing—my chest felt as though a weight crushed me, pressing me down into a nostalgic longing for childhood, beautifully painful.

Deep breaths, and I retrieved my journal and a pen, and the small lined paper with our cypher key I kept in a box of mementos on my shelf. Then sat at the desk and began the task. My hands shook with caffeine, and lack of food, and the nervous certainty that my life was about to shift.

The papyrus was not intact. Both the years and my hasty

retrieval had disintegrated the edges, and some of the hundreds of tiny black symbols faded into shadows.

But incomplete as it was, less than twenty minutes later, most of the message was lettered in my journal, in words that left me even shakier.

SAHARA

...our mother and I left you with those
   who search for this tom..
   and know you were destined for Egyp...
   ...pray this message reaches you,
   miraculous as that would...
   We cannot explain all here. We had to try
   to change it all, and then could not...
   but it is our greatest hope to reunit...
   By now you have surely discovered
   your ability to trav...
   ... must use his coin...
   meet us under his statu...
   ...n the Domus Aurea
   on the day of his deat...
   We love you beyond words, miss you
   ...ond reason and live for the moment
   ...see you again.
   ...r loving father
   PS Trust no one, especially G...
   ...etti

At the translation of this postscript, the hair lifted on the nape of my neck. I gripped the edge of my desk, as though the already-crumbling foundation under my feet might now shatter with a tectonic shift.

At the rap of a knock on my door, I shot to my feet, ready to run.

"Sahara? It's Jack."

Ready to run, yet frozen to this little spot on my floor.

My hand still clutched my desk, clammy and white-knuckled.

Trust no one. Especially...

CHAPTER FOUR

March 15, 44 BC
Rome, Italy

Giada Moretti opened her eyes by degrees, taking in the sun-warmed stones under her feet, the sandals and ankle-length belted *stola* she wore, then followed the footsteps of the passing citizens of ancient Rome. Dozens walked along the wide, tree-lined avenue that led to the soaring columns of the Theatre of Pompey.

She barely noticed the bit of nausea she'd experienced in her first two jumps through time.

Third time's the charm.

She inhaled a deep breath of Roman air and smiled.

Truly here. And on this day.

What would her mother say if she knew? Her older sister?

Too bad.

At only twenty-one, she'd surprised them both by developing her ability to travel earlier than they. Both warned her of the dangers. Her mother's decline had been rapid the past few years. Her sister seemed destined for the same.

Giada shook her head, dislodging their critical voices.

Just because they had been foolish with their gift did not mean she would ignore hers.

She studied the coin warming her palm. Flipped it over. Nothing to distinguish it from any other coin, probably. She patted her *stola*, a brightly-dyed yellow, and pulled aside its voluminous folds, but there was no place here to secret it away. Improvising, she untangled the corner of the elaborately wrapped costume, tied the coin into it, and tucked it back under the draped fabric.

She'd done enough research in the early morning hours, after hearing where she was supposed to show up, to know that the Theatre of Pompey was a mid-sized amphitheater that hosted both stage plays and gladiator games inside. All she could see from this angle was a huge stone arch, and beyond it, the steps to the marble-columned portico.

She made her jump at about 7 AM, but the avenue leading away from the Theatre was already busy with shoppers, merchants, and travelers. How long did she have to explore? History didn't tell her exactly what time of day Julius Caesar was assassinated, nor did that oily Chapter President, Eugene. She was supposed to be on the steps of the Portico of Pompey before the first dagger-thrust, to retrieve the answer required by the pock-marked Eugene and the Tempus Vigilia.

She neared the arch, eyes taking in everything at once, searching for any sign of the dictator, headed for his last Senate meeting.

Her timing mattered little, however. She already knew the answer Eugene asked, the moment he placed the coin in her palm and gave her the question.

She reached the steps, unremarkable at this hour, with only a few Roman men, presumably Senators, climbing to the porch, chatting amongst themselves.

A group of gladiators loitered just inside the first set of columns.

Across from her position, a young man, about her own age,

A TIME TO WEEP

stood near the top of the steps, also watching each ascending nobleman.

And watching her.

He wore a toga, but it was wrapped snug enough to see he was well-built. The strong jawline and confident set of his shoulders were also appealing.

She smiled, fleeting and vague, then looked away.

When she returned her attention to him, he was still watching her.

So why not get to know the locals a little bit?

She sauntered across the platform until she'd reached his position, but stayed a step or two above him.

"Beautiful day, isn't it?"

Not exactly a stellar first line, but the best she could think of.

"Are you Spurinna?"

She frowned. "Am I what?"

He shook his head, and his eyes moved away. "Not *what*. Who. But I guess not."

Was he waiting for a blind date?

"I'm Giada."

He nodded, but his attention remained on the men crisscrossing the street below them.

"She must be special, this Spurinna, to have you waiting for her so eagerly."

He shrugged one shoulder. "Just need some information."

"Hmm. Yes. So do I." She surveyed the wide marble steps once more. "But I guess he's not here yet."

"Who?"

"Julius Caesar."

The man eyed her now, suspiciously. "What do you want with Caesar?"

"Oh, so *you* are allowed to meet any woman you like, but if I am waiting for a man, it's a problem?"

He pulled back from her tone, eyebrows raised.

She swatted his shoulder with an open hand. "I'm only teasing you."

He blinked. "So. Why are you waiting—"

"Here to see the action, that's all."

"The… action?"

Was it against the rules to tell the locals their future? But then, nothing she did here would stick, so what difference did it make?

"What would you say if I told you Caesar's about to get stabbed to death this morning?"

His lips parted. "How do you know that?"

"And not by who you'd expect, either—"

He shot to his feet, jumped the two steps, and towered over her, studying her like a slide under a lens.

"How-do-you-know-that?" Every word a sentence, punctuated with a breath and glare.

The first flicker of unease tickled in her chest. Was he one of the conspirators himself?

He leaned closer, his face mere inches from hers. "Are you— are you from Tempus Vigilia?"

She jolted back, stared up into his eyes. "How did—are *you*?"

He swiveled a glance in all directions. "Yes." The words were a rasped whisper. "Or at least I shall be, when I return from here."

"You are being initiated, too? By retrieving information from this day?"

How crazy! What were the odds?

Or, wait. Perhaps the odds were quite high.

The realization seemed to occur to him at the same moment.

They shared a grin, then a laugh.

He stuck out a hand. "I'm Alexander."

She grabbed the outstretched hand. "Giada." She laughed again. "Oh, I guess I already told you that."

"Do they send everyone back here, to this day, do you imagine?"

She shrugged. "Maybe. I don't know."

Alexander was scanning the steps, the platform, the street below. "There could be many more of us, then. Each traveler, from different times—different *centuries* even—all converging upon an identical point in the historical record."

She joined his search. "That's so weird."

"There," he pointed to a woman about their age, near the bottom of the steps. She looked lost and uncertain. "Perhaps she is one of us?"

Giada was already headed down the steps. "Only one way to find out!"

The girl was extremely pretty, with big, brown eyes under thick lashes.

Her eyes grew even larger at Giada's aggressive approach. She took a step or two backward, clutching her stomach as though sick.

Giada grinned. "Greetings, Roman woman."

The girl said nothing, but glanced over Giada's shoulder to Alexander, still descending the steps.

He stepped to her side. "Giada, you are frightening the poor girl."

She laughed. "Sorry. Still getting my sea legs, I guess." She touched a finger to the girl's *stola.* "This is pretty. Where are you from?"

"I—I am not from—"

"Or maybe, *when* are you from?"

Those big eyes. A dead giveaway.

Giada nodded toward Alexander. "Definitely. Tempus Vigilia."

The girl gasped. "How did you know?"

"Hmm. Maybe it was the look of total bewilderment on your face."

"Come," Alexander pulled them both to the side of the stairs. "Let's step out of the way, where we can better observe."

"You're initiating?" Giada asked the girl. "What's your name?"

"Yes." Her eyes never stopped moving, taking in the two of them, the city, the sky. "I'm Renae."

"Giada." She thumbed her chest. "And this is Alexander. We just met."

Renae exhaled as though settling herself into the first century, then reached her arms outward, as though to welcome herself to Rome, and laughed. "This is amazing! And this—" she swept an arm toward the steps, and above them, the Theatre of Pompey—"is *really* amazing! I want to see it all!"

"Whoa, there." Giada held up a hand. "I don't know about you two, but I have an assassination to witness. Although I already know the answer to my question." She didn't even try to disguise the bit of pride that crept into her voice.

"You know where Marc Antony's facial scar is?" Renae seemed impressed.

"Scar?" Giada frowned. "No, I know Julius Caesar's last words."

Alexander crossed his arms and squinted up toward the platform. "And I'm tasked with learning the color of toga a woman by the name of Spurinna is wearing." He turned to the women. "It would appear they give each initiate a different question." He frowned at Giada. "But, how do you already know Caesar's last words?"

Giada smirked. "*Et tu, Brute?*"

Alexander smiled and studied his feet. "I'm afraid that phrase is not from the historical record. It's from Shakespeare. His third tragedy, *Julius Caesar.*"

She bit her lip. "So—you're saying it's not true?"

"I am saying that the last words of Caesar are a hotly-debated topic among scholars and historians."

"Huh. Oh well, I guess I'll have to get close to the action, then."

"I can tell you where to look for Spurinna."

This from Renae, her wide doe-eyes trained on Alexander.

He leaned toward the girl. "Can you? Truly?"

"For one thing, Spurinna is not a woman. He was the seer, the 'soothsayer' Shakespeare portrayed—"

"—who predicted Caesar would die by the Ides of March!"

Giada snorted and rolled her eyes. She'd spotted Alexander

first. But here these two were, finishing each other's sentences, having their own private history party.

"Of course." Alexander was nodding. "I'd completely forgotten." He imparted a bright look on Renae. "You are a historian, of course?"

She laughed. "A university student only."

Alexander half-turned to include Giada. "Where are you both from? And, I suppose… when?"

"Oh, let's not say!" Renae touched a hand to Alexander's forearm and smiled up at him. "Just for fun. Let's have today, explore the city, and not say a word about our real lives."

A day of anonymity in ancient Rome. Giada could definitely get behind this idea. Although it seemed likely all three were initiating into the same Tempus Vigilia chapter. It was too coincidental, the way they'd all been assigned to travel to the same day, to retrieve the answer to a question, and thereby prove themselves. So it stood to reason that Alex and Renae were also both from Philadelphia, perhaps even students at the University of Pennsylvania as she was, at some point since its founding in 1740.

"I suppose we could do some sightseeing," Alexander said.

"Yes!" Renae seemed ready to launch at any moment. "We can stay all day, right? When we return, we'll return to a fraction of time before we left, but we'll have our answers."

It seemed more like a question than an explanation. Perhaps Renae was even more new to all this than Giada herself.

The whole thing had been strange—seeking out the Society through whispered information among other travelers she had met through childhood, showing up at one of their meetings and asking to join.

The requirements to be part of the Tempus Vigilia were simple. You need only *prove* you could travel through time. University student initiates were brought to a historic location while doing a semester of study abroad, where the history went farther back. In a secret meeting, the highest-ranking member of the chapter who was present placed a coin in your palm and bent to whisper a question in your ear. If you could truly do as you claimed, you'd travel back in time, get your answer, and return before your interrogator took his next breath. Then, simply open palm, state your answer, and you're in. Theoretically, you could stay years in the past before returning if you wanted. Not recommended, however, since the moment of aging instantly upon your return did nasty things to your body.

"So, no last names? No birthdates?" Giada glanced between the two.

"Right!" Renae swept the area with a wide glance. "Just three strangers, who will likely never meet again. Besides," she blinked up at Alexander, "what if I looked you up when I got home, and you were dead already? That would be so tragic!"

"Or worse," Giada elbowed Alexander, "the Professor here could be *old*."

He nodded, brow furrowed. "It is true you might return to your time, which could be my future, and find me somewhere, much older. But I don't see how that would be worse than if I were dead. Also, I am not a professor—"

Giada sighed. His good looks weren't exactly matched by quick social skills. "Right. But something tells me you can show us around this city as well as any tour guide."

Alexander turned to study the Portico of Pompey above them. "We should wait here, I feel, to get the answers to our questions. Then we can explore."

"Then let's go!" Renae grabbed Alexander's arm and pulled him along, up the steps.

Giada followed, flexing tight fingers against her thigh. The girl was somehow charming and annoying at the same time. All that radiant energy—it made you want to both stare and look away.

And Alexander was mostly staring.

CHAPTER FIVE

"*S*ahara, Minnie told me you're in there."

The crackly rectangle of papyrus on my desk seemed to scream a warning at me.

I lifted it by one edge, positioned it carefully between two blank pages of my journal, and stashed the volume on my towering bookshelf, between Titus Livius and Herodotus.

"Coming." Was the room hot already? The day was still young.

I opened the door to Jack, glanced into the empty hallway, then grabbed his arm and pulled him into my room.

"Whoa, okay, then." Jack grinned, eyebrows raised.

I slammed the door and whirled to face him.

He took a step backward, hands raised. "What did I do?"

"What are you doing here? What do you want?"

"Just wanted to see if I could actually sneak into a girl's room in this place."

My years at boarding school came flooding back. What would Headmistress Hughes have said, if I had brought a boy into my room?

I planted my feet and crossed my arms.

"Sahara, what is wrong?"

The message stuck between the pages of my journal might as well have been painted across the back wall. All my suspicions about Jack's Aunt Giada had been accurate.

"Why are you really here, Jack? Here in Egypt, following me? Did your aunt send you?"

"I've already told you, I'd wanted to meet you for years."

He circled me, dropped into the creaky black chair I'd shoved against my scratched and secondhand mahogany desk, then tipped the chair backward, its front legs hovering in mid-air.

I paced the room. In my early morning start to the day, I neglected to make my bed, and the hills and valleys of my rumpled powder-white sheets tempted me to crawl back in and pull the blankets over my head.

The words of my father's message, the thoughts crowding my mind since reading it, all of it threatened to spill from my lips. I clamped them shut, holding back the foolish inclination to trust this man.

He picked up the pen from my desk and tapped it against his thigh. "You're going to have to tell me at some point, Sahara."

I flexed my fingers and lifted my chin. "I don't have to do anything you say."

Jack dropped the chair legs and leaned forward, his eyes warm. "Now you're worrying me. What's happened? Did you get to the tomb? Did you get inside?"

"Oh yes, I got inside!"

He was right. I was going to have to tell him. For better or worse, he was my single ally, and no matter how much I tried to avoid it, my heart kept connecting with his.

I crossed to my bookshelf and reached for my journal, but hesitated. Let my hands fall on my early edition of Livy, bound in velvety, rose-red leather, and traced its raised gold title with my fingertips. Even with my back to him, I could hear the tap, tap, tapping of that pen on his leg.

The loopy scrolls of Livy's *History of Rome* invited an afternoon of leisurely reading. The room felt warm and close and drowsy.

My chair creaked again, and Jack was behind me. His hands wrapped my upper arms.

"Tell me." His voice was low in my ear.

I replaced Livy, and pulled out my journal. "Sit." I pointed to the chair.

Jack obediently returned to sitting.

I pulled the coin from my pocket and placed it on the desk.

Jack glanced at it. "Looks old. A reproduction?"

"No. And it is old. Roman. About two thousand years old. Eve found it in the tomb and brought it to me last night."

Jack's forehead furrowed. "But only two thousand? Roman? That doesn't make sense."

"It doesn't. But there's more." I fluttered open the pages of my journal until I reached the letter from my father, then let the papyrus slide gently onto the desk. "This message was also in the tomb. With the coin."

"This looks more Egyptian, right?"

"It may look that way, but it's actually a code created by my father and me when I was a child."

Jack studied it for another moment, then lifted his eyes to mine, understanding dawning there. "Your father left you a message in Tut-ankh-amun's tomb?"

"A message. And this Roman coin."

Jack's lips tightened, and he nodded sharply. "That proves it then. A message left in the tomb before it was sealed, found three thousand years later when it was opened? One of your parents was a Revisionist."

I stared through the window. What was their life together like? I thought I knew them. Clearly, I did not.

"So, what does it say? The papyrus?"

I read him the translation that I penned in my journal, stopping after the phrase I assumed was "your loving father," and leaving off the postscript.

Jack whistled through his teeth. "Wow. So they want you to meet them. But I don't get it. Where? When?"

I pointed to the coin. "It was minted in 68 AD, the year of

Nero's death. I think that's what the message means, that they want to meet me in the Domus Aurea on the day of Nero's death."

"The Domus—?"

"It means 'Golden House.' It was the palace complex Nero built after the fire of 64."

"So they're not dead."

I exhaled and dropped my shoulders.

"Sorry." Jack reached to touch my arm again. "Didn't mean to be so abrupt."

"They're not dead. I think you must've been right. They went back to meet Belzoni, and got trapped in the 1800s with my sister. And this was their idea of hoping to get a message to me."

"But how could they possibly have known you would be here—"

"I don't know. Perhaps they thought this message would never be translated correctly, that it would be published and I would see it."

"Or perhaps they knew their daughter. Knew you'd be with Carter and Carnarvon, looking for this tomb."

I shrugged. It was hard to imagine the leap of faith it would've taken for my parents to believe both that Carter would find this tomb and I would be here to see their message.

"One thing I don't understand—"

"Only one thing?" Jack smiled.

"I didn't think it was possible to bring things back and forth from the past. I tried taking my journal, some small items, back with me to Hatshepsut, but it didn't work."

"Revisionists can bring things they find in the past back with them, to their present time, like souvenirs. But they can only take an object *back* in time if it existed in that past time. So nothing from the modern world ends up in antiquity."

I'd found an Egyptian headband in my mother's trunk at Highclere, so much like the one I was wearing when I appeared at Hatshepsut's Mortuary Temple. At the time, I believed its pristine condition meant it was a reproduction. But perhaps it had been authentic. Not that any scholar would have declared it so, given its apparently new condition.

I lifted the coin from the desk and held it aloft. "So I can bring souvenirs back with me, to my real time. But still, explain how my father brought this coin, minted in 68 AD, into an Egyptian tomb sealed nearly fifteen hundred years earlier."

Jack frowned. "I can't. I can't explain it at all."

I rubbed the coin between my fingers. "And what about people? How did my sister get back to ancient Egypt, if she's still too young to have developed her ability to time travel?"

"That one I can answer. Two travelers can take the hands of a third person who will eventually be a traveler and bring them to a different time."

"So you can't bring modern *items* to the ancient world, but you can bring modern *people?*

"Right."

It made sense, in the weird way most of the Codex principles of the Tempus Vigilia made sense.

"So?" Jack took the coin from my fingers. "Are you ready to go to Rome?"

I turned away. "There's no way I'm going to Rome in 68 AD. I can't afford to take weeks to travel to Italy and back, not right now, with the tomb cataloguing just beginning. And I don't know enough about that time or place."

"Ack, Sahara, always the need to know everything. And always the work first."

"Besides," I ignored his criticism, "I wouldn't go to Rome to visit them. I'd go to Venice, try to meet up with them in the 1800s when they went to visit Belzoni. See if I could figure out what went wrong and warn them. Get them back to 1905 before my sister is born."

"Whoa, hold on there. I knew you wanted to meet up with them in the past. Have a visit. Maybe plan another time and place to meet. But you're talking about changing history—"

"What's the use of being a Revisionist if I can't change the awful parts of my past?"

41

"For one thing, it's against the rules—"

"I don't care—"

"For another, it's really dangerous!"

"Dangerous, how? Am I going to break the universe or something?"

"No, just your mind."

I leaned away from that bombshell.

"You think you're going to meet up with your seventeen-years-younger father and pregnant mother, and divert them back to the England of 1905, so they won't disappear and be believed dead? Then return to '22, where you would never have been separated from them? What do you think happens to your mind, then?"

"I—I don't know."

"I'll tell you. You have two sets of memories—the ones you have now, and others that are somehow shoehorned into your brain beside the old ones, until you're not sure what's real."

"That sounds… confusing."

"More than confusing! Damaging. Devastating." He spit the words like curses. "The few who've been stupid enough to keep risking it have bought a one-way ticket to dementia, depression. Even worse."

Something in his tone, the tight clench of his jaw.

"Jack? Someone you cared about?"

He turned away, to the sound of laughter filtering through the window.

I crossed to it and flattened a hand against the glass.

A small group, the Winlocks and Burtons, along with Frances Breasted, wandered up from several cars, laughing and chattering as though coming from a party. Was it lunchtime already? The smell of baking bread and curried lentils filtered into my senses. I leaned my forehead against the warm glass, and watched the dust particles floating in the sleepy, buttery-yellow sunshine.

"How do you even keep track of the places you've been, the years you've visited?"

"I don't. As you so eloquently said—just heading out on every lark that strikes my fancy. It's not like it's a systematic thing."

An image intruded of my father's "travel journal," as he called it. A wide roll of paper tacked to his office wall.

I crossed to a large trunk near my bed and rummaged through the supplies I stored there.

"What are you looking for?"

"Keep your voice down. The others will hear you. I don't want their judgment about having a man in my room."

I pulled a stack of blank paper from the trunk and a little bottle of rubber cement.

"I'm going to make a timeline."

I adhered the first sheet to my wall, then positioned the second beside it.

Jack stayed my hand. "Do it vertically."

I frowned.

"Just trust me."

Within a minute I had five of the sheets glued to my wall and was inking a straight line down them.

Jack tapped the top sheet. "Put 1922 here, at the top."

I followed his instructions. "Explain."

"It's the best way to think of the travel, because of the way the return works."

We stood shoulder-to-shoulder.

"It's more like descending into the shaft of a well than going back and forth across a line. You go deeper, farther back," his finger traced the line from 1922, downward, "and then you can go even deeper still, but each time you down farther, you must return back up to the place you left most recently. Before you can get back up the shaft, to your original time."

I tapped 1922. "So you're saying I could go back, say, eighty years, to 1842, and then from there I could go down deeper, another eighty, to 1762?" I followed the line downward in two segments.

"Well, I can't do math that fast, but yes. And when you left 1762, you'd have to return back up to where you left—1842—

before you could return to 1922. As though you were climbing
out of a deep well. It's the only way to visit the same time twice
—if you've never yet gone *above* that time, back to a more recent
year or the year in which you belong."

"And it's the return to the year in which you live that erases
your changes in the past?"

"Technically, no." He traced a finger up the line. "As soon as
you climb up the shaft of time to the future date you left, that's
when you undo any changes to the past. Or in your case," he
grinned, "that's when you revise history forever."

I would rather forget that reality. The face of the guard I'd
pushed into an ancient Egyptian bonfire still haunted my
dreams.

"OK. So, my very first accidental travel, when I was still in
my twenties, in the tomb of Seti the First. What year did he die—
1279, wasn't it?"

"You're asking me?"

I grabbed a volume from my shelf and looked it up, even
though I knew the answer. Then wrote *Seti I* and *1279 BC* on my
timeline, choosing the second sheet from the bottom.

"And Hatshepsut's Mortuary Temple on the day of her
funeral commemoration. Most likely 1458 BC." I added it to the
bottom page, under Seti.

"And then just weeks after the death of Tut-ankh-amun, in
1325 BC." I added Tut-ankh-amun and the date, between
Hatshepsut and Seti.

None of the dates anywhere close to Nero's 68 AD, nor the
early 1800s, when I suspected my parents got stuck in Venice.

"That can't be." Jack tapped my Seti date. "Here, 1279 and
1325. These aren't eighty years apart."

Oh yes. All of the rules and principles of Tempus Vigilia. It
was not possible to jump to dates within eighty years of each
other.

I stood back and frowned at my timeline. "These two dates
are fairly well-established."

"Could you have them wrong? Egyptologists, I mean. Not accusing your memory of failing, for sure."

"Even if we were off by a few years, these dates are only forty-six years apart. We would have to be *quite* wrong for them to have been actually more than eighty years apart."

I studied his eyes, watching for any trace of deception. "Are you sure about the eighty-year thing?"

Jack laughed. "Why does it not surprise me that if you can't read a fact in a book, you're unsure if it's true?" He tapped the timeline's dates. "Trust me. Travelers have been experimenting with targets for years, and less than eighty years—it can't be done."

"At least not that you believe."

Jack glanced at me sideways. "Someone thinks she's pretty special, doesn't she?"

"You're the one who told me I was special! If I'm a Revisionist and not an Observer, maybe I can do less than eighty years."

"I don't know. I've never heard of that ability, even with Revisionists. And you all are the stuff of legend, so I feel like that fact would have been in the stories somewhere."

A sudden realization fluttered in my belly, and I grabbed Jack's arm. "But what if I can?" It was like finding the final puzzle piece under the edge of the carpet and clicking it into place. "A few weeks ago, you said I was 'amplified' into being a Revisionist, because both my parents were time travelers. But now we know one of them was not only a time traveler, but a Revisionist as well. Maybe that gave me… even more."

Jack blinked. "Wow."

"And if I can do less than eighty years, I wouldn't even need to find them in 1800s Venice. I could go back to 1905, before they even left England. I could undo this whole thing. All of it, from the moment before they left for Venice."

"Sahara, I told you, it's dangerous—"

"You said 'keep risking it' —people who 'keep risking it' damage their minds. But even once? Maybe it'll hurt me a little, but—how much?"

"It's unpredictable. And cumulative. There are stories, but it's hard to say how many of them are true. Revisionists don't exactly advertise their ability, nor their actions when they change things. The Society brings consequences down on them pretty hard."

Fantastic. Would I get my family back, and then end up in an asylum?

"Sahara, I'm not going to let you find out firsthand—"

But his words rolled off me. Instead, the warm room, the laughter outside, the delicious smells of lunch, all brought a sense of calm, like a burden lifted, like the sun breaking through dark clouds.

The past was fixable. That was all that mattered.

"I have to test it out here. I have to find out if I can travel within the eighty years, before I would go to England and find them in 1905."

I turned back to my timeline. Then jabbed a finger just below my Seti date of 1279 BC. "Here. I'll go to Seti's tomb, and try to travel back to when it was still under construction. Before he died, which would be a different time than my first visit to his funeral, but even closer to Tut-ankh-amun's burial down here." I tapped the 1325 date. "If I can get to the construction of Seti's tomb, I'll be less than eighty years from both Tut-ankh-amun's and Seti's burials, both of which I've already visited."

Jack sighed. "Well, you're not going alone."

CHAPTER SIX

"*L*et's go."
    I stepped from my room without waiting for Jack to follow. This late in November, the days were getting shorter and the Valley would be dark in a few hours.

There was no time to waste, if I was going to test my theory that my amplified abilities allowed me to travel to a time less than eighty years away. That truth would change everything. Could fix my past.

"Wouldn't it be better to wait until morning?"

"No."

"Sahara, when was the last time you ate something?"

I continued down the hall, and called over my shoulder. "I need to get to the Seti tomb right away, Jack. I don't have time for sitting around the dining room."

He caught up and pulled me to a stop, then tilted his head with a look that shouted disapproval. "Wait outside for me."

I pressed my lips together, gave him a quick nod, and headed for the verandah.

No one sat in the wicker chairs this time of day. Likely they were all in the dining room, enjoying their midday meal. I ignored the chairs and braced a hand against one of the stone arches, my mind already across the scorched desert, in Seti's tomb.

I had tried a repeat in that tomb last February, after Eve brought my mother's journal page. But in that attempt, I aimed for the exact moment I visited in '14. Once I returned to 1914, that moment was no longer open to me. Would targeting a year or two earlier work?

Jack emerged in minutes, a brown paper-wrapped parcel and large silver flask in hand.

"Ready for a picnic?" His camera had materialized on a strap around his neck as well, and he looked like a proper tourist, ready for an adventure. He pushed his tan fedora back on his forehead, blue eyes twinkling.

"How did you put that together so quickly?" I pointed to the package.

"Oh, those women love me in there. All I had to do was mention taking the beautiful Sahara Aldridge on a date, and they were falling all over themselves to make us lunch."

I shook my head and descended the steps in quick succession. "Well, I'm not carrying it."

"Fair enough."

"And this is not a date."

"Of course not."

I squinted down the road and shielded my eyes from the sun. Again, no drivers waited. How would Herbert Winlock feel if we borrowed his motorbike?

But Jack was holding something aloft, metal jangling. "I also got Burton's motorcar keys from Minnie."

"Well, then, I guess we are all set."

I climbed through the passenger door of the old Buick.

Jack cranked the engine from the front. "She's got the steering on the wrong side, you know."

"Should I be worried? You'll have the road to yourself at this hour."

"Then hang onto your hat." He jumped in and punched the accelerator. The motorcar lurched forward, sputtering exhaust and kicking up dust.

Harry Burton was probably choking on his lentils.

"You manage to make everything into an adventure, don't you, Jack?"

He shrugged one shoulder. "And you manage to turn every adventure into work."

My fists tightened in my lap, and I watched out the window as the empty landscape slipped past.

Despite Jack's barbs, I would admit I was on a mission, yet again. The fluttery excitement in my belly, becoming typical in the moments before my time travel adventures, mixed with a larger, heart-pounding hope that I could recover my family by learning of another new ability.

Jack drummed his fingers against the steering wheel. "Speaking of work, I saw Callender in the dining room and he said you should be at the tomb first thing tomorrow."

"Finally! I thought they'd never let me help."

We reached the Valley in minutes, parked the car as close to the tomb as possible, and headed down the sandy path toward the entrance.

Jack carried our lunch, but stopped three times along the way to shove the wrapped package and flask into my hands and take photographs.

"I wish I had one of my camera lamps, to get some shots in the tomb."

"Howard would throw a fit. All that flash powder on the tomb walls."

A tiny tent stood outside the entrance, with supplies from the small team that had been working there stacked on a metal table and piled on the ground. I grabbed an electric lantern and signaled Jack to follow me.

We descended the steps and I pushed open the gate, a double of the one Callender had installed at the entrance to our new tomb, but this one cast in a more permanent metal.

Jack tilted his head, eyebrows raised. "Unlocked?"

"This tomb has nothing to steal. It was all raided thousands of years ago. There's little need for security."

I flipped the lantern to the On position and held it aloft as we entered the tomb. "Have you visited this one before?"

Jack shook his head. "I've been waiting for the prettiest tour guide I could find."

I stopped short and turned. "What about the time? I didn't think to ask you, how close have you been to 1279 BC?"

What odd questions I was asking these days.

But Jack didn't bat an eye. "With you, at Tut-ankh-amun, of course." He looked into the distance. "And then there was that time I went back to play checkers with a pharaoh in the Great Pyramid…"

"Are you—yes, you are kidding."

He grinned.

We stepped into the entrance, moving slowly as our eyes adjusted after the sun-blindness of the bleached valley.

I pointed to first set of steps, only a few meters away, to make sure Jack didn't misstep.

"So this is the famous Belzoni's Tomb?" He scanned the interior of the small chamber. "Doesn't seem like much."

I shrugged. "Just wait. KV17 goes deeper than any other tomb in the Valley, with more finished chambers than any other." I held the lantern to two figures on the time-roughened wall. They stood in the typical Egyptian fashion, bodies forward, legs striding, faces in profile. "Here's Seti himself, praying in front of the sun god Ra, in his falcon-headed form."

"Good-looking guy."

"This tomb was the hallmark of all his building projects, and that's saying something, in a reign known for a huge step forward in arts and culture."

I extended a hand toward the narrow steps. "Ready to descend one hundred and twenty meters into the earth?"

Jack squared his shoulders. "Ready as I'll ever be."

The passage grew cooler and mustier as we traveled down

the first ramped corridor, then the second stairway and into another corridor.

We walked slowly, the lantern playing over the ancient walls, every one of which displayed figures and animals in vivid colors of turquoise blue and honey gold, jade green and scarlet red. Scenes from ancient Egyptian texts like the Amduat—the Book of the Secret Chamber— and the Book of the Dead.

"Here. This is from the Litany of Ra." I held my fingertips just above the surface of a mural-covered wall. "It shows the sun god, unified with the king, in over seventy-five different forms." I inhaled, tasting the staleness of the air. "It's as good a place as any. I can try to travel to the day this mural was completed."

"No lunch first?"

I pressed the fingertips of one hand against the wall. "Can you try to stay focused, please?"

"Hey, a guy's got to eat."

"After."

"Fine."

"Besides, I'll get back before I leave, right? So, you'll be even less hungry when I return."

"Hey, you made a joke!"

I set the lantern down.

Jack placed his bundle and the flask of water beside the lantern.

"Ready?" I flattened a palm against the hull of a royal barque traveling toward the setting sun.

Jack placed his palm beside mine, overlapping our thumbs.

I smiled in spite of myself. The man really was a flirt. "You're not actually expecting to go, right? You've already been too close."

"Who knows? Maybe I'm special, too."

I frowned. "What happens if I get there, and for some reason I need to stay? And then decide to revise history when I come back? Do I disappear in front of your eyes, and come back later?"

"I don't know."

"How can you not know?"

51

"Sahara, I feel like you're still not getting it. Revisionists are really discouraged from using their ability. It's all kept very secret. Like a taboo subject to even talk about."

"OK. Well, if I disappear—"

"Just don't. Whatever happens, come back without revising. Please."

"Alright. I promise." I studied the wall under our hands.

"I'm aiming for the day this mural was completed. The last brushstroke."

Jack nodded. "Don't stay long."

CHAPTER SEVEN

I closed my eyes, fixed my mind, bent my head. Then concentrated on visualizing the artists, their brushes of bundled and frayed reeds, paint pots of reds and golds and blues. The artist standing back, then reaching to put the final touches on a masterpiece that would remain for millennia.

I waited for the vertigo, for the world-shifting spin that would come.

Nothing.

I could see the artist in my mind now, paint-spattered white kilt, bare chest, torch aflame to light his stony canvas. But only in my mind.

Still, nothing.

I opened my eyes and glanced to Jack.

"It's not working."

He shrugged and grinned. "Not for you."

"You were *there*? 1279?"

"Yeah, the artist painting this mural," he ran his fingers over a red lotus flower, "she was crazy about me. Much nicer than you. She actually fed me lunch—"

I jabbed my elbow into his ribs. "Very funny. Maybe I should try again."

But the effort failed. Just as when I'd returned here months ago, trying to repeat what I'd believed was a hallucination eight years ago, I could not get back.

"What if it's the place? Maybe it's impossible to also visit the same place twice? Not only the same time?"

"You can visit the same place in many different times. That's not the problem. I told you, it's not possible to travel to two times within an eighty-year span."

I sighed. "Then our dates must be way off. For Seti and Tut-ankh-amun. It's the only explanation of how I could have been in both times."

"So then, let's eat."

"For glory's sake, can you think of nothing else?"

He grinned.

I grabbed the wrapped parcel and dropped to the floor of the tomb.

"Right here?"

"Oh, now you want to wait for a better spot?"

Jack dropped beside me and opened the metal flask.

"That had better be water."

"Please. Do you think I'd try to get you drunk with all these jackal-headed gods looking down on me?"

I pulled waxy paper from a sandwich, the crusty white roll stuffed with thinly sliced pink ham, and handed it to Jack.

He pulled three oranges from the package. And proceeded to toss each into the air, until he had all three going at once, like a circus performer.

"Did you ask those ladies to pack three oranges, just so you could impress me with your juggling?"

"Is it working?"

"Oh, you're amazing."

He caught one, then two, but dropped the third. "Your high praise threw me off." He pulled a pen knife from his pocket, sliced the top of the rind, then pulled it away in one piece. The fresh scent of oranges spritzed into the mustiness of the tomb.

"So, why do you do it?" He handed me a section of orange. "Turn everything into work?"

"I'll relax once my career is certain. Right now, I'm still trying to prove my value to the team."

"To the world."

"Yes. I suppose."

"And do you think if you allow yourself any personal time, you'll fail?"

I chewed a bite of the salty ham sandwich before answering. "Not sure that's fair. Earlier this month I spent nearly a week as a tourist in the ancient past."

"Oh, come on. You were there on a mission, and you know it. Haven't you ever done anything simply for fun?"

"I've had fun." A memory rose, unbidden, and I forced it back. A face, a name, I'd avoided thinking about for years. "It didn't end well."

Jack barked out a laugh. "That's the saddest thing I've ever heard: *I've had fun. It didn't end well.*"

"What about you, Mr. Jolly-All-The-Time? What's the most *serious* thing you've ever done?"

He swigged at the flask, then held it to me.

"Thanks." The water was lukewarm, but washed away the dryness.

"I won a contest once."

I set the flask on the stone floor. "My turn to laugh! Winning a contest is the most serious thing you've done?"

He shrugged. "Yeah, I guess that's ridiculous."

"No, wait. You meant it. Tell me about the contest."

"It was just a photography thing. In the town newspaper. My dad gave me my first camera for my eighth birthday, and I entered a photograph of the Town Hall, taken at dawn with the sun coming up behind the clock tower."

"And you won. At age eight? That's amazing."

He smiled into his sandwich. "Thanks. I think that might be the only time I've felt like a real photographer."

"You're a real photographer."

"Thanks," he said again, still looking down. "After my... after I went to live with my Aunt Giada, I put the camera down for a long time."

Could I ask about his parents? We had shared so little of our pasts.

"Was your father—could he—travel?"

Jack shook his head and pulled at another section of orange. "My mother. And she never would have defied the Society by marrying another traveler. She would have believed it was too dangerous to bring the child of two travelers into the world."

"Yeah, I guess my parents were crazy that way."

"Sorry."

"And your aunt. Giada. She was your mother's sister?"

"Right. I wouldn't have made it without her."

Trust no one.

"Did—did your parents die?"

"My mother," he said again. "Suicide."

I gasped. Reached instinctively to clutch his hand in mine. "Oh, Jack."

"The traveling, it was too much for her. She saw things, and... I don't know. I was young, and Giada has never spoken much about it. I'm not sure which is worse, the dangers to the mind for Revisionists or the dangers to the body for Observers."

He tapped a rhythm on his leg, and looked away.

"What dangers? Did our trip to Tut-ankh-amun hurt you?"

He shrugged. "Traveling through time, even for Observers, is not without risk. Returning to a fraction of a moment before you left your present, it ages the body instantly. So while to everyone else it appears you were never gone, in reality your body has aged for the same amount of time spent in the past."

"So, my time in this tomb back in '14, and my time at Hatshepsut's funeral—"

He nodded. "And your four days spent with Senamun in 1325 BC. Each took a small toll on your body, but not likely too significant. It's the longer trips, when people go back and find they don't want to return home. They get too involved. Stay too long. When they finally come back, it's a jolt to the system. Not to mention a shock to everyone else who knows them, if they've visibly aged."

"And that's what your mother did?"

"I'm not certain. But yes, in my memory she seems far older than she should have been."

"What about your father?"

"That's another story. After my mother's death, my father went on a bender. Giada took me in. Changed my last name to Moretti, instead of my father's, as if he never existed. We haven't seen him in years."

"I'm so sorry. I'm sure that's… difficult."

He shrugged. "You keep moving, don't think too much about it."

Yes, and don't slow down long enough to *feel* it, either. Jack's strategy was obvious.

He elbowed me. "So, tell me about the fun that didn't end well."

I tried a nonchalant laugh. "Just a fella at university, and then for a time after. I thought it would be permanent. Gave up a few early opportunities that wouldn't have included him. But then he decided to move on to someone more appropriate."

"Appropriate?" Jack raised his eyebrows, clearly indignant on my behalf.

"Yes. Her father had a peerage. A viscount, if I remember correctly."

Oh, but I remembered correctly. Every painful moment of Roger's halting, apologetic explanation, before he slunk out of my London flat one drizzly September morning, leaving me to figure out the next phase of my life, after I'd given up so much and banked on being his wife.

"What an idiot."

"The viscount?"

Jack laughed. "No, your 'fella.' I'm certain he's still kicking himself over losing you."

"Yes, I'm sure."

"So now, let me guess, you're focusing on your career, making sure you don't let love get in the way again?"

"You know me so well."

"Yes. I think I do." Jack's tone had grown serious.

The moment lengthened, and I brushed at a speck of dust on my trousers.

"Well, anyway," I said, "I also need to focus on getting the past resolved. Maybe that's meant to be my purpose right now."

"So you would—what? Just jump back to 1905, surprise your parents at how you've aged, tell them you're from the future, and convince them to forego their trip to Venice?"

I took a deep breath, contemplating my next words for a moment. "Jack, there's something I need to tell you. It's about Giada."

He raised narrowed eyes and studied my face.

I hated myself for what I was about to do, but it couldn't be helped. We had to have honesty between us.

"I think she had something to do with my parents' disappearance."

"What are you talking about? I thought they took a vacation in Venice, and then got stuck there after your sister was born, and they couldn't bring her back to 1905?"

"They may have been stranded there, but they were in Venice for a reason, and it wasn't a holiday. I believe Giada followed them there, after she visited me at Highclere and learned where they'd gone. I think it was because of Giada they couldn't return."

Jack clapped sandwich crumbs from his hands and began to gather up the remnants of our picnic. "That makes no sense."

"There's something more."

His hands slowed and his gaze returned to me.

"I didn't want to say anything before now, because it was only a feeling, a hunch. But then I got my father's message."

"Telling you to go to Rome. What does that have to do with—"

"I didn't read it all to you. There was a postscript. A warning."

I described the words to him. Explained my certainty that the "G…" and the "…etti" could mean nothing other than his aunt, who was not to be trusted.

The muscles of his jaw worked silently and he looked away.

"I'm sorry, Jack. I know how you feel about her."

"It's not possible. She's my family. No matter what your father might have said, I trust her completely."

A pang twinged in my chest at the fierce loyalty in Jack's voice. Oh, to belong to someone who would be that loyal to me.

I searched for a change of subject. "Do you think it was hard for them?"

"Who?"

"My parents. To have to stay in the nineteenth century, with my sister there and me here?"

"What do you think?"

"I think it must have been torturous. To be forced to stay in a time not your own, separated from everyone you care about, for the sake of someone else you love."

Jack nodded and rubbed at the back of his neck. "We should be getting back. It's late."

I sighed at the closed-off sound of his voice. I'd offended him with my accusations about Giada. Alienated him, even.

Jack stood, then extended a hand to help me up from the ground.

We retraced our steps up the sloping corridor, ascended the first set of stairs, and reached the entrance of the tomb with its metal gate.

Jack pushed against the gate, but it didn't budge.

He pushed again.

"What's the problem?" I reached past him.

He extended a hand. "Please, be my guest."

But the gate refused to move.

I bent to the latch. Had something gotten stuck?

"It's locked!"

Jack leaned in, his head touching mine. "What? How?"

"Someone must have come and locked up after we entered."

"I thought you said—"

"Hey!" I yelled through the bars. "Is anyone out there? We're still in here. We need you to unlock the gate!"

My frantic shout was met with desert silence.

CHAPTER EIGHT

I paced a short route, back-and-forth, in front of the metal gate.

Jack continued to rattle the lock, and even threw his shoulder against it a couple of times, to no avail.

"This is insane." The words hissed between my clenched teeth. "We never should've stayed this long. A picnic, for glory's sake!"

"Hey, if we'd come tomorrow morning, this wouldn't have happened. You're the one who insisted this experiment couldn't wait!"

"Which would have been fine if, if—"

"If what, Sahara? If you didn't take a minute to enjoy yourself? Have a conversation with me, instead of avoid me like you've been doing the past two weeks?"

"Argh!" I shook the gate myself. "Who knows when someone will be back to let us out? Howard is expecting me at the dig site first thing in the morning!"

Jack sighed and slumped against the wall. "You'll get there."

"You don't understand. I have to be there, I can't disappear again. Not after last time. Between the missing days and... you... Howard's already suspecting everything I do."

"Me? What have I got to do with it?"

I scrubbed my hands over my face. "You're a reporter. That's enough."

The sun was already low in the sky. No one would be at the site this late. And our KV17 was too far from KV62, even if Howard was working late. No one would be anywhere close to the gate until morning.

"So," Jack put his hands on my shoulders to stop my pacing, "it would appear we are stuck here for the night. Anything in Archaeology Training School prepare you for spending the night in a creepy tomb?"

I breathed against the tightness in my chest. Was I more nervous about my surroundings, or about spending the night with Jack?

"'Archaeology Training School,' as you call it, teaches you to be smart enough to *avoid* spending nights in creepy tombs."

"Well, then, that's on me."

"Howard is going to kick me off the team." I raked my hands through my hair.

"Don't get ahead of yourself. We could still be out of here first thing in the morning. Besides, Howard likes you too much, appreciates your work too much, to kick you off the team just for being late."

"You don't know him like I do."

"And is being part of this team that important to you? Even now? Now that you know the world is open to you in a way you never imagined?"

"Yes! Yes, it is. You don't understand."

"Enlighten me."

"It's hard to explain." I turned away, lifted the lantern from the floor and held it against the murals that marched in timeless rhythm toward the stairwell. The mother goddess Mut, from which all life was supposedly born, gazed down on me.

"Ever since my parents died—disappeared—I've felt lost. Like I've been waiting for someone to tell me who I was supposed to be. What I was supposed to do. These past few years, digging here in Egypt, I've known this is it, this is where I'm supposed to leave my mark. The only thing that matters is the work."

"All work and no play."

"It's the only way to make a difference."

"Sounds like a good way to destroy yourself in the process."

I sighed. "Can we talk about something else?"

"Sure. How about a better tour of this place?"

"That's it? We're going to resign ourselves to being stuck in here?"

"You have a better idea?"

I growled, but he was right. What else could we do but wait until morning?

"So, isn't there a sarcophagus or something?" Jack glanced toward the corridor.

I sighed. "There was."

Secretly, I was glad for a change of subject. I swung the lantern to the steps and gave my tour-guide lecture as we descended.

"The sarcophagus is gorgeous. Carved from one huge piece of alabaster, but only about five centimeters thick, so it's nearly translucent. Belzoni tried to sell it to the British Museum, but his asking price was too high. Sir John Soane bought it, for £2000, and put it in his own museum in London."

We passed through the Well Room, with its ritual shaft dropping into inky oblivion beneath us. I held the lantern near our feet as we crossed the stone bridge.

"Belzoni sounds like a character."

"He was, for sure, but in his defense, the sarcophagus truly was a treasure. The entire piece is carved, inside and out, with glyphs from the Book of Gates, showing the king's *ka* passing through the twelve gates of the underworld."

We entered what archaeologists called the Four-Pillared Room.

"Wow." Jack slowed and took in the pillars, covered floor to ceiling with paintings. "Is this where it was?"

I smiled. "This is nothing, compared to the burial chamber."

I skipped the small chamber at the side of the room, and led him down yet another set of steps and another corridor.

Jack sucked in a deep breath. "Is it just me, or do you feel the weight of the entire earth on you?"

"It can be a bit suffocating, yes. You have to avoid thinking about it."

Finally, we slipped into the first part of the burial chamber, its six painted pillars dwarfing the last room.

"Wow," Jack said again, then laughed. "Feels like I should find some alternative words, but I'm a bit speechless."

I grabbed his hand. "Come. Back here."

I led him to the crypt that opened from the back of the burial chamber, then handed the lantern to Jack. "Hold it as high as you can."

The light flickered against the vaulted ceiling, high above us, with its complex gold splashes of starry constellations, a gilded treasure, far out of reach.

Jack turned a slow circle, wordless.

"This is where it happened the first time, eight years ago."

"The first time you time traveled? Accidentally?"

"I was standing here, with my hands against the wall, and I bent over to pick up a stone while thinking about the last time Seti's mummy was seen. That's when—"

I froze, mid-thought.

Wait, could it be...?

"Sahara? Where did you go?"

"Jack, that's it! That's why I was able to travel to Tut-ankh-amun's 1325 BC, even though I'd already traveled back to see Seti here."

"I'll need more information."

"The Royal Cache! TT320." My mind raced through facts, putting pieces together.

Jack waited, head tilted and eyebrows raised.

"Keeping the king's body safe was incredibly important to ancient Egyptians. They started burying pharaohs in pyramids, but a pyramid was like a giant red X on a treasure map, begging to be looted. So eventually they switched to burying kings here, in the Valley, underground and hopefully hidden. But it still didn't work out very well." The words tumbled from my lips, like water racing downstream. "Tombs were always getting looted. When Belzoni discovered this tomb, Seti's sarcophagus was here, but it was empty. His mummy had already been moved, to a cache with more than fifty mummies, many of them royal, not far from here."

"Did Belzoni find that cache, too?"

"No. It wasn't found until probably about 1870, and not by archaeologists. A tomb-robber named Ahmed Abd el-Rassul found it, supposedly when his goat fell down a shaft. He and his brother Mohammed started systematically selling off the treasures in the tomb, living off the profits for years."

Jack chuckled. "Smart guys."

"Yeah, until the authorities finally figured out the source of all the illegal artifacts on the market, and tortured the brothers into giving up the location of the cache."

"Nice."

I shrugged. "Different times."

Jack scratched his jawline. "The whole thing reminds me of something... a story Aunt Giada told me, maybe. About her early adventures in time traveling." He gazed at the celestial ceiling, then shook his head. "My memory's nothing like yours. Can't remember, exactly. But I'm still not getting what this has to do with you."

"Because when I was here in '14, and was wishing I could have seen the tomb in ancient times, I was wanting to see Seti's mummy just before it was lost for millennia. But that wasn't in 1279 BC when he was buried. It would have been about 1075 BC, when his mummy was moved to the Royal Cache."

"So then, your two trips were... two-hundred fifty years apart, not less than eighty."

"Exactly!"

But then reality hit me. "Right. Guess I'm not super-special after all."

In an odd counterpoint to my sudden illumination, the lantern flickered and died.

The immediate darkness, even in the spacious burial chamber with its vaulted ceiling, pressed down on me with the weight of countless tons of stone above our heads.

"Jack?"

"I'm here."

His arm slid around my waist.

I turned into him, forehead against his warm shoulder. "I won't be able to stop them in '05."

"That was never a good idea."

I took a minute to process my disappointment. "We need to get back to the gate. At least we'll have a little light there."

I pushed away from the security of his embrace and stepped toward the unseen stairs, feet sliding against stone and hands extended.

"Hey," Jack's voice echoed off the chamber walls, "can we at least stay connected? I don't want to lose you."

"The first set of steps is right here." But I misjudged, and slammed my foot into the bottom step, pitched forward and scraped my shins into the steps.

The lantern smashed against stone, and the glass shattered.

I braced a forearm against the steps. "Aaahh!" Glass pricked my hand.

"What happened?" Jack's voice was tinged with panic.

I felt his hands on my hips.

"Are you alright?"

"No, I'm not alright! I'm stuck in this stupid chamber."

"Well, at least stick closer where I can keep an eye on you! It's as dark as a tomb in here!"

"Funny."

"Come on. Let's get to the top of this place."

We moved more carefully this time. In the second corridor, we scuffled against the remains of our picnic. I rummaged like a blind woman through the discarded paper wrappings from our sandwiches, and chose one to wrap my hand, still bleeding.

Jack gathered the trash and the flask, and we continued feeling our way upward.

After the utter blackness of the pit, even the glimmer of moonlight caught my eye. "We're nearly there."

We settled down at last, backs against the tomb wall near the entrance, and shared the final orange. I rubbed the rind between my fingers, preferring the citrusy smell over the stale air of the tomb.

Jack handed me the silver flask, glinting under the moon. "There's only a bit left. You finish it."

I took the last swig of the tepid water.

"Thanks."

No food, no water. Someone had better find us soon.

The night stretched, and we talked sometimes of little things, of unimportant things, and very occasionally of deep things.

As much as I wanted to prove myself courageous in the face of a dark and empty tomb with nothing but the sounds of scuttling insects around us, I found myself, partway through the night, curled against Jack with his arm holding me tight against his chest.

I awoke from strange dreams and fitful sleep to the sound of shouting.

Jack was already pulling away, carefully leaning me against the wall.

I clamored to my feet.

We both lurched for the metal gate, hands wrapped around bars that were still cold with the desert night air.

"Hello? We're in here!"

"Sahara? Where are you?"

"Here! KV17! We've been locked in."

"Goodness, girl, I thought we'd lost you!"

I'd never felt so overjoyed to see someone as I did when Harry Burton's face, alongside his wife Minnie, appeared outside the metal gate.

"What on earth?" At the sight of Jack with me, Minnie managed to look both shocked and concerned at the same time.

This event was sure to make it into her diary.

"We came to see the tomb yesterday afternoon, and someone locked the gate."

Burton took the situation in stride. "Let me find someone with the key." He disappeared.

Minnie stayed at the gate, tut-tutting. "When we realized this morning you hadn't returned with the car, we could not *imagine* where you could've gone. Where you could've spent the night."

Her waggling eyebrows spoke volumes about where she suspected I spent the night.

"Harry insisted we go searching. That we all go searching."

"All?" My heart sank.

"Yes, of course. Everyone is so worried. They are all gathered at KV62, deciding on how to divide up and start looking for you."

Wonderful.

Burton returned a minute later, with Herbert Winlock in tow.

"Sahara! Are you alright? Have you been hurt?"

Now all we needed was Howard and my humiliation would be complete.

"I'm fine." I held up the wrapped hand Winlock was eyeing. "A little scratch, that's all. Just get us out of here."

Word of our miraculous "discovery" spread ahead of us to the mingling group of a dozen or so bystanders at the digsite, and by the time we reached them, concern had shifted to amusement.

Burton clapped Jack on the shoulder. "You'll go a long way for a story, won't you old man?"

Helen Winlock seemed to be blushing on my behalf. Good grief.

But it was Howard's thunderous expression I wanted to avoid.

Jack slunk away, toward the edges of the crowd.

"Sahara, this nonsense must stop." Howard's ears had gone red and his mustache twitched. "You cannot keep disappearing—"

"I'm sorry, Howard. It won't happen again. I had no idea the tomb would be locked—"

"We have important work here, Sahara. If you cannot be serious about your role, then perhaps you should return to England."

Harry Burton stepped up and circled my shoulders with a comforting arm. "Give the girl a break, Carter. She's had a rough night. And she's more of an asset to this team than you're willing to admit."

I tried to smile my gratitude at Burton, but tears were too close to the surface.

Howard grunted and turned away.

"Don't worry about him." Burton squeezed my shoulders and then released me. "He'll forget all about you as soon as he starts into that tomb again today."

Yes, that's what I feared. That Howard, and everyone else on this team, would forget all about me.

And where was Jack?

He had disappeared to the other side of the gathered group, and now stood gesturing to a man who faced him. From this angle, with both faces in profile, they seemed to be arguing. The stranger wore a smartly-cut suit and hat that looked newly purchased. He removed his hat to run a hand through a wavy mop of orange hair, shaking his head.

I started toward them, then hesitated. Something about the way they huddled together…

I circled the group of archaeologists, engineers, and their wives, and slid along the back edge of Howard's tent. I stepped close to the dirty-white canvas, one eye peering past the corner, around the rusted metal tent pole.

"I'm telling you, I'm not leaving." Jack's words, though hushed, were clipped and sharp.

"She's worried—"

"Then tell her I'm fine."

"That doesn't make sense, and you know it."

"Well, nothing else makes sense, either!"

I was having trouble following this exchange, but a coldness was creeping into my throat, even as the sun rose above the horizon, blinding and hot.

The red-haired fellow crossed his arms. "And what about the parents? And the other one? Have you learned the whereabouts yet?"

Jack's head pulled back. "The parents are dead. And what do you mean, the 'other one'?"

"The other child, the sibling."

I wrapped a hand around the tentpole, trying to absorb its sun-warmth.

"No, I don't know—why is she asking?"

He shrugged. "Just doing my job, man."

Jack shoved forward and grabbed his suit lapels in tight fists. "There's more you're not telling me."

"She insists on getting *one* of them, okay?" The man yanked Jack's fists from his jacket. Your girl isn't the only one. Either one of them would do."

Either one of them.

Me?

Persia?

"If you're not going to help, you know she'll find another way."

The subtle threat to a sister I'd never met was like experiencing phantom pain in an amputated limb.

"Another way to do what?"

"Look, I'm not going back empty-handed. She's waited more than fifteen years for this, and who knows what she'll do if I don't bring back the information she wants. Not to mention, you're clearly not safe. She'll send someone to help, as soon as she knows what's happened."

I moved out of the shadow. "Jack? Is this a friend of yours?"

The stranger eyed me and glanced back to Jack.

"I'll see you soon," he said, then turned and headed for one of the waiting drivers.

A TIME TO WEEP

I joined Jack and watched in silence as a motorcar took him down the road.

"Explain, please."

He inhaled and moved to rejoin the group near the work tent. I put a hand out to stop him.

"Just a colleague of my aunt's. She's wondering how I'm enjoying my visit to Egypt."

I focused on his face, his eyes. Stepped close to him, my chin raised to his. "The truth."

He rubbed a hand across his jaw. "I don't know, Sahara. I'm as confused—"

"You were talking about my parents. About Persia. Your aunt is tracking them!"

He turned away, stalked toward the road, as if to escape me.

I ran after him. "Jack, how could she even know about my sister?"

He was still walking, head down.

"She must have gone to Venice in '05! Found them there and learned my mother was expecting a baby."

I grabbed his arm and yanked him backward. "Jack, stop!"

He whirled on me.

The ashen color of his face frightened me.

"Jack, did you tell your aunt that I am a Revisionist? Is she after me, because of what I can do? Is she after my sister?"

"Sahara, I don't know anything!" He broke free from my grasp. "Just let me think!"

But I was finished with thinking. Finished with suspecting.

My sister was in danger.

I would not trust Giada Moretti. And I would not leave my family stranded in the past, for her to find and use for some nefarious plan.

Back in my room at the American House, a coin minted in the year 68 AD invited me into action.

It was time to stop resisting.

It was time to go to Rome.

CHAPTER NINE

March 15, 44 BC
Rome, Italy

Giada followed Alexander and Renae up the marble steps, toward the towering Theatre of Pompey, where Julius Caesar was apparently scheduled to be assassinated some time that day. The early morning light had warmed, the day advancing with its doomed conclusion. How long would they need to wait, before the action started?

"So, where and when does this thing happen?" Giada called to the pair ahead of her.

Renae slowed and pointed upward. "Inside the Theatre, in a chamber to the side. Caesar will be heading into the start of a Senate meeting."

Of course Renae knew. Had she studied before her initiation test?

Giada received the news that her initiation test would take place at the famous Roman square, the Campo d' Fiori, only last night. Maybe she should have grabbed a late-night study session about what happened here in history, instead of the late-night bottle of wine with the Italian student she'd met at a cafe in the Piazza Venezia.

"Caesar is currently funding renovations in the Forum, where the Senate usually meets." Alexander spoke over his shoulder, apparently for her benefit since Renae seemed to have all the answers. "So today they are meeting in a chamber inside the Theatre of Pompey. Just a side chamber, not in the theater itself, of course."

"Of course." She rolled her eyes at their backs.

A pack of heavily-muscled men, sporting tanned leather vests, strapped with swords and daggers of varying sizes, loitered at the top of the steps. They strolled or leaned against marble pillars, attempting without success to look casual. The smell of leather and sweat was overpowering.

Gladiators? Something was definitely afoot.

The three travelers positioned themselves a few paces from the yawning entrance into the Theatre complex. Alexander held them back, warning they'd be caught in the chaos.

But wouldn't she and Renae need to be fairly close? To find a scar on Marc Antony's face and hear a dying man's last words?

A shiver of excitement ran through her. She was no history buff—she'd done this semester in Rome because of her family's roots here, and mostly for the Italian men and unlimited gelato —but still, to actually *see* Julius Caesar assassinated! Crazy stuff.

"So what did the guy do, to get himself killed?"

Alexander eyed her with surprise in his expression.

"I'm not a historian," she said in answer.

"Caesar's reforms were quite popular with the people, and his soldiers loved him. But the senators felt he was gaining too much power. Drifting from the ideals of the Republic they'd built. Treading dangerously close to becoming a tyrant, even toying with the idea of monarchy. They decided to keep his reforms, but get rid of the man himself."

"So, any idea when he'll get here?"

Alexander met the curious glance of a passing gladiator, then spoke under his breath. "The texts tell us Caesar's wife warned him to stay away today, because of a bad dream, an ill omen. At first he complied. But when the conspirators heard he wasn't coming, they sent his longtime friend and general Decimas Brutus to convince him. Decimus taunted him, really, for paying too much attention to the dreams of women and omens of foolish men. So he came along after all."

Giada kept her eyes trained on the courtyard below and the long tree-lined avenue beyond, bordered by bubbling fountains. "Decimus Brutus—that's the *et tu, Brute* from Shakespeare?"

"Well, the Brutus from *history*, but yes. Probably. There was another man involved, Marcus Junius Brutus, so if Caesar's final words were anything like Shakespeare's line, it's unclear to which of the 'Brutuses' he spoke."

"Great." Was she going to be able to pull this off? What if she missed the moment, missed the dying words, and had to return to the Tempus Vigilia chapter without an answer? Would she get a second chance at this bizarre scavenger hunt?

A small contingent of men coalesced in the courtyard below. Something about the way they all walked together was hard to miss.

The three waiting on the platform straightened as one.

Giada didn't take her eyes from the man at the forefront of the little group.

The men ascended the steps slowly, a group of five, most of them broad and imposing. They followed a tall, athletic man with the bearing of soldier. Despite being in his fifties, he had wavy dark hair, thinning on top and combed forward to cut a line across his forehead.

To their right, a bulky man descended toward the group, wrapped in abundant, multi-colored robes.

The leader looked up, caught the eye of the rainbow-hued man, and smirked. "Well, Spurinna," he called, "the Ides of March have come."

The large man bowed slightly. "Ah, but they are not yet gone."

At this, Julius Caesar scowled and glanced toward the clot of gladiators at the top of the steps.

Giada elbowed Alexander once more and jutted her chin toward Spurinna. "Trick question. He's wearing just about every color."

Alexander nodded, but did not pull his attention from Caesar. He had his answer, but clearly was not done absorbing this historic moment.

Caesar passed the three of them, close enough to touch, and entered under the wide doorway.

Giada followed.

Alexander held her arm.

She shook him off. "I'm getting in there!"

The group of men headed to the right, once inside the entrance.

From the other side of the portico, a younger man, perhaps in his thirties, stalked toward the entrance.

Caesar was disappearing into the Theatre. She had to go now.

Most of his friends who looked like bodyguards remained outside the door. One of the men with him peeled away from the group. He intercepted the younger man who approached from the side.

Giada was on the heels of Caesar. She could feel Alexander and Renae following.

"Antony!" Caesar's companion called across the portico.

Behind her, Renae gasped.

Giada stopped, turned. Which way? The approaching man must be Marc Antony. Renae needed to see him up close. But Giada couldn't risk missing the action inside, where Caesar would speak the words she needed to hear.

Renae glanced at her. "Go," she whispered, nodding.

Giada hesitated for only a beat, then slipped into the Theatre behind Caesar and his men.

Alexander stayed with Renae.

Inside, she followed Caesar as he marched toward the double doors of a large chamber clogged with buzzing men in togas. A crowd circled Caesar immediately.

She hurried to get in, before the doors might close, but was waylaid at the entrance by a pair of soldier-looking men. With sharp-looking swords.

She snarled at the expression of disdainful amusement on their faces. But whether it was because she was a woman, or simply a commoner, she wasn't getting in that room.

The chamber was high-ceilinged, with a ring of tiered stone seats. Men in white togas sprawled over the tiers, some seated and some standing in clusters, talking in urgent tones.

At the entrance of Caesar, all speaking stopped.

Immediately, a man rushed him. "Imperator, I have the petition we spoke of," he held up a scroll, "to recall my exiled brother Publius—"

Caesar waved him away.

Unexpectedly, the man grabbed at Caesar's shoulders, and ripped his tunic downward, exposing his bare chest.

Caesar stepped back, shock playing across his face. "Truly, this is violence!"

Another came at him from the side, dagger in his upraised hand. He thrust it toward Caesar's neck.

Caesar's military training showed. He caught the attacker by the wrist. "Casca, you villain! What are you doing?"

The man's eyes bulged. "Help me, my brothers!"

And then, chaos.

A surge of attackers, knives loosed, surrounding Caesar.

Giada growled under her breath. Too far. She was too far to hear any last words.

But the soldiers at the door were paying no attention to one woman trying to get in where she didn't belong.

And a mob of terrified senators were fleeing the chamber.

She slid between two escaping men. Dove toward the cluster of Caesar's attackers. Hunched her body downward, toward the floor where the dictator was bleeding out.

The ring of togas still surrounded him, a tiny arena watching a gladiator game.

She dropped to her knees, threaded her way between legs and sandals and a sea of white.

Inside the circle, bright red speckled the white togas and pooled on the marble floor.

Julius Caesar thrashed on the floor. He wasn't going willingly.

But then a dagger appeared in the hands of one who bent over him, and Caesar's eyes locked onto this man's.

Giada could almost feel the pain, the betrayal, in those eyes.

Caesar sagged, exhaled, and the words came in a whisper, with a slight nod. "*Kaì sú, téknon.*"

Kaì sú, téknon? What did that mean?

A stab of panic. Why didn't she understand the words, as she did everything else she'd heard spoken around her?

Caesar reached a limp hand toward the man.

The new attacker caught his hand almost reverently, released it, and pulled Caesar's toga over his head. Then drove his dagger deep into the dictator's chest.

Giada scuttled backward.

There would be no more dying words. She mouthed the foreign phrase to herself, over and over.

A moment later, she was free of the chamber. Moving the opposite direction of the crowd again, with senators now streaming toward the assassination.

"Giada!"

Alexander and Renae, there at the entrance.

She stumbled toward them, hands outstretched.

"You are hurt!" Alexander caught her, held her upright.

"What?" She took in the blood, spattered across her *palla*. "No —no, it's—it's his blood—"

"Come," Alexander pulled her toward the steps.

On the opposite side, Renae supported her by the arm as they descended.

"I cannot believe you did that!" Renae was shaking her head. "It was like you had no fear at all, diving into that mob!"

Giada tried to smile. Her legs felt wobbly.

"*Kaì sú, téknon.*"

Alexander nodded. "Interesting."

They collapsed in the grassy courtyard, nearly oblivious to the madness surrounding them as news spread.

"What is it? What did he say?"

"It's Greek. One of the theories of his last words. It means, 'You too, child?' Historians speculate his last words were the incredulous realization of his betrayal by Brutus, causing him to give up."

Giada took a deep breath to quiet the blood pounding in her ears. "It wasn't really a question, though. More like a threat."

"Fascinating."

Giada started laughing, knowing she sounded more crazed than amused.

"What is funny?"

"You are. With your 'interesting' and your 'fascinating'—as though you're reading a textbook. Do you realize we just *witnessed* that?"

Alexander looked toward the Theatre of Pompey, and his face took on a glow. "We did, didn't we?"

"So, what's next?" Renae was eying the city beyond the main avenue leading to the theater.

"Seriously?" Giada loved a challenge, but this girl didn't seem to take a breath.

"What?" Renae shrugged. "We got our answers, right? Spurinna in all the colors. Marc Antony has a scar over his right eyebrow, by the way. And Caesar's dying words. So... time to explore!"

Giada looked down at her clothing. "Maybe we could find me something less... bloody... first?"

But in the end, Renae simply helped her wrap the fabric so Caesar's blood was neither visible nor touching her skin, and the trio headed off toward the Forum, where Renae insisted they visit the Temple of Vesta to have a conversation with some Vestal Virgins. At which suggestion, Alexander blushed deeply and both women laughed.

All in all, it was one of the best days of Giada's life, violent assassination notwithstanding. The three made an excellent combination. Renae knew how to have fun, Alexander knew all the answers, and Giada was willing to take whatever risks needed to encourage an experience none of them would forget.

By the time the sun lowered over the Forum they were exhausted, but they lingered on a stone wall, watching the city wind down, unspoken resistance to the coming separation hovering in the air.

"Still no last names? No dates?" Giada glanced sideways to Alexander at her side, and Renae sitting beyond him.

Renae shook her head. "Today has been perfect. I want to remember you both, just this way. I want to believe you're always here, always this... alive." Her eyes shone in the twilight. She took Alexander's hand in her own.

Alexander returned the grip, and the smile, and then clasped Giada's hand. "Thank you, both. For... everything."

As if by mutual agreement, they lowered themselves from the stone wall, and each pulled a coin from where they had it hidden away. They stood in a tight circle, palms facing up and nearly touching. Then closed their hands around their coins, bent heads forward, with eyes closed.

Later, when Giada parroted the Greek words she'd heard Caesar whisper, Eugene grinned but said he needed more. Said she could have looked up those words in any history book. She was forced to replay the entire incident for the hungry audience of Tempus Vigilia members. It wasn't until she related the way the man who must have been Brutus pulled Caesar's toga over his head that Eugene nodded and held out a hand of welcome. Apparently that little detail hadn't been in the textbooks.

She was in.

Let the fun begin.

CHAPTER TEN

December 5, 1922
Valley of the Kings, Egypt

$\mathcal{I}$n the hall inside the front door of the American House on Tuesday morning, Minnie Burton grasped my arm with her a petal-soft hand. "Sahara, don't go out there. You'll be simply *attacked.*"

If we thought news of a sealed door in the Valley of the Kings had brought a frenzied press to our doorstep a few weeks ago, we had foreseen nothing of what was to come once the tomb of Tut-ankh-amun was opened.

Madness had descended on the Valley.

A reporter by the name of Arthur Merton broke the story on the thirtieth of November, writing for *The Times of London.* Within hours his column was picked up by *The New York Times* and every other news outlet across the United States and Europe. Every reporter within reasonable travel distance grabbed his press badge, ink pen, and notebook, and raced for Egypt. One could only imagine what the King's Valley would look like, once American reporters began to disembark from steamships even now speeding across the Atlantic.

I smiled at the older woman. "Thanks for the concern, Minnie. I'm only going to meet Jack for dinner at the Winter Palace. No reporters for me."

Her eyebrows rose. The obvious lack of logic struck me.

"Yes, I know. Jack is a reporter. But he's not writing a story, I promise."

At least, hopefully not. After our night in Seti's tomb, and my honesty about my suspicions, something felt freed up inside me, enough to agree to dinner with Jack. Nothing more.

Though it had taken nearly a week to get a night free from Howard's insistence that we work nearly 'round the clock on the preliminary work needed to catalogue the tomb's contents. I hadn't seen Jack since he refused to explain his argument with the angry, red-haired stranger.

I patted Minnie's hand, still on my arm. "Have a good evening."

I opened the door and stepped through, into a swarm of buzzing voices, clicking camera shutters, and general chaos.

I pressed my back against the door, which Minnie had already sealed behind me.

"Is your husband one of the ones working on the tomb, ma'am?"

"Do you want to make a statement for *The Observer?*"

"What was it like, miss, stepping back in time?"

This last question landed like a slap. I searched for the speaker.

There—a squirrelly little man—pen in hand, poised over a spiral-bound notebook.

He waggled bushy eyebrows. "Did you feel as though you were stepping back into ancient Egypt when you entered the tomb?"

"That's enough, boys." Jack's voice tunneled through from the back of the crowd, and then his upper body, shoulders first, and arm holding his press badge aloft. "Coming through for an exclusive with the famous female archaeologist Sahara Aldridge."

He jogged up the steps onto the verandah.

A few intrepid reporters followed him onto the steps.

He turned on them and scowled. "I said exclusive!"

"Jack," I whispered, "don't give them any more to go on. Now they'll be putting my name in the papers!"

He winked at me. "Somebody has to be your publicity agent. You don't get enough credit around here."

"Still—" I eyed the mob beneath us, "I'm not sure I want the notoriety."

"Then let's go for dinner."

But ten minutes later, when our car to the ferry had been chased by a string of reporters in other cars, and it looked as though they'd stalk us across the river and maybe even into the Winter Palace dining room, I balked.

"This is crazy, Jack. Let's just go back to the American House. I don't want to deal with this."

We hurried back to dighouse, grabbed a plate of curried lamb and pita from the kitchen, and secreted ourselves in a corner of the empty sitting room at the front of the house. Only a single, carmine-fringed lamp cast its wine-colored glow from the opposite corner, leaving the scattered chairs, tables and towering bookshelves across the back wall in shadows.

"Sahara, I'm worried about you." Jack studied my face between bites of lamb. "Those dark circles under the eyes are getting worse. You push yourself too hard."

"Yes, as you keep telling me."

"And when will you believe me, that you don't need to work like this, to prove yourself?"

"Don't I? Besides, it's not only about proving myself. I need to be ready for Rome, to fix the past."

He wrapped tight fingers around my hand and peered at me from those arctic-blue eyes. "Listen to me. There is no need for you to undo the past, nor do some important work for archaeology, to be a valuable person."

I tried to smile. "I appreciate that, Jack, but—"

He released my hand and waved away the rest of my rebuttal.

"This obsession, driving you to exhaustion, it will only lead to more trouble."

I bit my lip and pushed the spicy meat around my plate. "I haven't been sleeping since your aunt's goon arrived. If I don't get to Rome soon, I think I will go mad."

"I wish you would let me go instead—"

"I've told you, there's no way."

"Because you don't trust me." Jack's jaw muscles tightened and he tapped a finger against the arm of the chair. "You *still* don't trust me."

Did I? I'd known the man a month now, and had experienced as many feelings toward him as there were days in that month.

"I believe you. I believe you don't know why your aunt was looking for my parents in 1905, or why she's looking for my sister now."

"But?"

"I know how important she is to you. I know how important family is."

Jack set his fork down.

For a moment, I half-expected him to say *you're my family.*

"Yes, she's my family, all the family I have. But if she's trying to harm you, or your sister, or your parents, I would never let that happen."

"I want to believe that, too."

"At least let me loan you some money. To pay for your trip to Rome."

This lack of money, along with my fear of being kicked off the dig site team, had been my main concern the past two days. The trip north would cost a pretty penny. First to Cairo, then to Alexandria on the northern coast of Egypt, then a boat ride across the Mediterranean to an Italian port above Rome, and then whatever it took to reach the statue of Nero at his Golden House by sunset of June 9, 68 AD. It was money I did not have.

I shook my head. "I won't take your money. Or hers. And I don't want you to even tell her what I know. I will get there on my own. I'll do whatever it takes to find them, to save my sister.

You keep telling me I have a higher purpose, that I'm meant to somehow go back and make something right. This is it, I know it is."

Even if it meant I'd never dig in Egypt again.

The sitting room slowly filled with tenants of the American House, finished with their dinner and ready to socialize.

Helen Winlock put a record on the phonograph, one that was all the rage, apparently. She waved the album cover like a prized trophy. "It's the Original Dixieland Jazz Band. My sister sent it. She says this *jazz* is positively catching fire across America."

Herbert Winlock pulled the drapes shut so we could pretend the reporters didn't exist. Or perhaps to ensure they didn't witness his wife Helen and Frances Breasted rollicking to the scratchy tumult of "Tiger Rag" in the corner. Winlock kept to the bookcase, chatting with James Breasted over smoky cigars, and the Burtons started into a game of bridge with the Lythgoes at a round table by the window.

I watched the socializing for a few minutes, trying to let the upswing of the ragtime music lift my mood, but my thoughts were full of Rome. Jack and I didn't do small talk very well, especially not in the presence of others. And I wasn't about to discuss my next adventure in front of an audience.

"I think I'll turn in," I said. "Get an early start in the morning."

Jack stood, grasped my hand, and gave me a quick kiss on the cheek. "Until tomorrow."

I slipped through the darkening hall, the feel of Jack's kiss lingering on my cheek, and entered my room, still smiling, closing the door to the music and conversation drifting along the hall.

"Miss Aldridge, if I could just get a few quotes from you—"

I backed against the door, heart pounding.

A figure shifted in the darkness.

"Who are you?" My palms slid along the door, scrambling for the knob. "How did you get in here?"

But the curtains fluttering at my open window told the tale.

It was the little man who asked me about stepping back in

time. Porch light seeping through the window reflected off his oily hair and the oversized, wolfish canine teeth of his leering smile.

"Get out of here!"

I yanked the door open.

"Mr. Burton? Mr. Winlock?" I yelled down the hallway. The sound of jazz filtered from the sitting room. Surely the music was too loud for me to be heard.

The little reporter shot through my door, pressed up close until my back was against the rough wall of the hallway, and wrapped ink-stained fingers around my forearm.

"You owe the world a story!" His voice was a raspy hiss. "You can't keep all of this to yourselves!"

I twisted my arm from his tight grip, pulled away from the smell of that oily hair. "Get out of this house!"

"Sahara? What is this?"

Lord Carnarvon's voice boomed from the other end of the hall. Frail man that he was, his voice could still strike fear.

The reporter backed up, hands held in surrender. "Just trying to get a quote for my paper, your Lordship."

The earl stalked down the hall, cane tapping an angry rhythm, grabbed the man by the lapel, and dragged him toward the front door.

A moment later, Porchy returned to the door of my room. "I was just arriving to speak with Burton when I heard your yell. Did that rascal hurt you?"

"I'm fine. He only surprised me, hiding in my room."

Porchy huffed. "This is beyond madness. It's not safe for you here."

"I appreciate your concern." I tried to steady the annoying tremble in my voice. "But I am fine."

"None of this is fine. Eve and I are leaving in two days, going back to Highclere while Howard makes preparations. We'll be back once the work starts in earnest, perhaps in a couple of months. You're coming back to England with us."

Not a chance.

"Your Lordship, I appreciate your concern, but—"

But he was already turning away, striding down the hall to join the others.

I returned to my room, slammed my window shut, then checked the box that held my father's Roman coin, tucked between two copies of *Five Years' Exploration of Thebes*, the book Howard Carter and Lord Carnarvon published together ten years ago.

I sketched in my journal, chewed my pencil, tried to read a few pages of an Arthur Conan Doyle mystery, took down and replaced a half-dozen other books that couldn't hold my interest.

Lord Carnarvon was right, I needed to get away from here. But not to avoid pushy reporters. I needed to get to Rome and save my sister.

Two days later, the answer presented itself.

Howard and I were inside the newly-opened tomb, his sleeves rolled up above the elbows, jacket off and sweat already dampening the back of his shirt.

"I'm going to Cairo," he announced. "To start purchasing supplies and meeting with officials. And I'll arrange for more workers. I will likely be there a few weeks."

I kept sketching the lion-headed bed he'd tasked me with and nodded. "I'm coming with you."

"Not necessary."

"Porchy wants me to return to England, to avoid all this craziness. But I'd be better off in Cairo, waiting it out."

Howard slid a clay jug onto a tray. "Suit yourself."

"I could be of use to you in Cairo, you know."

Why did I say that? I had no plan to stay in Cairo. But his casual dismissal irked me.

He said nothing, only scribbled on a little notepad he carried everywhere now.

So, the first leg of my journey was arranged. If I traveled to Cairo with Eve, her father, and Howard, I'd have no need to purchase my own ticket. It wouldn't occur to either of the men to ask me.

Over the next two days, a bit of deception ensued. I let Porchy believe I would be returning to England with them. Sticking with him and Eve would get me on the train from Cairo to Alexandria. But in Alexandria, I would not board the ship bound for Marseilles with them. My ship would head for Rome. I had a little money of my own and it would have to be enough for the rest of the venture.

Once I reached Rome in 68 AD, I would have only one ancient coin that could never be spent. But with luck, I would only be there for less than a single day, and would find my family at sunset.

The night before we were to leave, I packed a few necessary items into my battered steamer trunk. A few dresses, for both day and evening. No sense in packing my work clothes and risking the attention of any reporters sniffing for traces of archaeology news. I surveyed my room. What else did I need? A couple of books to read on the journey, my hairbrush.

A twinge tightened my chest, something like a premonition. My mother's hairbrush, stashed in a forgotten trunk at Highclere. Did she pack for her trip to Venice in just this way? Believing she would return in a few weeks, back to her daughter and her life?

Would I return?

A sharp knock at the door sent my pulse racing.

"Sahara?"

I opened the door a crack. "Jack, I thought I would see you in the morning—"

"Can I come in?" He glanced down the hall.

I widened the door opening and stepped back.

"Are you sure about this?" Jack closed the door behind him.

"We've been over it." I continued my packing, folding a floral silk kimono, a gift from Almina, Countess of Carnarvon, into my trunk. "If Giada is still searching through history for my parents, for my sister, then I need to find them first. Need to warn them. And if all goes well, I'll find out what really happened, go from Rome to Venice, jump to the eighteen hundreds, and undo whatever happened there. Perhaps in only a week, I will have my family back. They will never have left."

"So you're still insisting on risking your sanity, on top of your physical health."

"Only this one time. One trip, to fix everything. It's worth the risk."

I finished the last of my packing. I would leave my journal until the morning.

"That's it, then. All finished." I struggled to pull my open trunk to the floor.

Jack took it from me and laid it beside my bed.

"I should probably get some sleep. We can say goodbye now. No need for you to come in the morning, since we'll be leaving early."

I'd avoided thinking about this moment. Hadn't asked Jack if he would still be in Egypt when I returned. It seemed unlikely. So perhaps this was more than a temporary goodbye.

Jack turned from my bed and took both my hands in his. "I hate the thought of you doing this alone. There's still so much you don't know."

I tried to smile. "I'll be fine."

"But wouldn't it be better if I—"

"Jack, I can't ask you to come with me."

Not that I hadn't thought about it.

He clasped my hands and pulled me to his chest, his forehead nearly brushing mine. Those eyes pouring something into my own. "Ask me." The words were a whisper.

I inhaled, summoning courage.

"Come with me." My own words emerged half-strangled, barely audible. But I had said them.

Jack released one of my hands and cupped my cheek. "I'm coming with you."

CHAPTER ELEVEN

December 7, 1922
Cairo, Egypt

"We couldn't have chosen a worse time to spend the night at Shepheard's."

Porchy's dim pronouncement was delivered to our party of five in the lobby of the posh Cairo hotel.

The stained glass above our heads splintered the morning light into shards and spilled a rainbow over the Persian carpets at our feet. But no amount of opulence, even the massive rose-granite pillars reminiscent of my visit to The House of Rejoicing, could blunt the impact of the seething unrest in the street, beyond the buffer of hedges and palm trees in front of the hotel.

I shrugged. "We could have been here three years ago, during the Revolution."

Porchy frowned at my contrary opinion. "Well, of course, Sahara. Of course."

The demonstrations and strikes of 1919 had cut across all classes, genders, and even religions, as Egyptians everywhere protested to end the British Protectorate of Egypt. The declaration of Egyptian independence had finally come nine months ago. But with the British Empire still holding so much power in the country, Egypt's so-called sovereignty was nominal. At Shepheard's Hotel, the elegant nightly dances for French and British officers hadn't missed a beat.

And outside this morning, the Wafd Party whipped protestations into a frenzy, calling for support of its new constitution and parliamentary representative system.

"It's nothing but a dust-up." Howard waved a vague hand in the direction of the hotel entrance. "We'll have you at the station in no time."

Eve smoothed her hair behind her ears and straightened a pink cap that matched her blush-colored traveling suit. "The sooner we're back in England, the better. I simply *despise* trains and ships. All that rocking and swaying."

Behind me, Jack remained silent. He'd figured out weeks ago that both Howard and Porchy disapproved of his presence in my life, and his best course of action was to remain in the background.

Eve, of course, thought Jack dashingly handsome and insisted I marry him at once and begin producing babies.

"Nothing for it, but to go, then." Howard checked his watch. "We have just enough time to get you to the train."

Howard led the way, and the rest of us followed like ducklings behind their mama, with six porters carrying luggage at the rear.

I'd told Howard this morning I wouldn't be staying with him in Cairo, and instead would be boarding the train to Alexandria. He shrugged and said it was probably for the best. Which gave me little confidence he would miss my expertise and welcome me back to the project when I returned from this crazy Roman adventure.

The Ramses Railway Station sat about three kilometers east of the riverfront Shepheard's Hotel, but we needed to thread our way to a taxi location, three blocks away.

"It'll take longer to fetch a ride to the taxi stand than to walk,"

Howard said, pointing through the crowds in the general direction of the unseen taxis.

We set off into the heat of the morning. Beyond the hotel courtyard, we descended to the chaos of the paved walkway along the street.

The street roared with the chants of countless citizens. The flutter of white ankle-length *galabiyahs*, white turbans, and red *tarbushes* blurred together. The churning mob was like a frenzy of angry fish in a gravelly ocean, under the cloudless Egyptian sky.

One of the young porters scuttled past me, to approach Howard. "I can find you private car, *sayidi*. Very good car to take you to the ferry."

"We're not going to the ferry, man! We need a taxi to the train station. Ramses Railway. These folks need to get the 9:02 to Alexandria."

The porter shook his head. He was perhaps only sixteen, but enthusiastic about his job. "No, no, *sayidi*. The 9:02 does not come. It is the 8:50 now."

Howard pulled a pocket watch from his waistcoat and glanced at it. "Dash it all. You may have to get the afternoon train, Porchy."

Lord Carnarvon flourished his cane in the air. "Can't do that, old man, or we'll miss the ship in Alexandria."

"Well, come along, then." Howard's pace increased.

Eve tugged at her father's arm, but he wasn't moving quickly these days.

Jack stepped to his side, offering an arm.

I stayed behind the father and daughter, to make sure we didn't lose anyone.

But I should have feared for myself. Or perhaps someone should have been watching me. The push and shove of protesters forced our party into fragments. Only minutes into our trek to the taxi station, I spun and searched and saw no familiar faces.

I wrapped my arms around my belly, clutching my satchel to

my middle. The bag held too many books, and the leather strap cut into my shoulder and across my chest.

The crowd around me surged and carried me along. Was I headed in the direction of the taxis? I had only two pounds sterling on my person, enough for the ship passage from Alexandria to Rome, but little more. Not enough to hire my own taxi, buy my own train ticket. If I even made it to the train on time. What little guilt I felt about letting Porchy pay my way was swallowed up by thoughts that my trip might be doomed before it began.

I cursed my own stupidity. Why did I think I was up for the challenge of navigating the sprawl of ancient Rome, when I couldn't stay with my party for three blocks through Cairo?

I fought the surge of the crowd. Which way? We'd left the Nile behind us, and without it I had nothing by which to orient myself.

A shout to my right gave me a flush of hope.

Jack?

No.

I was attuned to every sound now, every touch. The smell of the sweat and body odor of the crowd mixed with the ever-present smell of spicy Egyptian cumin hanging over Cairo in a haze.

The swell carried me, unable to break free.

I planted my feet. I must get my bearings.

A shove from behind knocked me to my knees.

The crowd did not stop. I would be trampled.

I scrambled on my knees toward the wall of a shop. Pulled myself to standing, hand scraping against the grey cracked stones of the wall.

The taste of mint tea I drank at breakfast mingled with a salty taste of sweat, or perhaps I was crying.

A thick-lipped bearded man tried to grab my satchel.

Political protestation had turned to looting.

I thrust an elbow toward the would-be thief, the satchel's strap biting into my palm, and slid along the wall of the shop until I reached the corner. Then folded myself into an alley.

How far from the taxis?

I slapped a hand against the alley wall. Curse it all, I had to be on that train!

Down the sliver of alley behind me, I glimpsed the minarets of the Umar Mokram mosque in Tahrir Square. I spun, and scanned the cityscape in the other direction. Yes. Should only be another block to the right.

I rushed from the alley, toward the street, but at the curb I went down, a shot of pain through my twisting ankle.

Oh, for glory's sake.

I hobbled forward, the hot dampness of the crowd pressing around me, my own dress clinging to my skin.

There! Just ahead. A cluster of taxis.

I shouldered forward, all elbows and no apologies.

"Sahara!" Eve stood on her toes, waving frantically.

Howard was already inside one taxi, glaring through its open window.

Lord Carnarvon glanced at me, bustled Eve in beside Howard, then climbed in himself.

Jack held the door of the second taxi.

I dove through.

Jack remained quiet, but his pale expression and shadowed eyes said enough.

The taxis honked and weaved through the three kilometers of insanity until we were at the Ramses Railway Station, disembarking.

Howard glanced once more at his watch. "You've only a few minutes."

Porchy handed Howard a wad of notes. "Run and get the tickets for us, old man. I'll never make it."

Howard melted into the crowd.

The rest of us twisted our way through the more genteel crowd of travelers, following signs to the track for the 8:50 to Alexandria.

I breathed in coal fumes and winced at the piercing whistle of a soon-departing train on the next track.

Minutes later Howard was back, handing out crisp, white tickets, shaking Porchy's hand, accepting Eve's embrace.

I reached to embrace him myself, but he extended a hand, and I ended up with a double-handed awkward patting of the scratchy arms of his tweed jacket.

And then we were climbing the steps, the gold handrail smooth and cool under my palm, against the blistering scrape left by my satchel strap in my flight through the mob.

We squeezed through the aisle in single file, then sank into four seats, with Jack and me facing father and daughter, our knees nearly touching theirs.

"Oh, that was such an adventure!" Eve fanned herself with her tiny ticket. "I didn't know if we'd make it. And Sahara! We almost lost you!"

Her words were reminiscent of Howard's when I reappeared after four days in the ancient past, and Harry Burton's words after Jack and I spent the night in Seti's tomb. Was I destined to keep making a nuisance and a fool of myself?

We rode in silence for nearly an hour, all of us still recovering from our race through Cairo.

Perhaps I was recovering from even more. The exhaustion of the past few weeks seemed to be hitting me at once.

But as Alexandria neared, it was time to face the music.

"Lord Carnarvon," I swallowed and smoothed my dress over my thighs, "I need to tell you something."

His eyebrows waggled an invitation.

"I'm not going with you to England."

Eve gasped and covered her mouth with her fingertips. "Oh, I knew it! You two are running away together, aren't you?"

I sighed. "No. Well, not exactly." I glanced at Jack, reddening. "We are going to Rome. There's… there's something I need to do there. Some… research I want to do."

Eve's jaw dropped. "Going to Rome—together—not married?"

Porchy huffed. "What nonsense is this? What research?"

I exhaled slowly, through pursed lips. "It's just, I'd like to take some time researching my family history."

"In Rome."

He said it as a statement, not a question. As if he'd already concluded my idea was ridiculous.

"Yes."

"And this chap is going with you?"

"Yes."

Porchy gazed out the window, lips tight. Then turned back to me.

"Sahara, I must say I am disappointed in your erratic behavior over the past several weeks. I was your champion, as you know, with Carter. Insisted he let you join his team. But my faith in you has been shaken."

I licked dry lips and studied the slums of Alexandria's outskirts, sliding past the window.

Jack leaned forward. "That's not exactly fair—"

"Young man, if I want your opinion, I will ask for it."

I glanced sideways in time to see Jack's eyebrows shoot up, but fortunately he kept his thoughts to himself.

"Your Lordship, I promise when we come back in two months, to open and start the project, I will be fully here, ready to give it my best."

He studied me. "You know Albert Lythgoe has been talking to me about publishing some of your sketches?"

My heart leapt. "I did not know that."

"Yes, well, I was waiting to see how it all turned out. But now… Perhaps you're not ready for this kind of opportunity."

I was ready. More than ready. Publication of my sketches of the process to unearth and catalogue the most famous Egyptian tomb ever discovered? This chance would give me a purpose and legacy, justify my entire life, be my gift to the world.

But first I simply needed to travel back a couple thousand years, save my sister from Jack's creepy aunt, change history so my parents never abandoned me, and get back in time to pick up where I left off.

Good gravy, who did I think I was?

CHAPTER TWELVE

December 11, 1922
Rome, Italy

our days later, we stumbled onto Italian ground from yet another train, this time in the great terminal station of Rome itself, the *Stazione Centrale delle Ferrovie Romane.*

The stormy days on the ship from Alexandria to the port of Civita Vecchia, seventy kilometers north of Rome, had taken me to the brink of exhaustion, unable to keep food in my stomach or sleep more than a few hours at a time.

I barely saw Jack, who weathered the crossing of the Mediterranean with his usual good-natured ease, spending the rainy days reading under a deck canopy or chatting with other passengers, while I sprawled on a cot in my claustrophobic stateroom, praying for the end.

He visited me several times, but I only cracked the door, and refused the scandal of letting him in.

Now we paused on the train platform, and Jack took my trunk from my hand. He squinted at me through the spattering rain. "You're looking better. But I still say we should wait a day or so to recover before doing this."

TRACY HIGLEY

I headed for the narrow station house at the far end of the platform. "Not a chance. Your aunt—"

"I get it. You believe she's looking for Persia for some purpose you don't trust. You're here to stop her, perhaps even change what happened in '05." His tone sounded weary, as though he'd given up arguing with me.

"And you're here to prove her innocence." I didn't stop moving, just tossed the statement over my shoulder.

His purpose was no secret, but I didn't resent him for it. The truth was all that mattered. And using the truth to fix the past.

"This pace is going to kill you, Sahara." Jack was jogging to keep up, a trunk in each hand.

I slowed. "Sorry."

"I'm not talking about how fast you're walking! You've barely slept in weeks, you spend every free moment researching ancient Rome or worrying about your family. Even when you emerged from your cabin, I don't think you spoke to more than two people during our entire crossing!"

"There will be plenty of time for relaxation and socializing after I've put everything right."

"Ha! I don't think you even understand the meaning of those words."

His tone wasn't entirely jesting.

I winced, but kept walking. Why was Jack always trying to help me, if he found me so uptight and boring?

We crossed into the station house, crowded with travelers clamoring for tickets. Several tired-looking men with grand mustaches slouched behind metal grates, stamping and sliding tickets across the counter. To the right of the counters, a young boy stood guard at a narrow door.

"Here," I nodded toward the boy. "We can store our trunks."

The boy took the luggage, scrawled a little ticket for us, and grinned at the tip I slipped into his hand.

We headed for the street, and I rehearsed my mental list. Luggage safely stashed away. Check.

"Let's get a map."

Minutes later, we emerged from the station's stone arches to a steadier rainfall, a map of Rome's streets and ruins in hand. The square opened before us, with tourists and locals alike braving the rain.

I pinched the edges of the unfolded map between wet fingers and held it close to my chest to keep the rainfall from soaking it.

"Hey, an obelisk!" Jack was pointing left, to the stone needle erected outside the station. "I didn't know they had those in Rome."

I frowned. "Only because they brought them here from Egypt. That one's from Heliopolis, when Ramesses the Second was pharaoh. They brought it here about thirty years ago, to commemorate the soldiers killed in the Battle of Dogali during the Eritrean-Ethiopian War."

"You really do know everything, don't you?"

"I don't know how to stay dry while we walk two kilometers to the Domus Aurea."

Jack pointed to an awning along the street outside the train station. "Ah, there's where my expertise can be of use."

A clever businessman huddled, stoop-shouldered and hugging his chest against the chilly wetness, behind a table littered with a muted rainbow of colored umbrellas.

"Brilliant discovery."

We crossed the busy street to make our first purchase out of the quickly dwindling supply of my funds.

Jack snapped our new umbrella upright, and we put our heads together to study the map.

"Here." I jabbed a finger at the outline of the Colosseum. "This is where the Domus Aurea stood, in the narrow valley between the Palatine and Capitoline Hills. Most of it is under the Colosseum now."

My father's code, scratched out on papyrus and left in a pharaoh's tomb, instructed me to meet them in the courtyard of Nero's "Golden House" under the statue the narcissist emperor erected of himself.

"Once we're there, the thirty-meter bronze statue should be

impossible to miss. It's the centerpiece of Nero's three-hundred-acre palatial complex."

"And that's where the grotto was found?"

"Right." One of the corridors of Nero's palace, now underground, had been discovered in the fifteenth century. Referred to as a "grotto," it had sparked a renaissance in art, and an artistic movement eventually known as *Grotesque*.

"Have you ever painted in that style?"

I shrugged. "I'm not a real artist. I sketch and doodle what I see." I smiled up at him. "You're the true artist—because you can bring out what no one sees."

A wave of emotion, unreadable, passed across his eyes. He lifted a hand and brushed a damp curl from my forehead, then ran the back of his hand down my jawline.

The gesture was so unexpected, and so tender, I had to swallow to keep my own emotions under control.

I pointed to the map again, to the Colosseum. "So, we can't make the jump at the Domus Aurea itself. It doesn't currently exist in this time. Besides, we need to find somewhere quiet." I traced a path down the Via Cavour to the northwest corner of the Forum. The massive plaza, crowded with statues, monuments, governmental buildings, and marketplaces was sure to have a quiet corner we could slip into. "Maybe somewhere in here."

"Seems risky. No matter where we do it."

"I know we need to find an out-of-the-way spot, but it also needs to be relatively intact today, as it was in 68 AD."

"Listen to you, talking like an experienced time traveler."

I shrugged one shoulder. "Doesn't take too much experience to realize you don't want to materialize in the ancient past under a pile of rubble, in a building that didn't exist at all, or in front of spectators."

"So, where? Something tells me you have that question already answered by now."

I refolded the map and started walking.

Jack strolled alongside, holding the umbrella over both our heads.

"I think the *Curia Julia*. In the back corner. It's one of the best-preserved buildings right now, and served as the Senate House before and during Nero's reign."

"Senate House? Sounds like a busy place."

"Perhaps. But we should be able to find a back room tucked away somewhere. It's as good a place as any, since there's no way to really know."

Jack checked his watch and glanced at the sky. "Under these heavy clouds, meeting your family at exactly sunset is going to be tricky."

"You forget we are traveling from December to June."

Jack laughed. "The expert speaks again."

I leaned into the chilly rain. Too bad we didn't have the money for a taxi. The umbrella helped, but I was already regretting the choice of my wool suit. What I gained in warmth was lost in the heavy material's absorption of every raindrop. All around me, the city smelled like wet wool and wet stone.

At least it didn't smell like gunfire and violence. Only six weeks ago, Benito Mussolini's Fascist Party took over the Kingdom of Italy, without even an armed conflict after their march on Rome. To my eyes, the city seemed unchanged since my visit years ago. No doubt there were political undertones invisible to Jack and me.

We reached the Forum in about twenty minutes, stopped at the tiny ticket booth manned by a woman who looked ancient herself, and shelled out yet more cash.

Between the low tourist season of December and the driving rain, only a few straggling visitors walked ahead of us through the gate and down the crumbling steps into the sprawl of ruins.

Nearly all the original buildings were now roofless, creating a maze-like feeling as one looked down across the rectangular plaza, with only a few restored. The impressive structures of this ancient civilization should've inspired me with the confidence mankind could do anything we set our minds to. Instead all I could see was collapse. As if to echo my morbid thoughts, thunder rolled across the Palatine Hill, rumbling down from a sky the color of old gravestones.

I pulled the map from my jacket pocket and unfolded it, careful not to tear apart the soggy folds. The black ink of building outlines blurred into white spaces.

This close to traveling, and to possibly finding my family, my nerves were starting to sharpen, and a queasy feeling tripped through my stomach.

Jack seemed to sense my hesitation, and slipped an arm around my waist, to pull me into the crook of his arm under our umbrella.

I inhaled and nodded toward the far end of the Forum.

"Let's do this."

CHAPTER THIRTEEN

September 18, 1737
Rome, Italy

R enae peered over the lip of an indistinct hole in the ground, excitement building along her veins.

"Is that really it? That little opening?" Alex's dubious question was fair, given the unimpressive location.

Renae shrugged. "In another hundred-fifty years, the place will be crawling with tourists." The new day's sun filtered through the streets and cast a shadow from the Colosseum, but under their feet the grass sparkled in the morning dew.

Persia pulled a length of rope from Alex's hand and began uncoiling it into the man-sized hole.

Alex tied off the other end to a stake that had been rammed into the ground by previous explorers.

"Are you sure this thing's going to hold?" Renae jiggled the post.

"You're getting overly cautious in your old age." He patted a hand against the small of her back.

Did Alex share her anxiety?

"Well, this has to work."

Please, please work. They had so little left. No more ideas. No more chances.

"I'll go first." Persia wrapped two hands around the white rope tied into evenly-spaced knots.

"Ha!" Renae elbowed her daughter out of the way. "Not a chance. You'll go between us, just like always. She grabbed up the end of the rope.

The breath in her chest caught and held. She gripped the rope with tense fingers, then turned her back to the hole and began a slow descent.

"What do you see?" Persia's voice filtered down from the ground above.

"Nothing. Too dark."

Minutes later, Persia and Alex stood beside her in the famous grotto that fired the imagination of artists like Michaelangelo and Raphael, and set off the Renaissance in the west.

Alex struck a match and held it aloft. The flame flickered and bounced off the ceiling of the cavernous vault, catching a glimmer here and there of burgundy or indigo splashed across the muted multicolor frescoes of the corridor and domed ceiling.

"Even in the dark, you can see it's different than Egypt." Persia touched her fingers to the smooth wall reflected under Alex's flare.

Renae skimmed a glance over the murals, but couldn't focus.

"I can't wait to see it restored to glory!" Persia looked upward to the opening they'd left above. "Do you think Sahara will be there as soon as we arrive? Even though we're going early? Or not until later, closer to sunset?"

"We don't know that she'll be there at all!" Renae winced at the bite of her own words.

Persia sighed and rolled her eyes at Alex. "Cautious *and* pessimistic."

"Well, it's a longshot, and we all know it."

Alex circled her waist with an arm.

She pulled away. Her skin felt like it was on fire.

They came early, to give themselves the day in Rome. For Persia, it would be all about sightseeing. The Circus Maximus was high on her list of ancient places to visit. But Renae agreed to the extra time solely to ensure they could be where they needed to be, at the right moment. The statue of Nero. Sunset.

Persia rubbed her hands together in the chilly cavern. "Well, maybe Sahara is an Amplified, and she'll find a way to beat the odds." She shrugged. "Or maybe I am. And then I'll be able to fix everything I put wrong."

Renae turned to study the wall. Persia shouldn't have to see the spark of hope in her eyes, even if it was snuffed out by a curtain of guilt.

All her life Persia had felt responsible for separating their family.

"Stop, Persia. You can't think that way. It's too much pressure for anyone. And you're only seventeen."

Persia grinned. "Right. At least three years of freedom left, before I have to take on saving the world, or die trying."

"Not funny."

"Enough." Alex pulled a pouch of coins from his pocket. "Let's get there, before the rest of the tourists show up for the day."

Persia held up the rope they'd climbed down. "What happens if we come back later, and someone's taken the rope away?" She looked around the underground subterranean chamber and shivered. "I don't want to spend the night in this eerie place."

"We're not coming back *later*, Persia, and you know it." Renae frowned. Hopefully the girl could see her expression in the dim light. Persia's casual willingness to revise history was like a stone in Renae's belly. Revisions got them into this mess more than thirty years ago, and they'd been fighting their way out ever since.

Persia shrugged, but didn't challenge, for once. It was an old argument, like well-worn grooves in a rutted street.

"Are you ladies ready?" Alex lifted the satchel strap that crossed his chest and handed it to Persia.

She strapped it across her own body and nodded.

He held out a hand to Persia and placed a flat palm against the wall behind him.

Renae took Persia's other hand, mimicking Alex's posture against the wall.

Persia stepped backward between her parents.

Yes, at least three years, before Persia would start jumping through time on her own, not needing to be anchored between her parents to make the jump. The stone in Renae's belly shifted. She and Alex had given up everything to stay with Persia, but it would not surprise them if their daughter chose a different path. Chose to find her way through history without her parents.

Even now, the girl was practically bouncing on her toes in anticipation of the adventure to come.

Renae tried to share her excitement, tried to believe everything would work out, then bent her head, leaned in, placed her thoughts on the day of Nero's death, and felt the year 1737 dissolve around them.

These days, she barely noticed the spinning, the free-falling. And the nausea was a thing of the past.

Her feet gained solid ground, the air shifted, and she opened her eyes to seek out the reassurance of her husband and child still with her.

Alex smiled and nodded.

Persia let out a quiet *whoop* of delight, pulled her hands from her parents' grasp, and pointed to the frescoes. "I knew it! I knew they would be amazing!"

She ran her hands over the art, pointing out details to Alex.

Renae stepped away from the distracting buzz of their conversation.

The freshly-constructed corridor was silent in the early morning light, but they shouldn't wait too long.

"Let's get out of the palace, find the statue."

Persia glanced at her and started laughing.

"Something funny?" She put a hand to her hip and cocked her head.

Alex was laughing as well.

"Your hair." Persia pointed above Renae's head. "I've never seen it so... high."

Renae touched tentative fingertips to the hairstyle bequeathed to her in ancient Rome. Elaborate curls piled six inches above her forehead, woven with strands of what felt like pearls.

She allowed herself a smile. "Well, your father looks like he's wearing enough bedsheets to outfit a dormitory."

A few minutes later they slipped through the halls of the palace, passing only a few servants who paid little attention, and twisted their way toward what was hopefully the courtyard of the massive palatial complex.

Sunlight greeted them at the end of a long hall, and they increased their pace toward it. The courtyard opened before them, more like an expansive public park, lined by the columned far-off wings of the palace, and filled to bursting with fruiting trees and flowering shrubbery in cotton-candy pinks and shades of purple. The air seemed honey-scented, and the sound of trickling fountains surrounded them.

The entire vista was a study in contrasts... bright sunlight striking marble statuary and throwing deep shadows, sharp-edged flagstones surrounded by fragrantly-soft flower petals. A gentle, warm light bathed all the ostentatious excess.

But the centerpiece of it all would not be refused attention—a ninety-foot-tall bronze statue of the naked emperor himself, holding a rudder and directing a globe.

How many peasants had been taxed to death to pay for all that bronze?

Renae turned her head from the disgusting display.

Unfazed, Persia clapped her hands like a tour guide. "Where to first? Too early for the Circus Maximus, right? Shall we explore the Forum? Just meander through the streets?"

Alex was already striding forward, pointing toward the House of Caesar Augustus on the bordering Palatine Hill, commenting on the locations of the Capitoline Hill opposite.

Renae followed in their wake. How could Alex and Persia be so casual, as though this were simply a sightseeing trip?

The three emerged from the palace complex within minutes, into the streets of Rome, already beginning to fill with merchants, citizens on their way to meetings or entertainment, servants scurrying to purchase and return with bread and cheese needed for their masters' morning meal.

The chattering of people, assorted animal noises, and squeak of wagon wheels on the stones grated on Renae's nerves.

"Who's hungry?" Persia glanced at both her parents. "I'm hungry."

Alex laughed. "Renae, I don't think we brought enough coin for this girl's holiday in Rome."

At that comment, he patted the leather of the satchel Persia had returned to them, lines deepening between his eyes.

Renae stopped, watched. Bringing things back was always tricky, never guaranteed.

But then his hand stopped searching, and he met her glance and nodded.

All good.

In the street ahead of them, the crowd thickened and seemed to pause as one. Beyond the heads of the crowd, dust filled the air with the noise of drum beats.

Some kind of ancient parade?

But then Renae caught the words *Praetorian Guard* on the air around her. Not drumming they heard. Hoofbeats.

She glanced back at Persia and Alex to make sure they were staying well clear of the busy street.

But where was Persia?

She fought down a familiar spike of panic.

Her daughter stood among a stall of food merchants, between hanging hanks of raw meat and piles of melons, apples, and pomegranates. The eyes of several young children were on her, as she juggled three bright yellow quince.

The children laughed and clapped.

Persia caught one quince in her palm, then the next, and the third. Handed them back to the vendor, who shook his head and held up a hand for her to keep them.

She returned to Renae and Alex, handed a quince to each, and started biting into her own before Renae had a chance to scold her for wandering off.

Wandering off? *Renae, you sound as though she's still five years old.*

But with one daughter lost to her as a girl, and the other becoming a woman, Renae was caught between.

She and Alex followed Persia's stroll along the crowded edge of the street.

The Praetorian Guard's cohort was almost upon them.

"Let's cross." Alex pointed to the other side of the street, with its wider promenade.

They hurried, ahead of the leading horses of the mounted Guard, then stood in a tight cluster to watch the pageantry. The leader of the cohort, assumedly a prefect, rode a few paces ahead of the tight line of horses.

It seemed odd to see military men in formation without uniform or armor, but Augustus had years ago imposed the formal toga as the required clothing for his soldiers while in the city, to reduce the chance of alienating the citizens.

"Beautiful, aren't they?" Renae glanced to Persia, who loved this sort of thing.

But her daughter's attention was across the street, on one of the children who had been watching her juggle moments ago.

The little girl was hopping on one foot and laughing, as though competing for her mother's attention with the oncoming Guard.

The woman beside her ignored the girl's antics.

A moment later, the child broke from her mother and darted into the street, her eyes on the horses. Oblivious to their high-stepping hooves.

"No!" Renae and Persia called in unison.

At the warning, the girl halted in the center of the street.

The prefect's horse shied left at the intrusion, then pawed

backward. The line of horses behind jostled into the back of the prefect's mount.

The animal snorted, kicked its front legs into an upward spiral.

And then the heavy hoofs crashed downward, toward the child's upraised face.

It all happened in an instant.

A child's wide eyes. Thick forelegs and split hoofs poised above.

And Alex, swooping in, under the horse, to pluck the child off her feet.

CHAPTER FOURTEEN

The *Curia Julia*, Rome's third Senate House, stood at the opposite end of the Forum. We picked our way through the dripping ruins, and I pointed out buildings and recited their names from the map, mostly to take my mind off the desperate anxiety building in my chest.

After the systematic damage I'd done to my career in Egypt, this plan had to work, had to be worth it, to save my family.

And the thought had occurred to me—saving my family could also save my career. If my parents never died, never disappeared and left me alone... how far could I have gotten in my profession, with a father to advocate for me?

Even Jack's warning about two sets of memories possibly damaging my mind was not enough to discourage me from wanting to remember a different past.

A rivulet of water ran down my cheek and into my mouth. I leaned closer to Jack, huddled under the umbrella.

Why had I worn a skirt and these low heels? My toes squished inside the wet shoes, and I shivered.

Jack stopped abruptly and handed me the umbrella.

"What?"

He stripped off his suit jacket and spread it over my shoulders.

"No, I'm fine—"

He ignored me, retrieved the umbrella, and resumed walking.

We passed the Temple of Divus Iulius, paused for a moment to gaze at the six marble columns, placed so narrowly they made the temple seem to tower over the Forum.

"Divus Iulius?" Jack asked.

"Divine Julius. The Senate deified Julius Caesar a couple of years after he was murdered."

"Hmm. I'm guessing he would have preferred to be alive and mortal than a dead god."

When we finally reached the Senate House, the rain let up enough to lower the umbrella.

"The exterior has been rebuilt and restored a few times," I pointed to the marble facade. "After it was destroyed in various fires."

Jack nodded, as though the information were important.

We both knew I was stalling.

He nudged my shoulder with his own. "Ready?"

"As I'll ever be, I suppose."

We ascended the single flight of steps and pushed open the bronze doors, replicas of the original doors which now resided in a Catholic basilica across the city.

Inside, three broad steps ringed the large room, tiers which would have contained chairs for about three hundred senators. The decorative floor drew all the attention—a grid of repeated rosettes and leaves in red and green, on a background of purple and yellow.

A young couple wandered the far end of the hall, in front of the pedestal of the now-missing Altar of Victory. The twenty-something girl, layered in abundant frills of peachy organza with a matching cap smashed over her curls, circled to stand behind a headless red marble statue. She positioned her face above its empty shoulders.

"Look, Tony, I'm an ancient Roman!" She saluted, knocking her hat to the marble floor.

Her companion whooped as if it were the funniest thing he'd ever seen.

Jack scanned the room, then inclined his head toward the southwest corner. "How about over there?"

In front of the silly couple?

But we already discussed that I would not be doing any history-changing on this trip.

Go back, see my parents, meet my sister. Give information, get information. Then return here the moment before we left. All of my history-changing would need to happen in the Venice of the 1800s. The couple here in the Senate House would never miss us.

I followed Jack along the tiered steps, into the corner and beyond, behind a pillar.

Jack set the umbrella on the floor at the base of the column.

I dug the only thing that mattered from my pocket. The ancient coin about to become new.

I held it flat in my palm, then flipped it to show the splotch of black tar Jack adhered to it during our sea crossing.

"So we don't accidentally spend it on ancient gelato," he'd said.

It was a good plan. If we ended up with more money for any reason, we wouldn't want to lose track of the only way we'd be able to return to this time.

I pinched the coin between my thumb and forefinger and held it toward Jack so he could do the same.

Instead, he took the coin from me, tucked it into the center of my open palm, then covered my hand with his own and intertwined our fingers.

The coin felt warm between us, connecting us.

He drew me close and circled me with his other arm.

"June 9, 68 AD," I said. "The day of Nero's death."

"June 9, 68 AD."

And then, as though we had joined in some kind of strange,

ritualistic dance, we tightened our handclasp, closed our eyes, and bent forward as one.

Here we go.

Spinning. Less nausea than the last time.

Knees nearly buckling. I put a hand out for support, but felt only empty air.

And then the world steadied. The wave of vertigo receded.

I blinked my eyes open, straightened, and sucked in a ragged breath.

I was in the Senate House. And I was alone.

"Jack?" It was only a whisper, but it echoed back from the gleaming marble walls, too loud. I clutched the coin in tight fingers. "Jack?"

I took a step toward the main chamber.

The murmur of low voices, nearby, held me in place.

"I am telling you, we will never get close enough to take him."

"He has too many loyal, always around him."

"How is it possible the monster has anyone left who is loyal?"

"We need only one person to turn. Some poison, a dagger to the chest—"

"No! He cannot die a quiet death. They'll make a martyr of him. He must be executed, publicly!"

"We must see him arrested, and let the Praetorian Guard do the rest."

Three figures huddled only a few meters from me, heads together for this conversation. At the scuffle of my sandal, they turned as one.

A woman about my own age stared at me—petite, with her hair piled high into a sort of triangular shape, and gold jewelry tangled through it. Two older men stood opposite each other, one short and straining the seams of his toga, the other white-haired and tall with an aristocratic profile like so many Roman statues I'd seen over the years.

The woman took a step toward me. "What—where did you come from?" She looked me up and down with narrowed eyes. "Whose mistress are you?"

The disorienting mismatch of words and lips resolved itself quickly.

Mistress?

I glanced down at myself. My heavy, wet wool had disappeared, but its replacement was less than ideal. Rather than a modest *stola* wrapped over a tunic, I wore a revealing bit of purple and yellow fabric that reminded me of graffiti found in the brothels of Pompeii. My upper arms were bare except for gold bands that encircled them, each set with red garnets. A matching band wrapped around my ankle.

"Apologies." I dipped my head and started across the Senate House floor toward the door. A quick escape seemed the best course of action.

But where was Jack?

The woman stepped into my path. "Not so fast. Answer my question."

"I'm no one's mistress." I lifted my chin. "I was looking for a friend, who is obviously not here. Excuse me for interrupting you."

"Florin, run outside and fetch some guards to come and take this woman."

The portly one grinned stupidly, his thick neck wobbling. A mostly-bald head shone in the light streaming from high windows, and his wide smile reminded me of a circus clown. He hurried across the tiled floor to do the woman's bidding.

"Mistress or not, it's clear your being here is no coincidence. Who sent you?"

"No one sent me. I'm leaving now."

But she stepped in front of me again.

"Get out of my way. Please."

The please was a last-minute addition. Probably unwise to make enemies this soon into our day.

She slapped me.

She actually slapped me!

"As soon as my husband returns with guards, you won't be so bold."

I lifted a hand to my warm cheek, jaw dropped open. What was more shocking—that she'd struck me, or that the old circus clown was her husband?

The doors burst open and the man did return, guards in tow.

Unbelievable. Arriving in an ancient time, being suspected of being a spy. It was like watching the same film, but with different costumes. Instead of the Egyptian John Barrymore in the form of the Vizier Ay, we had this stooge from a vaudeville act and his terrifying wife.

Two guards grabbed me, each from one side, while another two stood by with swords drawn.

"Take your hands off me!" I struggled to free myself.

Behind me, a voice called across the Senate House floor.

"There you are, my dear. I thought I told you to meet me outside."

I exhaled my relief, at the most welcome voice of Jack Moretti.

"And I see you've been making some friends." He crossed the chamber to take the hand of the woman who slapped me between his own hands, smile, and lean forward until his forehead was nearly touching hers. "Thank you for taking care of my... *friend*. She sometimes gets away from me."

Was the woman actually blushing? Jack's gift with people was going to be legendary in every era.

"Might I have the name of such a lovely lady?"

Her lips twitched into a smile. "Decima Marcellus the Elder."

He bowed over her hand.

Jack's physical appearance was largely unchanged in this time, but he wore an elaborate toga he'd probably never be able to rewrap.

Her husband was less taken in by Jack. "I don't trust either of them." He glanced toward the aristocratic gentleman. "Epaphroditus, do you know him?" He thrust a weak chin toward Jack.

The taller man shook his head. "And I believe they've heard too much."

The woman pulled her hand from Jack's and spoke to the two guards. "Get rid of them. Somewhere they won't be found."

One of them abandoned my arm and grabbed for Jack.

"Wait." Epaphroditus peered down on me, salt-and-pepper eyebrows drawn together. "Have them searched first."

It took only a moment for one of the guards to pat me down, though he lingered far too long in some areas.

But it was the item he pried out of my clutched fingers that bothered me most.

He handed the coin to Decima.

She examined both sides, scraped at the black spot with her fingernail, then sniffed it. "Some kind of bitumen." She lifted a hateful gaze toward me. "Clearly a token to communicate where loyalties lie." She held the coin for the other two men to inspect. "Nero's coin. And this marking."

She flipped it into the air, caught it with a flourish, and just like that, my father's coin—our ticket home—disappeared into the elaborate folds of her *stola*.

"So, as I suspected." Her dark eyes glittered. "Loyal to Nero, and spying on those who want something better for Rome."

She flicked her head toward the guards, with a repeat of her previous command.

"Get rid of them."

CHAPTER FIFTEEN

June 9, 68 AD
Rome, Italy

A rearing horse, a frightened child, a screaming mother.
The commotion in the street blurred and all Renae could see was those hooves coming down, not on the child, but on Alex's shoulder, where he hunched his body over the frightened little girl.

The horse crashed against his shoulder with what seemed only a glancing blow, but enough to shove Alex to the ground.

Persia screamed and jumped into the street.

Renae grabbed her daughter and yanked her back before she suffered the same fate under the hooves of the next row of horses.

"Galeria!" The scream came from the other side of the street, followed by a stately woman in flowing sun-yellow robes. She dashed into the street, one elegant hand held aloft as if to stop the oncoming march of the Praetorian Guard.

A crowd gathered immediately, preventing the flow of chariot traffic.

The mounted prefect jumped from his horse and leaned over

Alex. "Are you hurt, man?" He reached for Alex's shoulder, where his robes were torn and muddied.

The yellow-robed woman pulled her child, crying, from under Alex's chest.

Renae fell to her knees beside her husband, palm against his face.

Alex pulled himself to standing.

"I am well." His voice shook.

Renae pulled his toga aside where the fabric had ripped. The skin just below the shoulder was already purpling under an angry red welt.

Beside them, the curly-haired child held a finger between her ruby lips and pressed her dark head against her mother's hip.

The sweet smell of oranges seemed to surround them.

The soldier dipped his head to the mother. "My lady, the Prefect Aurelius humbly asks you to forgive the near miss."

But the woman's eyes were on Alex. "How can I thank you? Surely, you saved my little one's life."

Nothing draws a crowd more than a crowd. The streets soon clogged with onlookers. With the matchstick lines of Praetorian Guards blocking one end of the street, a mob soon blocked the other and swelled behind it.

The young mother bent to her child, brushing hair from the little girl's face and then shaking her shoulders, in that motherly impulse to both soothe and scold, so familiar to Renae.

The prefect, Aurelius, leaned in to mutter to Alex. "You picked the right child to save, my friend. Do you know who that is?"

Alex shook his head, and rolled his shoulders as if to release the pain.

"Father, are you hurt?" Persia was at his side, gripping his arm.

Renae eyed the crowed. "Alex, we need to get out of here. We are causing a scene."

But the child's mother refused to let them go so easily. She turned to Aurelius. "This man is a hero. He should be lauded as such."

"As you wish, my lady."

Alex held up a hand. "That's not necessary, I assure you." He tried to move away. "We were simply passing by, and saw the danger." He pulled Renae and Persia toward a gap in the crowd.

A large hand descended past Renae's head and landed on Alex's unhurt shoulder.

"Not that simple, I'm afraid." Aurelius's grip steered Alex back toward the side of the street. "When a consul's wife insists you be lauded, it's not for a lowly soldier to refuse."

Consul's wife? Seriously?

Renae sighed.

Why could they never seem to enter or exit a location without drawing the attention of someone significant?

A nearby dais at the edge of the cobbled street seemed placed for such impromptu commendations. The prefect directed Alex up its wooden steps, motioning to Renae and Persia to follow in his wake.

The Romans did love a good speech. Stone platforms were not only for the public Forum, even the streets had an occasional raised dais for anyone to claim.

Aurelius was making good use of it.

"The wife of Publius Galerius Trachalus wishes to acknowledge this man…" he bent to Alex and awaited a name.

"Alexander."

Renae huffed, exasperated.

Alex shrugged and grinned at Persia.

"…wishes to acknowledge Alexander—aptly named after the great Alexander of Macedon—for his heroism in saving the young child of Trachalus from being killed by a spooked horse." He turned to Alex and extended a hand over the widening crowd. "Do you wish to address the people of Rome?"

Good grief. Were they so hard up for entertainment?

Alex held up a hand, shook his head and looked to his feet, the very picture of humility.

The crowd cheered. Hopefully the "lauding" was now sufficient.

Aurelius's attention had strayed, however.

Renae glanced at his eyes which had turned steely and serious, then followed his gaze across the heads of the crowd.

Some kind of disturbance closer to the palace. Soldiers running. Yelling.

The prefect was gone an instant later, down the steps, then mounting his horse and turning its head toward the commotion.

"Make way!" He waved a hand at the mob, nosed his horse into the thick of it, and forced the spectators to flee to the sides of the street.

The Praetorian Guard once again pounded through the Roman street, leaving a gaping hole behind them immediately filled in by the curious crowd.

Renae pressed hot fingertips against her gritty eyes.

"Please, Alexander, can we get down from here?"

Alex took her by the elbow and guided her off the dais, but at the foot of the platform, held her back from the street.

"What is it, Renae? You've been on edge since we arrived." His voice was low, with a glance at Persia.

Renae swallowed and rubbed at a spot on her throat. "I don't know. A premonition? Maybe just nerves. What if—"

Alex put two fingers over her lips. "We will find her."

She took a huge breath, let it out, and nodded.

"And until then, let's take our other daughter to see some chariot racing."

Persia brightened and fell into step behind them.

Alex directed them, up toward the crest of the Palatine Hill.

Persia had gaped when Alex first told her the Circus Maximus could host 150,000 spectators at its games and races. Growing up, first in tiny, water-locked Venice and then in the remote countryside of northern Italy, she'd seen little of large events. Ever since their plan took shape to meet Sahara in Rome, Persia insisted they see the stadium, which Nero had already restored since the fire four years ago.

Renae trailed her husband and daughter by a few paces as they crested the Palatine.

Persia drew up short and laughed aloud, as she got her first glimpse of the valley between them and the Aventine Hill.

"It's magnificent!"

Renae smiled despite the anxiety in her belly. It was good to see Persia happy. She joined the two and gazed down on the oblong arena, with its massive tiers of stone seating.

Persia led the way down a shrubbery-lined path, trailing her hand along the greens at the edge. "We will have to return to our time later now, of course." She pulled a leaf from a shrub. "For the child."

Alex kneaded his injured shoulder with one hand. "Persia, we've talked about this—"

The girl's glare could have melted steel. "If I hadn't been watching that child, seen her run into the street—you are *not* telling me we are going to let that little girl die."

"Renae, explain to her…"

But Renae said nothing. How could she tell Persia they would return to the moment before they left 1737, leaving their footprints here erased, leaving the child to the fate history had decreed for her?

Alex growled at her silence. "You are both too soft for this life."

Persia smiled. "Does that mean we will Revise?"

"No! No, it means no such thing! I've told you a million times, we are meant to only be Observers—"

"How can you say we are *meant to be—*"

"Because being a Revisionist has brought nothing but trouble!"

The girl slowed, head down, fingers tearing at the leaf.

"Persia," Alex drew to a stop and closed his eyes, then walked back and embraced her. "I did not mean—"

"I know what you meant, Papa." She ticked off clauses on successive fingers, as though the argument was as familiar as her own name. "I am not trouble. I did not cause the trouble. Nothing is my fault."

Renae squared off against her daughter. "Those are all true things, Persia."

"Really? Are you so certain? Not even that angry bruise on Papa's shoulder? Everywhere I go, trouble follows!"

She pushed past both of them and continued toward the arena, then tossed words back over her shoulder. "And we are going to return with our changes intact, revise history, and save that child!"

More statement of fact than challenge.

Renae glanced at Alex and shrugged. "She's your daughter."

But her dark thoughts belied the casual words. Perhaps that niggling premonition again.

Ancient Rome had the power to wreak havoc on their plans, and even their lives.

CHAPTER SIXTEEN

June 9, 68 AD
Rome, Italy

"Hold." The aristocratic gentleman called Epaphroditus held up a long-fingered hand. "I believe we could make better use of them than seeing them at the bottom of the Tiber."

Decima touched her fingertips to gold bands wrapped around her neck, inset with green stones. "Whatever you think, Epaphroditus. Certainly, I defer to your preference."

I watched Epaphroditus with new respect. Apparently Decima did not control the room as I had thought.

He returned my steady gaze. "If they are loyal to Nero, and sent to gain information by listening around corners, perhaps they could also be a *source* of information."

Decima's glittering eyes slid to me, and she looked me over as though I were a steak hanging in a market stall.

"Indeed."

Visions of torture chambers and medieval racks danced before my eyes.

Wrong era.

Decima's husband, Florin, rubbed his hands over his belly.

I truly was beginning to feel like their next meal.

The woman circled me, running a finger over my low-cut tunic. "So, what do you suggest we do with them, Epaphroditus?"

The older man waved a hand, as if the question were an annoying insect. "I care little. I only want to see us with as many assets as possible. And these two might provide some leverage that can be used against him."

Florin ran his tongue over his upper lip. "Let's take them home, Decima."

The hair on my arms rose at his gleeful smile.

"As always, your ideas are splendid, my dear husband."

Unseen by his wife, Florin rolled his eyes at the flattery.

Decima flipped a wrist at the guards. "Bind them securely, and bring them to our villa."

Epaphroditus bowed toward the strange couple. "I will take my leave, and send word once I have sought out the answers of which we spoke."

I reached for Jack and we grasped hands for only a moment before the guards pulled us apart.

Epaphroditus exited the Senate House, and in moments, the guards produced dirty, frayed ropes of braided flax, and bound our wrists behind our backs.

Jack struggled against the binding, but with four guards surrounding us, the odds weren't in our favor.

Decima and Florin, apparently satisfied, led the way into the sun-bright Forum.

The guards shoved us forward to follow.

Despite the circumstances, the Forum took my breath away. The effect of our time travel was magical. The same buildings we'd seen only a few minutes ago, but now as if they'd bloomed from the ruins, intact and gleaming.

The two conspirators disappeared into a waiting two-wheeled chariot pulled by matching horses.

We were shoved forward on foot.

We circled to the north and into the streets beyond the

Forum. The smells of the ancient city assaulted me—assorted animals trudging the street, unwashed bodies, food and smoke and rotting meat and the smell of incense from some nearby altar. I licked dry lips. When was the last time I had anything to drink? My mouth felt like I'd swallowed the gravel from under our feet.

"Keep it moving." The guard shoved Jack's shoulder.

Jack stumbled, righted himself, and spun. "Touch me again and I'll—"

The guard roared with laughter. "You'll what?"

The other guard joined the fun. "Oh, Decima is going to enjoy this one."

"And this one as well." He leered at me. "That woman is a special sort of vicious. Like a sharp-clawed cat with a little mouse."

We walked on and the sun beat down, sucking moisture from my skin. I kept my head down, avoiding the stares and jeers of the city's residents, families out shopping at market stalls, others trailing goats, perhaps to the temple for a sacrifice. A city full of happy families, doing what happy families did. I braved a glance at the harsh sun. How many hours until I would miss meeting up with my family? It would take at least an hour from the Forum to reach Nero's statue at his Golden House, and we were walking in the wrong direction.

Walking, and walking, and walking.

How far away did this woman live? The unfamiliar sandals scraped my heels into blisters, and the ropes at my wrists tore my skin raw. The ongoing exhaustion of the past weeks buckled my knees more than once.

Jack seemed always to be in the right place, supporting me with a shoulder, whispering encouragement to keep going. "They can't keep walking us forever. Just hold on until we get to the crazy woman's villa."

Once again I was in the most amazing place, in what should've been the most fantastic history lesson of my life, and instead was on my way toward disaster.

The buildings along the road thinned, until it seemed we were passing into the suburbs. Small monuments sprung up, some like altars or memorial niches, others little mausoleum buildings, a sure sign we were beyond the city limits.

To our left, the Tiber River snaked northward, the sun striking the water, brilliant as cut glass. Conical cypress trees poked like spikes from the hillside we trudged.

The slap of my sandals, in time with those of the soldiers, settled into a rhythm. I focused on the broad outline of the brute ahead of me, and ignored the one behind. The wavy lines of heat rising from the streets at the edges of my vision threatened to close in on me, in a dizzy wash of darkness.

I yanked my wrists apart, tried to force some slack into the ropes.

A scream of frustration built in my chest. A mounting desire to pound my fists against something, someone.

A villa grew on the hill ahead, looming larger as we climbed.

"Is that it? Have we finally arrived?" I spoke the words back over my shoulder, to the guard who followed us.

"You'll be wishing for your easy walk through the city streets soon."

I don't care. As long as they let me drink something.

Years ago, when I was new to the dig season, I neglected to drink enough water one day on the site. The dizziness, headache, the black spots before my eyes. I knew the signs of dehydration. No doubt the repeated vomiting during our ship's crossing hadn't helped.

Jack was walking sideways, his eyes not leaving my face.

"I'm okay. Just need something to drink."

The villa was more than a house. The country estate boasted multiple buildings, where the rich couple no doubt retreated from the heat of the city into the cooler hills. To own land in Rome was a sign of prestige, notice to your fellow citizens that you came from aristocratic ancestry. These two who'd taken us, from the size of their estate, seemed like an important part of Roman society.

The guards prodded us through a wide double-doorway at the front of the main building, past a narrow entryway, and into an open-air atrium with a columned peristyle running tight around the perimeter.

"In there." One of the guards shoved Jack's shoulder with a meaty fist to force him toward a side chamber.

I followed Jack into the villa's *triclinium*, the iconic Roman dining room, with its three-sided, bench-like table and masses of cushions for lounging.

In the corner of the room a bronze brazier, heaped with coals, burned hot and orange. The room needed no heat in the middle of a summer day, but the brazier light reached to the corners, the murals glistening as though they might melt and run.

Decima, Florin, and Epaphroditus reclined on propped cushions and took us in with interest as we entered. The table overflowed with platters of food and glazed pottery decorated in relief with fantastical animals. From their relaxed positions and fresh clothes, it was clear the three had taken faster and easier transportation than we.

"She needs water." Jack spoke the words through a clenched jaw. "Give her something to drink."

Decima smiled cooly and tilted her head to study Jack. "You both are a mystery to me. I assumed she was your mistress from the way she was dressed, but your care for her seems genuine."

Florin got to his feet awkwardly and lumbered across the triclinium to stand too close to me.

His breath was hot on my neck. Could his wife see the clammy hand he placed against my lower back?

My skin crawled.

Without warning Florin stepped behind me and put both hands on my shoulders, then shoved downward, slamming me to my knees. The stone floor shot pain through my thighs, into my hips, and through my spine.

"Hey!"

I turned to see Jack shoving his chest against Florin.

The man only chuckled, and stepped away.

Jack moved to put me behind him, where I still huddled on the floor.

Decima lifted an amphorae from the table and poured a slow, steady stream of glistening red wine into a jeweled cup.

I watched the trickle turn to a flow that filled the cup, overflowed and splashed in droplets onto the table.

I would've given much to lick the droplets she wasted.

Decima laughed. "Yes, look at the way she follows the wine." She lifted a cluster of plump, purple grapes from a platter, climbed to her feet, circled the table and held the grapes before my face. "Perhaps one of these?" She plucked a grape from a stem and popped it between her even, white teeth, then clamped down until the grape burst and spilled juice down her chin. She laughed and swiped at the juice.

I swayed on my knees, my vision darkening again.

Decima plucked another grape and held it near my lips.

Like a sharp-clawed cat with a little mouse.

I wasn't going to rise to the taunt.

I looked at the grape, then at her hand. "I prefer my fruit clean."

Decima's eyes registered surprise. "Oh, let me kill her, Epaphroditus. Please let me kill her."

Epaphroditus laughed. "Patience, my angry one. By tomorrow, Rome will be a different place, and we will not have to be so circumspect."

Jack pushed his way between us. "If you want to toy with someone, how about me?" His tone was an odd mix of hostility and flirtation.

Decima glanced at her husband, then back to Jack. "You seem to forget I'm a married woman."

Florin returned to his overstuffed cushion. "Oh, don't mind me, my dear. I don't care what you do."

Decima's back was to her husband. He didn't see the rapid blinking, the tightening of her lips. It would seem Decima wanted her husband to care.

Such a strange trio. Decima, young, beautiful, and petite, fawning over her aging, revolting husband, who didn't seem to notice. And Epaphroditus, cool and aloof, but clearly in charge.

"Please," I softened my tone to deference, "we are only here in Rome to meet my family. We will be gone by sunset. There is no need—"

"Family? Part of your group of traitors, no doubt?"

"No! My parents, my sister."

Decima's eyes narrowed. "Are you certain, Epaphroditus, that we shouldn't make an end of them right now? Our position is precarious. No one must know Florin and I have aligned ourselves against Nero."

Epaphroditus tilted his head and studied me. He would seem almost grandfatherly, if he weren't part of a plot to kill me.

"No, I suspect we will be glad we kept them alive."

"Well, if I can't kill her, I can at least make certain she can't identify herself to her fellow traitors."

From the folds of Decima's *stola*, a glint of bronze, and there was our coin, in her hand.

"Give that back to me!" I couldn't stop the words from erupting.

But she was already making her move, eying the brazier in the corner. With a flick of her wrist, like a coin toss at a carnival game, the coin spun and flipped through the air toward the fire.

"No!"

I barreled my shoulders against the back of her legs.

From behind, a sharp pain exploded between my shoulder blades.

The fuzzy blackness, threatening me all morning, fell with a muffling silence, and shut down all my senses.

CHAPTER SEVENTEEN

June 9, 68 AD
Rome, Italy

"*E*nough!"

A kick to my belly accompanied the harsh voice.

"Guests will be arriving soon. Time for you to take up your duties."

I blinked and rolled to my side. Reached hands around my body to get my bearings.

I was on the floor, a cold stone floor, lying on a dirty mat of woven reeds. In a dark room, with the only light coming from the courtyard beyond. Amphorae lay stacked against the wall beside me.

Above me, another woman, younger than I, glared down her nose. She wore a stained brown tunic, shapeless and unbelted, with a hand on her hip as if I were a troublesome child.

"Where am I? What's happening?" I searched the corners of the room. "Where is Jack?"

"Blood of Mars!" The girl's curse echoed off the walls. "Have you lost your wits? You're a slave in the house of Florin Appius Caecus. Now get up and act like one."

I got to my knees, then used a hand on the tiled floor to push myself to standing.

"There's been some sort of mistake. I'm not a slave."

The girl laughed, the sound abrupt and mocking. "Trust me, that's what we all say on our first day. You'll get accustomed to it."

Oh no, I won't. I was getting out of here. As soon as I found Jack. I followed the girl from the storage room, into the courtyard I glimpsed when we first entered.

She turned to the right, heading across the mosaic garden space.

I headed straight for the wide front doors.

"Slave!"

I kept walking. No matter what happened, I wasn't going to answer to that name.

But a quick escape was not happening.

Some kind of enforcer stood at the wooden double doors. His bearded face showed little more than a pair of flint-black eyes, boring into me, immodest neckline and all.

My shoulders fell and my chest seemed to cave in under me.

The enforcer touched a dagger strapped to his waist. "It sounds like you're being summoned to the kitchen."

Was this for real? Did people simply submit to slavery?

"I'm leaving. I am not a slave." I took several steps toward the doors.

He matched my movement, one step to my three. Fingers wrapping around the hilt of that dagger.

"The kitchen."

I had no choice but to yield.

Perhaps I could get more information in the kitchen.

I shuffled across the garden courtyard in the direction the girl took. The smell of cooking meat and the chatter of female voices directed me.

"Ah, there she is. Getting to know Lucius? He's a charmer, isn't he?"

The kitchen hugged the back of the villa, with a large

hollowed-out fireplace at the rear. A group of girls sat around the table, peeling apples and chopping cabbage. Like some kind of ancient sorority.

An older woman tended the fire and turned to me, scowling. She had dark gaps where teeth should have been, and her hair was patchy above her forehead. "Think you're better than the rest of us? Those clothes tell another tale."

I wrapped my arms around my middle and exhaled a thin breath. "I'm looking for my friend, the man who was brought here with me."

The women glanced between each other, heads shaking.

"We saw no one." The girl who had awakened me grinned. "But another male slave would always be welcome. The ones we have now are all old and ugly."

"What do you care, Nona? The master's got his eye on you, anyway."

Nona shrugged a dainty shoulder and gave a coy smile.

"I hear he's taken a fancy to this one, though." The older woman at the fire jabbed a thumb in my direction.

At this, Nona whipped her head toward me with a glare that could singe wood.

A woman of middle age, large and matronly, bustled into the kitchen, dusting something from her hands and scowling at the kitchen staff.

"Why is no one working?"

I gripped her arm. "Can you tell me if my friend is still here? Tall, with dark hair and blue eyes? He was brought here with me—"

"You're the only new slave today, girl." She plucked my hand from her arm. "And we've too much to do, to waste time with questions."

"But I need to get out of here. I have someplace I have to be soon."

The room erupted in laughter.

For glory's sake, it was beginning to look like I was truly trapped here.

No Jack. No coin.

A horrifying possibility wormed its way into my mind.

Had Jack somehow retrieved the coin, then felt he had no choice but to return to 1922 without me? It would explain why none of these women knew anything about him. If he had returned, it would be as if he were never here.

"Where is Decima? Florin? I need to speak with them."

And find out if I had been here alone or with a companion.

"You'll see them soon enough, when the meal begins." The newest arrival, clearly in charge, waggled a finger at me. "For now, the chamber pots need washing out in every sleeping chamber."

No, that is not happening. Not a chance.

"May I please have something to drink first?" I eyed the apples and cabbage on the table. "And perhaps something to eat?"

She pointed to a large earthen vessel in the corner, with a sort of ladle hanging from its stone lip. "Get your water, drink, then get to work."

The liquid in the jug was a watered-down wine, and I slurped it greedily. Hopefully more water than wine. I needed to keep my wits about me.

Perhaps there was a back entrance to this place, where I could slip through while they believed I emptied chamber pots.

"Nona, go with her. Make certain she does the job right."

"Yes, Junia." Nona rose from the table, a haughty smile playing about her lips. "With pleasure."

"And first, dress the girl in something more appropriate!"

I followed Nona from the room. Every contrary, conflicting goal fought for space in my brain. I needed to find Jack, or at least learn if he'd ever been here. Did the coin still exist? What would I do if it were melted to a glob of bronze at the bottom of that brazier? Could it still take me home?

And how many hours until I was meant to meet my parents at the Domus Aurea?

From the light, I would guess it was early afternoon. Thankfully, it was a long June day, but there was much ground to cover between here and Nero's Golden House.

Nona retrieved a rectangular white *palla* from a basket in the hall, then rolled her eyes at my obvious confusion over how to wrap it around my body. She jabbed fingers in various places, until my immodest tunic disappeared under the folds of fabric.

She motioned for me to follow, and stopped at the head of a long hall. "All of the bedchambers in this hall." She pointed. "Take every piss pot and dump it in the trough beside the house, then rinse them with water from a jug outside the front door. And don't get any ideas about walking away. Lucius knows his duties and enjoys them."

I nodded deferentially. "Understood. Thank you for your help."

Now get back to the kitchen so I can find a back way out of this place.

But she only stood there, arms crossed over her chest and eyebrows lifted.

I wandered to the first chamber. A well-cushioned wooden bedframe dominated the room, and in the corner beside the bed, a rusty, blackened pot sat in the corner.

Blood of Mars.

I picked up the pot with hesitant fingertips, and carried it from the room.

Nona remained in the hall.

"Please do not let me keep you from your duties." I smiled sweetly. "I am certain I can handle this task without supervision."

I pushed past her, circling wide with my body, but she half-stepped into my path and bumped my shoulder as I passed.

Memories surged of mean girls at boarding school. People were the same in every era.

Lucius seemed to have gotten the news I was low slave on the totem pole, and allowed me to pass. He wrinkled his nose at the pot in my hands.

"Where?" I lifted the pot.

He jutted his chin toward the north side of the villa.

I dumped the pot, but gagged as I did.

I tried to swallow, against the reflex, but it was pointless. The water and wine found its way out of my belly and joined the contents of the pot on the ground.

I stood, wiped my mouth with the back of my hand, and tried to inhale some measure of strength.

Was this the higher purpose I was chasing? Had I believed myself some kind of hero, traveling through time, gifted with special abilities to do the work of God?

The mess at my feet mocked all my grand delusions.

CHAPTER EIGHTEEN

Stomach empty but still heaving, I stumbled back into the house, across the courtyard, toward the hall of bedchambers.

In the corner of the courtyard, a boy, perhaps in his early teen years, watched me from behind the fronds of a small mulberry tree.

I averted my eyes. His arm was badly deformed and I didn't want him to feel I was staring.

I sensed him flit from behind the tree as I walked.

Another quick glance in his direction.

He stopped behind a pillar, but still watched.

I nodded toward him with an obligatory smile.

"Why are you following me?" He jabbed a finger in the air in my direction.

"I – I am only cleaning the chamber pots."

"No! You are here to spy on me!"

"Marius!"

Junia, the woman in charge of the kitchen—my supervisor?—stood at the kitchen entrance, a fistful of turnip greens in her hand.

"Don't mind him, girl. Nobody pays any heed to the idiot son."

Son?

"Cursed by the gods he is." Junia tapped her temple. "Not right in his mind." She turned back into the kitchen.

Marius slunk away.

I traversed the entire length of the back hall of bedchambers, but there was no entrance leading out of the villa. For now, it would seem slave duties were my only option.

I emerged from the second bedchamber to find Marius awaiting me in the hall.

"Hello." I bowed slightly. Would my deference put him at ease?

He stared at me.

"Can you tell me, Marius, did you see the man who came to this villa with me? Do you know where he has gone?"

Or *if* he has gone. I still feared Jack had erased his time in Rome.

Marius continued to stare. Then slowly shook his head.

I exhaled heavily and pressed fingertips against my forehead. My head ached from thirst and my skin felt taut, too tight for my body.

Five emptied chamberpots later, I crossed the courtyard for the last time, and this time stopped in the center to rinse my hands in the water of a central pool. Intricate mosaic tiles surrounded the pool, vines and geometrics in yellows and blue. A few lilies floated, white petals with pink centers. I touched one with a gentle fingertip. My mother, as much as she loved the desert sands of Egypt, loved water lilies.

Assigned duties finished, I returned to the kitchen. If nothing else, I needed more to drink, and hopefully some food.

The kitchen was blessedly empty, the table still covered with bruised fruits and wilting vegetables, scraps left behind from the preparation of a meal. The only things that looked edible were a few clusters of berries, green with a purple tinge. The unidentifiable fruit would have to do. I held a cluster aloft and sniffed. Hopefully the flavor would be palatable.

I plucked one from the stem, but just before I popped it into my mouth, a hand reached from behind my back and knocked it to the floor.

"Hey!" I spun to face Marius. "I was eating that!"

Marius shook his head violently. "Those are elderberries. Poison if you eat them unripe."

I glanced at the berry, now rolling across the floor and against the wall, then back at Marius. "Thank you."

Marius responded by reaching out to run two fingers down the length of my hair. His gaze traveled down my clothing.

Oh boy.

Junia appeared at the kitchen door. "Marius! Out of here."

Marius fled her wrath.

"This is what comes of these new laws."

I looked at her quizzically.

Junia glanced through the kitchen doorway at the disappearing Marius, then lowered her voice.

"I suppose the Emperor Claudius's reforms don't reach to wherever you've come from." She tut-tutted with a shake of her head. "Claudius changed the laws twenty years ago, when he wanted to marry his brother's daughter. That's what Florin's done. Married his brother's daughter."

Inbreeding. Known to cause mental and physical defects. Poor Marius.

I appreciated the few moments of respite, but Junia did not intend to spend the afternoon gossiping with me. Within minutes I was assigned kitchen duties—stirring a sloppy pot of something over a fire so hot I feared my sweat would mingle with the meal, scrubbing the bloody remains of raw fowl from the table where another girl had gutted it.

The kitchen had no window, but even without the sun I felt the afternoon slipping through my fingers. I eyed the doorway more than once, but it was a long way to the front of the house, and as far as I knew Lucius still hunkered there, with his angry stare and his ready dagger.

I would need to await my chance when I could get free of this kitchen.

Another hour vanished, before the sound of female laughter filtered through into the room and Junia straightened.

"Guests are arriving. Go and help the others."

Thirty minutes later, I was still helping to carry platters of food and amphorae of wine to the *triclinium*.

Decima and Florin were entertaining in style. The table sagged under the weight of all the food. Roasted pheasant, stuffed snails, glistening olives and sweet figs, pots of honey and plates heaped with rounds of bread. Cheeses and wine—so much wine. A second brazier was lit in the corner, matching the first which still burned, melting away the only way I could return home. A young boy played the harp in the corner, with another beside him, piping a tune on a reed flute.

I bent to place a final platter, an artfully arranged sea bass with a garum sauce, on the only free space on the table, directly in front of where Decima lounged on a pile of cushions.

"Ah, friends, I almost forgot! Look what we have found. A nobleman's prostitute, loyal to Nero. Of course for us, that simply means a new slave."

A dozen guests laughed at her joke.

But my heart surged with hope.

A nobleman. Jack?

One of the men at the end of the table raised a goblet in my direction. "A woman such as this, made to fetch and carry? What a waste. I can think of many more entertaining ways to put her to use."

Florin chortled beside his wife. "A man who thinks like a man." He eyed me greedily. "And I agree with your taste, Felix."

I watched Decima from under lowered eyes. She was not happy.

"What is your name, girl?" Florin's friend was already slurring his words.

I hesitated. Why did I feel unwilling to let him know my real name? As though it would somehow give him power over me.

"Deserta." Close enough to Sahara, but not quite, it was the Italian word for the hot and dusty desert most of them had likely never seen.

"Deserta?" He chortled. "Your parents were not kind. But then, you are foreign, yes?"

"Yes. From Britannia." Well, technically America. But that was harder to explain.

Florin steepled his fat fingers under his chin. "Britannia? I had thought them all barbarians. But you are a fine piece of work."

I flushed, hot and sick.

Florin's friend at the end of the table clapped his hands. "Let us see how they dance in Britannia."

Florin raised his own cup toward his friend. "Yet another good idea from our friend, Felix." His gaze slipped back to me, warm and wet. "Dance for us, Deserta."

The harp and flute in the corner picked up tempo immediately. As if part of the farce.

Oh, God, help me.

I swayed on my feet, a slow rhythm, and body rigid.

Florin laughed. "Oh, I hope that is not how the Britanniarum dance! You can start by removing your clothing."

Oh, no, no, no.

I spun to flee from the room and found the house-guard Lucius blocking the door, hand on dagger.

I looked to Decima. Would she object to her husband's revolting request?

Her face was a tight mask of anger, but she said nothing.

"I said strip, slave."

They were all laughing now. Reaching for food by the handfuls, drinking as though the wine might run out.

I pulled the *palla* from my shoulders, unwound the long stretch of fabric, let it drop to the floor. I still hid under the tunic

I'd arrived wearing. But began a dance before I could be asked to remove more.

Florin rolled to his side, lumbered to his feet, and circled the table to face his friends at my side. Then mirrored my movements, to the great amusement of the entire room.

His hand snaked behind me, grabbed the neckline of my tunic, and ripped.

The clothing fell away and hung limp from the corded belt tied at my waist.

I stopped dancing.

Florin's fingers tickled the bare skin below my ribs.

I jerked away.

"Oh, don't make her dance anymore, Florin. Look at her. She's too tall, not enough curves. Clearly, the Britanniarum don't know how to take good care of their women."

This from a gaunt man near Decima, who followed his comments with a scoop of currants pushed into the laughing mouth of the woman next to him.

Decima chuckled with the rest of them, but her eyes were stormy.

"Yes, Florin," she grabbed a poker that stood against the wall near the brazier, "let's not make her dance. She loves Nero so much, let's see if she can display him to us." She thrust the poker into my hands. "Here, here's your rudder." She pointed to a jug on the floor. "And there is your globe. Turn yourself into a statue."

Huh?

But then it came to me. The massive statue of Emperor Nero, waiting in the courtyard of his Domus Aurea as a landmark where I would meet my parents. Supposedly, it was sculpted to show Nero, striding forward and holding a rudder against a globe, to signify his divine dominion over both water and earth. The statue had not survived antiquity, only its descriptions in the writings of historians.

I struck a pose. Hopefully similar enough.

The partygoers went back to their feasting, their attention drifting from the half-naked woman-statue in the corner.

I lowered my trembling arm.

"Statue!" Decima's eyes flared with heat. "You are Nero!"

I resumed my pose.

"Better." She smirked. "Oh, and if you move, you die."

CHAPTER NINETEEN

*M*y legs trembled.

How much longer could I hold this ridiculous pose?

The fires blazing in the corners heated the room until sweat ran down my bare back.

How did this happen? How had I yet again fallen into some sort of political plot that threatened to kill me?

The party ebbed and flowed around me, and still I stood, with my poker and jug, imitating a statue I'd never seen of a man who was nearly lost to history. The *triclinium* had no windows. I lost all sense of time. Was it perhaps five o'clock? So little time left. My only chance to find my family.

Jack's words flitted through my numbed mind.

This obsession, driving you to exhaustion, it will only lead to more trouble.

Yes, Jack, you were right. And here I was to prove it, half-dressed and on the verge of execution, all for the entertainment of a madwoman.

Was I finally ready to let go? Give up the impossible task of righting the past?

Fine. I spoke the words to the empty air, to the universe. To God, if he were listening.

I give up. No more trying to prove myself worthwhile by fixing every wrong I've caused.

Play along, then. Bide my time. Focus on escape and get back to the Forum. After I found Jack.

The housekeeper Junia entered the *triclinium*, a large platter of roasted pheasant on her hip. She glanced my direction, scowled, and crossed to the low table to place her platter in front of Decima.

Her body hunched over the table and her lips moved in a quiet message for Decima only.

Decima's attention shifted from Junia to me, still listening with her head inclined. She nodded once.

Junia turned and motioned to me. "You are needed in the kitchen."

I glanced to Decima.

She gave that single, sharp nod once more.

I ran from the room, poker still in my hand, and using the other to clutch my ripped clothing to my bare chest.

Junia bustled ahead of me toward the kitchen.

I would have followed her anywhere. I thrust the poker into a nearby flower bed in the courtyard and pulled my tunic over my shoulders. The rip down the back gaped, and I clutched it around my neckline to keep it from falling again.

In the kitchen, Junia pointed to a jug on the table. "Drink."

I poured a cranberry-colored wine into a small bowl and lifted it to my lips. "Thank you," I breathed. Then gulped.

"Well, you didn't deserve that. It was his fault. He always knows how to get Decima's jealousy raging."

"What does she see in him? Why does she care?" *He is repulsive*, I wanted to say, but bit that comment back.

"I can tell you what *he* sees. Money. He sees money when he looks at her."

Ah.

"His brother was rich, and died young. Florin spent a lifetime jealous, so he took his revenge by marrying his brother's daughter, and getting the money anyway."

"But her? She truly cares for him?"

Junia pounded a ball of tan dough against the table. "That is a mystery to us all. Except for the fact that her father was also a horrible man, and likely she suffered at his hands. Perhaps she's trying to somehow gain his approval, his affection, even after he's dead."

The woman could have given Sigmund Freud a run for his money.

"It's about more than simply having money for him, though. He has political aspirations, and ambition costs. He would never be taken seriously in the Senate without money behind him."

She pointed to a scratched three-legged stool in the corner. "Sit. For a few minutes. Catch your breath. I can't save you forever. Just for today."

The small bowl of wine was heavy and comforting in the palm of my hand.

Junia offered me a plate of pheasant too charred to serve to guests, but the look of it threatened to gag me. She brought me a tunic, the color of dried mud, to pull over my torn clothes, and I grasped her hands in gratitude.

She pulled them away, shaking her head.

Body covered and thirst slaked for now, I leaned back on the stool and dropped my head against the wall. Tears welled up behind my eyelids and I pressed the palms of my hands to my eyes to stop the flow. I couldn't seem to formulate a coherent thought.

Jack. The coin. My parents. The statue. Howard and the waiting tomb of Tut-ankh-amun.

All the disjointed fragments of my life floated like black specks before my closed eyes. Nothing connecting, nothing making sense.

What was I to do now?

Not surprisingly, someone else ripped the decision from my hands.

Florin appeared in the doorway, hand on his belly, belching out wine and food.

"Oh, I see our little new little slave is finished with her duties for the day. I will take her now."

Junia frowned. "Master, I must warn you. You risk your wife's displeasure with your fascination with this girl. And an unhappy Decima is one likely to tighten the purse strings."

Florin worked at something between his teeth with a fat finger, his heavy eyelids slanted in Junia's direction. "Your chastisement is noted, Junia, and wholly inappropriate. I assure you I have the full approval of my wife." He turned on me. "This one is coming to prove to those above me that I can be useful, in the upheaval to come."

He grabbed my arm and dragged me from the stool.

The small bowl of wine flew from my hand and smashed on the tile floor.

I looked to Junia with an apology in my eyes.

Her expression spoke only sympathy.

Florin dragged me from the kitchen, across the courtyard, through the wide double doors of the villa, and into the gravel courtyard beyond.

I tried to pull my elbow from his pinching grip. "I can walk alone. You don't need to drag me."

He let me go, but swept aside the folds of his toga near his belly, revealing a short dagger on a belt. His fingers caressed the hilt of the dagger. "As long as you do not give me any trouble, we can walk alongside each other as friends."

His smile nauseated me.

Now that we were outside, I studied the sun's position in the sky. My guess had likely been close. Perhaps five or even six o'clock. A few hours until sunset. Not long. And now we were leaving the house, my only chance for retrieving the coin, or the molten lump of metal, should it still exist or be workable. But I could worry about that later, after I found Jack. If he were still here in ancient Rome.

"Where are we going?"

Florin grunted in answer, and then we walked in silence.

The villa was not as far from the city as it seemed when Jack and I walked with the guards from the northern end of the Forum. We approached the outskirts within minutes, mingling into the press of the crowd.

Could I slip away, turn enough corners to lose him?

As if reading my thoughts, Florin dug his fingers into my side and pulled me to him. "Just making sure you don't decide to go a different direction."

The press of his body against mine set my arms and legs to shaking. My fists clenched and unclenched at my sides, begging to be let loose on the man's face.

Perhaps sensing my tension, Florin yanked me sideways into a shadowed alley.

The narrow pavement ran between two slimy tenement buildings with windows cut high. Something splashed down in front of us from a window above.

Florin jerked backward to avoid the filth and let me go for an instant.

My reflexes were not so quick. The sewage splashed the tunic Junia gave me. I stood staring down at the mess beneath my knees, unable to take it in.

Florin laughed and spun me to push me back against the wall. "Oh, we can't have that. Let's get this dirty thing off you." His hands went to the tunic and he tugged upward. He reeked of wine and rotting meat—both his body and his breath. This close, with his face nearly touching mine, the black tooth in his lower jaw was like a dark hole. His puffy, inflamed cheeks and nose screamed of a lifetime of overindulgence.

I turned my face away, palms braced against the rough stone wall behind me. "Stop."

But he had one hand snagging through my hair now, the other hand fumbling at his own clothing.

"Do not bother to scream. No one will care. It's quite obvious what you are."

Yes. He was right. No one would care. Because no one knew

where I was. Not Jack, not my parents. They would never know I came to Rome. Howard, Lord Carnarvon, Eve. No one would know that I had died in an alley in the ancient past.

Because I was going to die. I was going to fight to the death before I let this happen.

But this is not really happening. I would make it all go away, when I returned to 1922 a moment before I left. I would make it all *not happen.*

But... did it matter? I would not forget. Florin would forget me, but I could never forget.

He was pulling up his toga now, his wide, hairy legs white in the shadowy alley.

I choked out a cry, and the tiny sound loosened something in my chest. A sweep of incoherence, as if all the shame and confusion of the past few hours retreated like a wave washing out to sea. And the next wave rolling in was one of rage.

Enough. Enough. Enough.

I had done nothing but run, hide, and cower since showing up in this ancient city.

It stopped now.

I was here to find my family, not play the victim.

No more thoughts of giving up. Such nonsense only led me further into danger.

A newfound resolved flooded my veins. Every muscle tensed, every tendon stretched.

I pummeled his chest with my fists. Kicked his legs with my sewage-covered sandals. Screamed like a wounded animal into his hairy ear.

He took a step backward from my crazed performance.

And laughed. He only laughed.

Without thought I grabbed the dagger at his waist. Held it, point toward his chest, in front of my own body.

He was still laughing. "You might howl like a cat, but you fight like a kitten."

He lunged, fingers spread, to clutch my wrist.

I thrust forward. The knife tip sliced through the skin of his upper chest like hot wax.

His eyes bulged. His fingers tightened around my wrist. Pulled at the knife.

I forced the counter pressure. Kept the knife in place.

My breath puffed out in torn little pieces.

Blood coated the knife. It slipped in my palm. I shoved my forearm against his body and gripped the knife again.

He started to fall backwards.

I shoved again, unwilling to let go of the knife even now.

A moment later he was at my feet, blood pouring out of his chest to mingle with the sewage.

The slap of sandals behind me turned me the other direction. I howled a cry of rage and fear.

At the end of the alley, Florin's friend Epaphroditus, the man who pulled the strings of this insane couple, charged toward me.

Still frantic with terror, I raised the knife to shoulder level and hurled myself at my next attacker.

CHAPTER TWENTY

June 9, 68 AD
Rome, Italy

*E*ven early in the day, the Circus Maximus pulled Roman citizens into its revelry, promising games and races, hot food and a glimpse of society from plebeian to patrician.

On the hillside path headed toward the arena, Renae reached for Alex's hand to keep them together, and clenched her other hand at her side to resist reaching for her daughter.

Already a throng headed toward the multiple entrances, hundreds funneling through narrow doors into the wider arena beyond.

Persia had the good sense to stay close, right?

Besides, they always had a plan. A failsafe, should they ever be separated. Two failsafes, actually. Before they'd left 1737 they agreed upon their meeting place in Rome, 68 AD, should they get separated today, just as they did before every trip into the past. Today's was easy—the very statue where they would meet Sahara at sunset.

Her hand convulsed in Alex's grip.

He looked sideways at her and smiled. The morning sun lit his back, painting a glow around his head like a Byzantine saint.

She tried to smile in return, as though she'd been squeezing his hand from affection rather than a bit of panic.

The other failsafe—a constant that traveled with them to every location—was a single place and time in history where they would rendezvous should they ever be lost to each other in the millennia of time. The time and place were suggested to them by a traveler they met years ago, before they were even married. She and Alex kept well clear of that year in all their travels, preserving it for an emergency, so they would always be able to meet there if necessary.

Persia would still have to wait years, of course, to grow into her ability to travel to that rendezvous. Which was why Renae had to clutch at her own *palla* to keep from clutching at her daughter in the press of the mob heading in to watch chariots race the oval of the Circus Maximus.

Just inside the doors, a murky corridor chased around the perimeter of the arena. Alex pulled her out of the stream of citizens pouring straight across the corridor into the sunlit stands beyond. He caught Persia's eye and motioned for her to join them.

They stood apart from the crowd as it flowed past.

Persia leaned to glimpse the stone seating area. "What are we doing? Aren't we going in? I don't want to miss anything."

Several horses emerged from the darkness of the corridor behind them, led by young boys. The animals stamped and snorted at the passing crowd, impatiently waiting their turn.

Renae absently patted the horse closest to her. She felt its unease.

"Hands off!" The young boy jerked the horse's head away from her hand and stared daggers at her. "Do not touch the contender!"

Renae laughed, and the laugh released a bit of tension. The boy's strident tone belied his young years, as though he were a schoolmaster reprimanding an errant student.

"Let's wait until most of the people have entered." Alex circled her waist with an arm and Persia's with the other. "I don't want to get separated."

Their daughter sighed—that loud, theatrical sigh every parent knows as extreme exasperation with one's over-vigilant parents.

"Papa, we won't get separated. And we always have a plan. I am going in."

There was nothing to do but follow her, though finding a break in the crowd proved difficult.

Persia was about to jump in when a woman's voice carried over heads toward them.

"There! There he is!"

A flash of sun-bright yellow followed the voice. The young mother from the street, accompanied by an older woman—slave no doubt—carrying the fortunate little girl on her hip.

The mother pulled on the arm of an older man, dressed in the gold-trimmed toga of patrician nobility.

"Here, this is the very man I spoke of, Galerius. The one who saved little Galeria from certainly being crushed under the feet of that terrible beast!"

Persia drew to stand alongside Alex and smiled at the family.

But Renae held back. There was a day, in her younger years, when she welcomed the attention of the "historicals," as she and Alex called them, just as Persia did now. But time, and traveling through it, had wearied her. Sapped the joy she once felt.

Or perhaps it was only the loss of Sahara.

"Well," the Roman consul—Publius Galerius Trachalus apparently—gripped Alex by both upper arms, his fingers flexing into the angry bruise on her husband's shoulder.

Renae winced for him, but he didn't flinch.

"You will come and sit with our family, in our reserved seats, to watch the races." He cast a glance over Renae, then let his attention linger on Persia, from hair to sandals. "You, and your own family, of course."

A coil of disgust wormed through Renae's belly.

"Oh, yes, Papa, can we?" Persia rolled on the balls of her feet.

Alex sighed and looked to Renae.

She shrugged again.

What was wrong with her today? It was as though she could not find the energy to care about anything except that statue, at sunset.

"Very well." Alex dipped his head. "And thank you."

"Oh, it is *you* I should be thanking, according to my wife. She would have been quite distraught if harm had come to the child." He waved an airy hand toward the little girl, as if she were no more than his wife's favorite pet.

Renae turned away to hide her expression, but then followed her husband and daughter, escorted by the consul Trachalus, through the wide entrance doors onto the main level of the arena.

Like any arena in the twentieth century, the oblong Circus Maximus boasted many tiers of seats, and a crowd filling them quickly in anticipation of the day's events. The parallel sides of the arena squared off for stables at one end. A low wall running down the center of the stadium sported decorative sculptures gleaming in the morning sunlight.

Trachalus guided them to what he called his "honorable seating"—a section apparently reserved for his personal use—elevated only slightly above the sand and gravel of the central competition.

"You'll feel the wind of the chariots in your hair, my dear." His head bent to Persia's and his voice was as smooth as olive oil.

Renae squeezed between Persia and the stone wall, brushing a hand against the draped festoons of greenery and coiled red ribbons. The consul would not be sitting directly next to her daughter.

His eyes roved Renae's face, his lips drawn tight.

She met his look with one of her own.

"Please," he extended a hand to the marble bench, "make yourselves comfortable."

His wife seated herself on his other side, spreading her

butter-yellow robes around her on the bench, then holding herself as erect as a cypress tree.

Trachalus nodded toward a few slaves behind their benches. Serving trays of crusty bread, ripe figs, and stuffed olives were conjured from nothing. Goblets of wine followed and were handed to the consul, his wife, and the Aldridge family.

Renae raised an eyebrow at Persia's eager grip on the offered wine, but it was likely too watered to do much damage.

"You are not Roman?" Trachalus leaned forward past Renae and Persia, to speak to Alex at the end of the row. The question was more of a statement.

"We are on holiday," Alex said. "Traveling through your great city."

"From—?"

A cheer went up from the crowd at the arrival of two chariots at the end of the arena, saving Alex from fabricating an answer.

Persia fitted two fingers between her lips and whistled loud enough to make Renae wince.

"Persia! What have I told you—"

"*Panem et circenses*, Mama! We are here!"

Bread and circuses. Yes, they were here.

The phrase hadn't even been written yet, had it? Another thirty years or so, perhaps, before one of their satirical poets would make the comment, but the practice was certainly in full swing. Cheap grain and cheap entertainment kept the Roman citizenry's bellies full and minds amused, while the power politicians like the one beside her did as they pleased.

As if in response to her musing, another man squeezed between their bench and the stone wall, clearly intent on speaking to Trachalus.

His wife leaned back to avoid being brushed by the man's bulk.

He bent to Trachalus, with a glance toward Renae.

"My lord, there is news."

Renae trained her eyes on the start of the race. At least a

dozen chariots burst from the starting area, horses charging at breakneck speed in their first lap around the track.

Trachalus inclined his head, as though to invite the visitor to pour information directly into his ear.

"You are familiar with the noblewoman Decima and her husband Florin?"

"The magistrate who thinks his money and her name will be enough to buy him a seat in the Senate House?"

"She has more than a name, my lord. She is determined to create a legacy for her family and has the vicious treachery and the ear of more than a few patricians to make it happen."

"Very well, what have these two managed to accomplish today?"

"For once, their efforts to impress have not gone awry. There was a commotion earlier in the streets outside the emperor's palace—a child nearly trampled or some such thing—" At this, the newcomer waved an impatient hand.

Renae glanced at Trachalus, but he didn't seem to even put the two events together.

"—Apparently Decima had people on the watch for the emperor, thinking he might try to escape. When the disturbance held up the flow of traffic, Nero's men thought it would be an opportune time to slip him from the halls of the palace, but Decima's men were watching and apprehended him."

Trachalus grabbed at the man's wrist. "You use a thousand words to give me what should have been said in twenty! The mad emperor has been taken?"

The visitor loosened the fingers around his wrist and leaned away from Trachalus, nodding.

Renae glanced sideways at Alex, on the other side of Persia who was engrossed in the race.

Alex was listening carefully, his brows drawn together.

"Nymphidius has taken custody of him, and Nero is being brought to the Forum. No doubt the people will call for his immediate death."

"Nymphidius! Yesterday he's spreading rumors that Nero

has absconded for Egypt, and today that scoundrel will have all the Praetorians calling for the crown on his own head by nightfall!"

"Indeed. And Galba still at least a week away."

Another man appeared at the end of their row.

Trachalus's wife sighed heavily. "My dear, you are missing the races."

"Duty first, my love." Trachalus stood and bowed to Renae and Alex. "You will excuse me for a few moments. I must..." His voice trailed as he turned away.

Alex was shaking his head by the time Renae turned back to him.

"It's fine, Renae. We aren't Revising. None of it will stick, once we get back to 1737."

The exchange caught Persia's attention. "What are you talking about? What's happened?"

Renae frowned and kept her voice too quiet for Trachalus's wife to hear. "Our little adventure in the street, with the child. Apparently we managed to entirely change the course of today's events. Instead of escaping to the outskirts of the city, Nero's been arrested because of the ruckus we caused. And instead of the governor Galba arriving in a few days to be made emperor in Nero's place, an official named Nymphidius is the hero of the day and likely to be crowned."

"All that, simply because of saving a little girl—"

"This is why, Persia. Why we say that only Observing must be our objective, always." Alex's voice had taken on the tone of tutor, the role he'd played in Persia's life since her birth.

"But your father's right, it doesn't matter, because we'll put it all back the way it was, after we meet Sahara and then return."

Persia's chin lifted and she folded her arms across her chest. "And let the little girl die."

"Lower your voice, Persia!" Renae turned to the middle-aged slave still minding the child in the row behind them.

"Why should I lower my voice? Are you ashamed of your actions?"

"Persia!" Renae's voice was a hiss. "You know better. You know we cannot make whatever changes we wish—"

"So you are always saying! But if we have put something wrong here today, we have also put something right!" She turned her head to wink at the child behind them. "And that cannot be ignored."

"What would you have us do, Persia? Singlehandedly undo the Year of the Four Emperors?" Alex was whispering as well, but surely those around them were beginning to wonder about their family squabble.

"Four emperors—three emperors—who cares?" Persia waved a hand at the packed arena. "Do you think any of them care?"

"It doesn't matter if—"

"Fine! Then we simply have to undo what we put wrong. Find a way to restore the correct history with Nero and all that, so we can save that child when we leave."

Alex wrapped a hand around Persia's arm and pulled her to standing. "We'll talk about this outside."

But Trachalus returned at that moment. "You are leaving, friends? I had expected you to stay until at least the footraces."

"Yes, do stay," his wife agreed. She eyed Renae wistfully. "And perhaps even come to our home for a visit... All of Galerius's visitors talk of nothing but politics."

Alex stepped forward to grasp the man's arm. "We thank you for your hospitality." He bowed in the wife's direction, then stepped backward. "But, yes, I'm afraid we must be traveling to our next destination."

"And your lovely daughter?" Trachalus's predatory smile roamed the end of their row. "Where has she gone?"

Renae's heart thudded. She turned, but was barely surprised to see empty air where their daughter had stood.

Never one to believe something could not be accomplished, Persia had no doubt headed off to find a way to bring the corrupted pages of her history texts back into alignment.

But what new disaster might she cause in the process?

CHAPTER TWENTY-ONE

"*S*ahara!"

My name filled the reeking alleyway, where I stood over Florin's body, in a familiar voice more welcome than air itself.

Epaphroditus caught my wrist, knife raised, before the knife found purchase in his own flesh.

But there was Jack, right behind him, circling, warm hands gripping my shoulders.

As if in the distance, the knife clattered to the rutted stone street.

"Jack."

And then his hands were on my face, holding my head, looking into my eyes.

A coldness stole over me, a strange numbness.

"Sahara."

He was kissing my forehead, still holding my face in his hands.

Kissing my eyes, my cheeks, as though willing me back to life.

Was the earth shaking? Or was that me?

Behind Jack, Epaphroditus shifted, peered to search the end of the alley. "We must leave. I believe we've been followed."

I watched Jack's eyes, not comprehending.

He smoothed my hair. "It's okay. He's helping us. I'll explain later. Trust me."

Epaphroditus went to Florin's body.

The man on the ground lay with eyes bulging, mouth agape. Blood dribbling from the corner of his mouth down into his ear.

There was no saving him, Epaphroditus needn't try.

But no, he was searching Florin. Pulling away folds of robes, revealing a pouch tied to the man's waist. Pulling something from it. He handed his find to Jack.

Jack glanced at it, a small bronze coin with a tiny splotch of tar, then pressed it into my palm and closed my trembling fingers over it.

It was warmer than my skin.

Jack led me down the alley in Epaphroditus's wake. A team of pawing horses idled at the end of the alley.

We emerged out of the shadows and Jack guided me toward a small chariot harnessed to the horses.

I hesitated, my back pressed against Jack's chest. Still shaking.

"Get in, Sahara. Get in. We need to get away from here."

I climbed into the chariot and a moment later Epaphroditus threw a rough canvas over the two of us and the world went dark.

The canvas left us in a cave, and I huddled against Jack's warmth. The coldness was spreading, through my chest, out to my extremities, numbing my fingertips. Tiny pinpricks of light, holes in the canvas, were like the spattering of Egyptian stars we'd studied in the desert. Perhaps we were still there. Perhaps Rome was all unreal.

Dear God, let it be unreal.

Jack rocked me against him, murmuring soothing sounds as though to a child.

Why did he comfort me? Was it about my parents? Had they been hurt?

No, no it was me. It was me who had been hurt.

No, not hurt. I hurt someone else.

The guard on the rooftop. Pushed, screaming, backward into a fire.

The sticky wetness. Wetness on my palms, between my fingers, under my fingernails.

I pawed frantically at my tunic, to get rid of that awful slickness.

"Let's take this off, Sahara. You're covered in blood." Jack tugged at the tunic Junia had given me to cover my first destroyed costume of the day.

No, no, no.

It was worse underneath, where they left me bare.

I crossed my arms over my chest, gripped my shoulders and shook my head.

Jack pulled me close again. "Okay, it's okay. We don't have to take it off."

The smell of blood and sewage followed me, clung to me. The chariot wheels bumped and jolted on the rutted streets, and a sour gorge rose through my chest and into my mouth. I pressed the back of my hand against my lips and curled my body in on myself.

Jack clutched at me with warm, firm hands and kept up his soothing sounds.

Still so cold, shaking and blinking and rubbing at my skin. The humid warmth under the canvas did nothing to combat the numbness.

I traced constellations in the canvas's pinpricks, a memory of the alley playing out before my mind's eye, one fraction at a time.

"What is happening, Jack? I don't understand."

"I've told Epaphroditus we must get to Nero, that we have a message for him. He says Nero is safe, that he will take us to him."

"He will take us back to them, back to Decima!"

"No, he's loyal to Nero." Jack swept hair from my eyes. "He's been pretending, to get information from Decima and Florin."

"And the coin, how—"

"Decima's aim was not so good. After you went down, Florin grabbed it from the air and gave his wife a public scolding. Epaphroditus offered to get rid of me. Said two Nero-lovers was one too many, and Nero was more likely to bargain for a woman's life and let me die. Florin told him to take a guard. Said I looked like I could snap Epaphroditus in half."

I pressed my head against Jack's shoulder. Still so many questions. But no strength to ask.

"They kept me locked up for the rest of the meal, but Epaphroditus passed me a message, told me to play along. Eventually they came for me, but once we were well away from the villa, Epaphroditus faked an argument and then pretended to stab me. He sent the guard away, since I was supposedly dead. We went back to Decima's villa, so Epaphroditus could sneak you out, but when we found you were gone, we followed."

"You followed."

"Of course I did."

Nothing made sense. Nero, still safe in his palace? Had we changed history somehow?

But I relaxed against Jack, somehow willing to cease questioning for now.

What was happening to me? Walls that seemed solid two months ago, protecting me from people who could hurt me, were crumbling away, stone by stone. How many times would Jack need to save me, before I could trust him fully?

Under this canvas, in the warm cocoon of his embrace, I let myself imagine. How it would feel, even though I walked this strange tightrope of time travel, searching for my parents, to know that all along I had a safety net beneath me, someone who had committed to defending me?

The relief was physical, coldness fleeing, warmth filling my body.

I exhaled breath I'd been holding for years, and blinked at the tears that came unbidden.

The chariot rolled to a stop, Epaphroditus clucking to the

horses. The chariot floor bounced as he jumped down, and his sandals crunched gravel.

He flipped the canvas back.

We blinked away the harsh sun, low in the sky. Too low.

I scanned the area. How far to the center of Nero's famous Golden House and the massive statue he erected of himself?

"Come. Follow me. Quickly." Epaphroditus sped across the gravel toward a magnificent villa.

I turned to look behind me, and my heart thudded an uneven rhythm. "Jack?"

He followed my gaze, across the rolling hills, with the city on the horizon.

No, no.

We were once again in the suburbs of Rome, and even from this distance, I could see the colossal statue of Nero poking against the orange orb of the sun, far, far away.

I closed my eyes.

Stupid, Sahara. I should have known. I'd studied the history before we stepped foot in this time. How had I forgotten? Whatever safety Epaprhoditus assured Jack about, it had done nothing to change this moment, here.

We followed through open doors into the vast central courtyard of the villa.

Cardinals and bluejays tweeted and fluttered. Their wings must have been clipped to keep them flying so low. Pools and fountains with rainbow-colored mosaics littered the courtyard, lush greenery muffling the sounds of birds and water.

I stood on the threshold of this paradise in my mud-colored tunic, covered with purpling stains drying to a crust, my ripped and immodest tunic beneath, my hair wild around my shoulders.

The sun was too low to reach the cool shadows of the leafy courtyard, and in the center of the greenery one man lounged on masses of cushions, wine goblet in hand, swathed in robes of purple and gold.

He lifted suspicious eyes at our presence.

Behind me Epaphroditus poked us forward into the atrium.

"Imperator, it is good to see you have escaped the palace."

Nero Claudius Caesar Augustus Germanicus, Emperor of the entire Roman world, pulled his graceful body to standing, and peered at me with dark eyes as piercing as a raven's.

No doubt he recognized the bloody stains drying across my chest for what they were.

I bit my lip, trying to ground myself in this moment, here, and not a darkening alley in the city, where a body lay on the stones.

"Well, I very nearly did not. It was only with the help of the gods I was able to make it here to our meeting place. I've arrived only moments ago."

Epaphroditus nodded toward Jack and me. "I have brought these two, who are loyal to you and have a message. Surely, they have news from the Senate. A way for you to be restored to your throne."

Nero waved a hand over us both, his nostrils flaring. "Well, I am filled to the top of my head with false hope." He flung himself back to the cushions. "Speak nothing but truth to me. If I learn that you have lied, I will slit your throats myself."

CHAPTER TWENTY-TWO

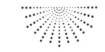

*I*n the center of the atrium, Nero stared up at us, waiting for his delivered message.

I gripped the bloody tunic in the tight fingers of one hand and held it from my body. The crusty blood cracked within my grip. I still clutched the coin in my other hand. I would not be letting it go.

Behind us, through the double doors of the villa, the sound of chariot wheels on gravel echoed into the courtyard.

Epaphroditus spun and squinted into the sunlight. "I feared the usurpers might be following." He glanced at me. "They will have found Florin's body. News travels in this city faster than sewage through gutters. They will kill you on sight."

Jack still held my hand, and pulled me to the left. "Sahara, come."

The ousted emperor lunged forward. "No!" He grabbed my other arm and yanked me toward himself. "You must tell me what you know!"

His face, the garden, all of it blurred before my eyes. Smells of blood and flowers, trickling sounds of fountains and Nero's whining voice. The soft lines of sculpted fountains and circular pools in the fringy greenery.

I swayed on my feet, back-and-forth between the two men.

Jack growled, deep in his chest, and crashed a fist down against Nero's forearm, breaking the emperor's hold on me.

Epaphroditus barreled toward Nero. "Imperator, we need to get you hidden."

I started to follow them toward the rear of the villa.

Jack held me back. "We are staying away from them."

We crossed the courtyard to the colonnaded terrace bounding the perimeter, then pushed through an unobtrusive door into a tiny chamber.

A bedroom, a *cubiculum*, with little more than an elevated sleeping couch. A wooden chest sat at the base, used as a step to climb onto the couch.

A three-legged stool in the corner held a jug and basin. I leapt toward it. Poured cold water over my bloody hands. My skin crackled with dried blood as my tunic had, and absorbed water like it was dying of thirst.

Jack opened the chest, found some sort of ivory *palla*, and held it up to me.

I ripped the blood-covered outer tunic Junia had given me over my head, then grabbed the *palla* from Jack's outstretched hand and stepped from the inner tunic Florin had ripped from my shoulders.

Jack averted his eyes.

I donned the fresh clothing, secured the coin in a pouch tied under the fabric, then turned to him. Free of Florin's blood at last, I suddenly had no other thoughts. My mind felt poured out and empty.

Jack kicked my discarded clothing into the corner, pulled me to the sleeping couch, and eased me down onto it.

He grabbed a woven coverlet, red linen shot through with metallic gold, slid into the bed next to me, and pulled the coverlet over both of us.

"Jack, a blanket is not enough to hide us."

He tucked me against himself, my head under his arm. "Then

I will have to do a better job than I did in the Senate House, of playing the part of a nobleman with his mistress."

"Perhaps I should have left the *palla* off, then."

He eyed me carefully, as though my flippant remark might be a sign I'd gone mad.

The bed was built for shorter people, with curved arms at both the head and foot. I turned on my side toward Jack and bent my legs to better fit into the overstuffed yellow cushions. My body seemed created entirely of sharp, jutting bones and tension, and the soft bed did little to absorb it.

"I'm sorry." Jack's lips brushed my ear, his voice a whisper. "I don't know how we ended up here. I told Epaphroditus to take us to the Golden House—"

"But Nero is hiding here, in Phaon's villa. Epaphroditus must have thought you didn't know, that you only wanted to see Nero."

The late-day amber sun through the high window bathed our hiding place and cast a pinkish glow over our bodies.

Jack's eyes burned blue in the rosy hue.

I locked onto those blue eyes, drawing strength, slowing my breathing.

"Phaon?" Jack's brow furrowed.

"He's a freedman of Nero's. Likely his Secretary of Finance. This is his house. Nero's hiding here from the Senate and the Praetorian Guard."

"When did you possibly have time to find out all that?"

"From a book on my shelf in the American House."

"Ah. So what happens next?"

Did I know? The certainty of so-called history had betrayed me already, and the past was not always what it seemed. Perhaps what history recorded as fact was incorrect. Perhaps my being here would somehow change it. Or already had.

"Others will come, loyal to Nero. They will try to bring him back to the Senate. But it won't work and he'll be dead before the day is out. That'll be the end of the Julio-Claudian dynasty, and after that, it'll be power-grabbing chaos for a year."

"Well, none of this concerns us. We have to get you out of here. Before the discovery of Florin's body has people hunting you, if it's not already too late."

"Jack, He—Florin—he was trying... I didn't—"

"Sshh." Jack's fingers touched my lips. "You owe me no explanation, Sahara. I know you. I know who you are. I am just sorry it happened at all. That you experienced something so awful, and I wasn't there—"

"I don't want to talk about it. Not now. We need a plan. Perhaps Epaphroditus would take us to the Domus Aurea."

Jack shook his head. "Not safe for you. I don't want you anywhere near the emperor's palace. I'll have him take you back to the Senate House where we traveled into this time, and I'll go to the statue to meet your family and bring them to you."

I wanted to do what he said. Or even hide under this blanket with him forever. At the very least, avoid any interaction with people of this time. Avoid causing any more harm than I already had. I had every intention of returning to 1922 without revising this history, including the horrible bloody moment in the alley, but this whole traveling-through-time thing was far more unstable than I'd hoped, and who could say what might happen when I left here?

My legacy in the past had thus far been only destruction.

"It's just logical, Sahara. Anything I do here can't be permanent. I can't mess with history. You should stay safe."

Everything I had been through, from fighting an Egyptian vizier and saving a widowed queen, to all that happened here in Rome—what good was any of it, what purpose did it serve, if I didn't complete what I'd come here to do, to find my parents and save my sister myself? This was my legacy, even more than the work I was doing in archaeology. Fixing the past—including the mistake I made telling Giada about Venice—was what I was meant to do, and without it, what was my purpose?

"How can I allow you to do the one thing that would give all of this meaning? I appreciate your offer, but—"

Jack brushed the back of his hand against my lips, my cheek.

"Sahara, you must understand that I can't let anything happen to you."

I felt the melding of our bodies, fit together so well, felt every touch of him against me, from his dark hair brushing my forehead to his sandals entwined with mine.

My breath caught at the look in his eyes, still rose-tinged under the warm coverlet.

And then his lips were on mine, completing the touch of our bodies, warmer than the blanket, warmer than my flushed skin.

The kiss was hesitant at first, as though he feared I would break.

Perhaps I would.

I clutched at his toga, and pulled him toward me. Returned the kiss with fear melting into abandon.

The kiss deepened and for a moment the world hushed.

But then reality intruded. The sounds of a shouted argument from the courtyard.

Jack broke away first, turned his head toward the unseen doorway.

Everything in me reached for him, to reconnect.

But the moment was over. It was time to face what came next.

I would not be a victim of Decima and Florin. Nor of Nero and his cronies.

I would not let Jack take my place at the base of the bronze statue before the Golden House.

A cold strength flooded my body, replacing the warmth of the moment with Jack. Anger that was icy rather than hot.

The resolve that hardened my muscles and my hand in the alley returned. Avoiding trouble ended now. I was here to find my parents.

The shouted argument burst into our tiny chamber. Someone ripped the covering from us.

The next act in this ridiculous play had begun.

CHAPTER TWENTY-THREE

The leader of the entire Roman Empire sprawled across his courtyard cushions once more, forearm thrown over his eyes, and the other arm extended in languid helplessness, fingers trailing over tendrils of vines that snaked from a blue-glazed pot.

Several new players had joined the scene. A young woman, on the other side of the courtyard under the peristyle. Twisting her fingers with the open-mouthed and wide-eyed look of numb shock on her face.

The two men who dragged us back to the courtyard each held one of us.

Epaphroditus stood beside Nero, arms crossed and glaring at us in the darkening courtyard. "You two, you must give Nero your message now. Tell him whatever you've come to say. Tell him the Senate might even now be changing their minds. He can throw himself on the mercy of Galba, even as he advances."

Nero moaned. "Perhaps you would have me petition the Roman people for the prefecture of Egypt, eh, Epaphroditus? Despite the fact they will likely tear me apart?"

He rolled over on the cushion to lay face down, his voice muffled by fabric. "Everyone has left me now. The Praetorian

Guards, my bodyguards." He lifted his head and looked at the woman across the courtyard. "You will not leave me, will you, my sweet one?"

The woman's face blanched, and she gnawed on her lip, eyes blinking.

"No, no, you will never leave me. You love me more than any other."

Epaphroditus jutted his chin toward Jack and me, still held by the two goons.

"Phaon, Neophytus, let them go. They are here to help."

Our conscription into this nightmare was unbelievable. I braced my palms against my thighs.

"What is your name, woman?"

"Sahara."

I gave it without thinking, but then Epaphroditus hadn't been present when I'd given Florin's drunken friend my name as "Deserta," so it mattered little.

"Then tell him, Sahara—"

"I have nothing to tell him! We want nothing to do with any of this. We must leave, and leave immediately."

On either side of us, Phaon and Neophytus stepped closer.

"You see?" Nero's voice was a high-pitched whine. He rolled himself to sitting and extended his hands toward us. "No one is for me. Everyone is against me. No doubt even these two flee to rouse my enemies, and prattle to them about where I have been forced to run, barefoot and in disguise like a common criminal."

If Nero had come here disguised, he clearly had packed some luggage. The elaborate silk toga he wore, edged in purple and gold, looked nothing like the garb of a common criminal.

I yanked myself away from the would-be captor next to me, and stepped closer to Nero. "We are not your friends, but we are not your enemies, either. We do not even call this place home. We are to meet my family at the Domus Aurea and then travel home. We don't want any trouble."

Nero scrambled to his feet, crossed to where I stood, and leaned in to search my eyes.

"You see, my sweet?" He turned on the younger woman with a hostile glare. "This is what it looks like to be a woman of strength. You should take a lesson from this foreigner."

"Imperator," the man next to me, Phaon it would seem, scowled. "Do not let this foreigner convince you she bears no ill will. Surely if you let them leave, they will take word directly to your enemies, and you will be executed before you have a chance to do the honorable thing."

Neophytus held his hands out to the emperor. "We beg of you, *Princeps*, to avoid such ignominy. End your reign while still under your own control, as any divine emperor should." He pulled a dagger from his belt, advanced on Nero, and pressed the dagger into the emperor's hand. "One quick thrust, up through the throat. It will be done in an instant. Your pain will be over."

Phaon elbowed in, pulled a matching dagger and held it flat on his palm. "I would ask the honor of *my* dagger being used." He shot a glance at Neophytus, teeth bared.

On the fringes of our little circle, the woman moaned and swayed on her feet.

I empathized with her. I put a hand out to open air to steady my own head at the sight of more daggers, like the one I'd left in an alley beside Florin's body.

"I will do it! Yes. I will do it. But I will not let those jackals have my body, desecrate it." He ran both palms down the length of his body, as if in supreme appreciation for it.

"You two," he inclined his head toward Phaon and Neophytus, "dig me a grave."

The two men each gave a sharp nod, pivoted, and turned toward the entryway of the villa.

"Not out there!" His shriek echoed from the atrium walls.

I winced and stepped closer to Jack.

"Someone will see! They will know!"

I grabbed Jack's hand. One way or another, we were getting out of here.

"We must do it back there," Nero raised an arm and pointed a long finger toward the rear of the villa. "In the garden. Dig it there."

The two men changed direction.

"No, no. Someone must watch the door. Someone must watch for my enemies." He looked at Jack. "You. You help Neophytus dig my final resting place. Phaon, you guard the door." He swiveled to rest his frantic eyes on me. "And you. You show my wife what it means to mourn her husband in the proper way."

Neophytus did not look as though he'd dig a grave himself. He prodded Jack toward the back of the villa.

I followed, with Nero, his wife, and Epaphroditus behind.

Vegetables and flowers tangled across an open plot in the center of the house. Deep shadows thrown by the setting sun fell on a central gnarled tree that suspended tiny olives like black pebbles over our heads.

Neophytus tossed a spade-like instrument to Jack.

Jack passed me, speaking low. "I'll cooperate, but keep watch for our chance out of here." He attacked the dirt beside Neophytus's spade.

Nero paced the garden, ripping blood-red grapes from a vine clawing its way up a trellis at the border, and grinding them between his teeth.

I pulled Nero's wife into the shadows. She should not have to be part of this nightmare, and she seemed to already be in shock.

At our feet, a square of asparagus spears spiked from the ground like lines of green soldiers at attention and beside them, a pile of purple cabbages stacked like dismembered heads rotted in the soil. I recoiled from the mess and sniffed. The smell of cabbage and the sweat of the men mixed into a foul brew that churned my stomach.

Nero pawed at his clothing, whimpering toward his wife. "Come, my sweet, let me rest my head on your soft shoulder."

She made a tiny sound, like a wounded animal, and shook her head.

I put a hand on her arm, a vain attempt to reassure her.

Beyond the garden, at the front door, Phaon barked a shout of surprise from his position overlooking the valley. "Someone is coming!"

Nero howled. "Not yet, not yet!" He still held a dagger, and pressed the point to his throat, eyes white and searching. "Dead! Dead!" He closed his eyes and threw his head back. "And what an artist dies in me!"

But his hand trembled on the dagger.

Jack and I stood transfixed, between the mad emperor and the incoming unknown.

Phaon was shouting outside the front doors. "What is it?" After a beat, he turned his head to call back to those of us among the vegetables. "Not the Guard. Only one man, riding hard."

Epaphroditus stepped forward. "Perhaps a message from the Senate even now. Surely most of them are still loyal to the bloodline of the Julio-Claudians. They would see an heir raised up, to preserve the future!"

Nero lowered the dagger to his side.

We filed into the courtyard.

Jack pulled me back to the rear of the group, eyes signaling we should be ready for whatever was next.

The sound of hoofbeats on gravel crescendoed, then a greeting from a male voice outside.

A moment later a short man, dressed in only a tunic and sandals, ran into the house, a tied scroll clutched in his hand.

"News from the Forum," he called.

Phaon snatched the scroll, broke the wax seal, and unrolled it as he walked toward the emperor. Then handed the page to Nero.

Nero snatched the scroll, held it open, and scanned the lines in silence.

When he raised his eyes, they were terror-filled.

"What is it? What news?" Epaphroditus advanced on him and pulled the scroll from his trembling fingers.

Epaphroditus read the message, then huffed a sound of frustration and tossed the page to the ground.

Nero paced, hands pulling at his hair.

Turning back to all of us who waited, Epaphroditus gave the news.

"The Senate has declared him a public enemy. Decreed the ex-emperor should be captured and brought to the Forum for execution." He glanced toward Nero. "Ancient style."

Nero moaned. "How ugly and vulgar my life has become!"

Epaphroditus searched the valley beyond the villa's doors. "Even now the guards will be coming to apprehend him."

"'Ancient style?'" Jack looked between the various men around us.

Epaphroditus tilted his head and spoke under his breath, as though Nero would not hear. "Meant for humiliation. Stripped naked, his head secured in a wooden fork, and then flogged to death in the view of all his enemies."

Nero still held one dagger, but at this utterance he rushed at Phaon and snatched the other from the man's belt, to hold one dagger in each hand.

He poked the point of each into the base of his jaw, on either side of his throat.

"Now, it must be now," he muttered and shook, dark curls falling into his eyes. "Come, you *coward*, do what you must."

But those eyes filled with tears, and the daggers clattered to the stone courtyard.

He turned on the young woman. "Empress, tell me you will mourn me. Someone must mourn me."

But she backed away, hands reaching behind to find support, until she reached a column holding the portico. She pressed her back against the column, then her head against it.

Nero yelped at her retreat and shoved his fist to his mouth. "Even you, Poppaea? Even you will leave me friendless?"

Poppaea?

Oh, son of a barnswallow. How did I not realize—?

I pressed a hand against my stomach in response to the rolling nausea.

Nero turned to Jack. "You! You are nothing to me. But you

can give me strength." He kicked one of the daggers across the stones. It slid to stop beside Jack's sandal.

"You must do it first." He lunged across the courtyard, snatched the dagger from the stones, swept it upward toward Jack's throat. "You must drive the dagger into your own neck, as an example and inspiration of true bravery."

Jack grabbed Nero's wrist in tight fingers.

But Nero wrapped his other hand around Jack's fist and nodded violently.

"Yes, yes, that is it. I will help. Drive the dagger deep. You must show me the way."

CHAPTER TWENTY-FOUR

June 9, 68 AD
Rome, Italy

"*M*ama, come!"

Renae heard Persia's words, as if they tunneled toward her from a long distance, through centuries, perhaps. Through strata of accumulated debris. Through a lifetime of wondering.

Seventeen. Persia was only seventeen. How was this possible? What Renae had just witnessed defied logic.

"Mama!"

A tug on her hand. Nearly pulled off her feet.

"Mama, we need to get to the statue. Look, the sun is nearly down. Papa will be frantic."

Renae shook her head, tried to dislodge the persistent fog. Her senses returned gradually. The murmur of crowds, the smell of markets and unwashed bodies. The tension in her neck and jaw.

"Mama," Persia drew close and gripped Renae's shoulders, "I don't—I don't understand it either, but we can figure it out later, together. Right now, we have to find Sahara."

Yes. Yes, we do.

Renae tightened her fingers around Persia's hand on her shoulder and nodded. "To the statue."

They pushed through the evening crowds, toward the ever-present bronze colossus towering against the bruised sky above the Domus Aurea, Nero's Golden House.

Persia clutched her hand, as though afraid they'd be separated.

Or perhaps she was equally as terrified by recent events as Renae.

From the moment she and Alex had turned in the Circus Maximus to find Persia gone, Renae knew the girl would create havoc out of the situation. But never, never had Renae dreamed she would witness her daughter's amplified abilities erupt in such a way, and so young.

Was it the intensity of the danger they'd fallen into that caused it?

Renae searched her memory as they ran toward the palace. In all their interactions with Tempus Vigilia members over the years, had they ever heard of someone manifesting so young, and with such an ability?

Danger seemed to lurk around dark corners as they ran through Rome's streets. Their handclasp broke apart in the midst of milling families, horses and chariots, merchants hawking everything from produce to prostitutes. They fought to regain connection, only to be forced apart again.

Renae ran behind Persia, keeping her eyes trained on Persia's shoulders. But if this—this extraordinary ability—was her daughter's destiny, the girl was going to need to grow up fast. Learn to control it. Learn when to use her gifts and when history was best left to itself.

Persia had done what she set out to do—free Nero so he could continue along the timeline known to them from history. By now he was no doubt hidden away at Phaon's estate outside the city, where the rest of his story could play out. Persia would believe she'd "fixed" everything, allowed them to revise history when they left. She'd believe they could now retain Alex's heroic rescue of the little girl in the street.

Renae would leave it to Alex to explain how nothing was so simple. How could they even know the ripple effect of all the changes they made today?

She and Persia slowed as they neared the slave-dug lake and its floating houseboat at the beginning of the three hundred acres of the palace complex. How could they find a way past anyone watching, all the way to the other side of the main palace building, to the courtyard statue? Alex would be waiting, for their only chance to find Sahara. He wouldn't come looking for Renae and Persia. Not until he had Sahara, or they found him first.

They slipped into the shadows of the colonnade running the length of the lake.

"Persia, wait." She pinched the fabric of the girl's *palla* and slowed her.

"We don't have time—"

Renae pulled the strands of pearls woven through her hair. She jutted her chin toward Persia's upswept curls. "Take your hair down."

Persia did as instructed. Without arguing, thankfully.

Renae held her pearls in one hand and pointed to Persia's throat. "Take off your jewelry."

Each with pearls and rubies in hand and hair hanging loose, they kept to the wall of the colonnade and strolled, heads down.

They did not have long to wait. Two women emerged from a doorway, one carrying a large serving platter and the other a terra-cotta jug on her hip.

Renae stepped to the center of the colonnade, blocking their path.

The older of the two, balancing a tray of roasted artichokes threatening to roll to the ground, scowled at Renae. "Who are you two?"

Renae took a chance and held up the pearls in her hand. "Someone offering you a trade. These pearls," she flicked a glance at Persia, who held up her gold chain with its central ruby, "and that piece, for your jug and tray."

The younger woman laughed. "Are you mad?"

Renae shrugged. "Perhaps."

The two glanced at each other, the older one gave a permissive shrug, and they handed the tray and jug to her and Persia, grabbed up the jewelry and scurried past them to disappear with their good fortune.

Renae led the way toward the main building. "Don't make eye contact if you pass anyone."

The "disguise" was sufficient. Alex would have needed to be careful, entering the palace without invitation or position, but two women were easily ignored if they were doing manual work. Even dressed in expensive fabrics, it would seem.

They glided through the palace, out the other side, into the courtyard. Sun still glinted from the bronze head of Nero high above, but the courtyard itself lay in the shadows cast by the surrounding buildings.

There—there was Alex, pacing at the base of the statue, eyes scanning the courtyard.

His shoulders visibly sagged at the sight of them.

Renae set the tray on the grass and ran into his arms. "Have you seen her? Is she here?"

Alex's voice was muffled against her loosened hair. "Not yet." He pulled away, held her by the shoulders, and studied her face. "What's happened? You're trembling."

She glanced at Persia, walking toward them slowly.

Her daughter set the large jug on the ground, expression sober. "I've—my—my abilities seem to have begun, Papa."

"What?" Alex looked between them. "So soon? I don't understand. And how could you possibly know—"

Renae shook her head. "Too much to explain. Later." She joined Alex, their backs to the statue, eyes roaming the palace courtyard. "Will we even recognize her?"

Persia wove her fingers through Renae's. "Of course you will, Mama. It's only been seventeen years."

"For us." Renae voiced the fear dogging her since they contrived this plan. "For us, it's been seventeen. But she could come to this day, June 9, 68 AD, at any time in her life. She might be… older than me. An old woman." Her voice caught. So many lost years.

Persia's hand tightened suddenly on hers.

Renae followed her gaze, to a woman striding across the courtyard, directly toward them.

Her stomach flipped, then righted itself. Her vision blurred.

But the woman was too petite, wasn't she? Sahara had been tall, even at fifteen. Hard to gauge the woman's age from this distance, but she moved like someone closer to Renae's age, perhaps early fifties. Was she misremembering Sahara's height? Could this be her?

The three waited in silence, heads lifted, hands grasped.

Renae forced herself to breathe.

The woman drew closer, her elaborate *stola* flowing around her ankles as she walked.

Was the soldier who followed with her? Some kind of bodyguard?

Her face was pinched, tight. Angry even. No, no, this could not be Sahara.

"You are waiting for someone?" she called to them.

None of them spoke.

"Your daughter, yes?"

Renae exhaled heavily and swallowed.

The woman nodded, eyes glittering. She stood opposite them, taking in all three. "Yes, she has sent me, your daughter. She wishes me to bring you to her."

"Where?" Alex took a step forward. "Where is she? Why did she send you?"

The woman extended a hand toward the palace behind her. "She awaits you in the emperor's dining hall. A feast has been prepared."

"Who are you?" Something about the woman felt wrong. She

was too… commanding. Not the sort of person to run errands for someone she hardly knew.

She smiled, but the warmth didn't reach her eyes. "My name is Decima. My husband and I were fortunate to meet your daughter earlier today."

Another soldier joined the first, both standing with legs in a wide stance behind the woman.

Decima. The name hit a familiar note.

Wasn't that the noblewoman Trachalus spoke of? What had he called her? *Vicious. Treacherous.*

Alex's tightening hand on hers signaled his recognition. "And our daughter? What is her name?"

Good, Alex. All of this could simply be part of the disaster they'd made of this day. Perhaps she didn't know Sahara at all.

Again the frozen smile. "Ah, you are suspicious, I see. The very sort of people who would give a daughter such a hideous name. Deserta."

Deserta. Renae's stomach churned. Italian for *desert*. But Sahara's Latin had failed her. *Deserta*, in Latin, meant *waste*. As in, wasteland. But still.

Decima laughed. "Yes, I see I have that correct." She flicked a glance at Persia. "And who is this one? Perhaps her sister, *Vomitus?*"

"Where is our daughter?" Alex's words were sharp, pointed.

She turned on him, gave him all the attention of her icy glare. "I have already told you—"

"Send this one," Alex jutted his chin toward the attendant soldier, "have him bring her to us."

"You will come—"

"We aren't going anywhere with you."

She stared at Alex for a beat, hatred oozing from the expression, then shrugged one delicate shoulder. "As you wish." She didn't turn, simply signaled with a casual hand to one of the soldiers behind her. "Take them. To the *Sala Ocula.*"

Alex stepped in front of her and Persia.

"Oh, do not worry. You'll see your daughter soon enough. Or her body, at least."

Renae curled tight fingers into the back of Alex's toga.

Decima chuckled once more. "Rome is a grand city, it is true, but did you think foreign treachery would go unnoticed?"

"What treachery? What are you—"

"Your daughter has helped a public enemy escape justice."

Beside Renae, Persia gasped and clutched her *palla* to her chest.

"Do not pretend you did not know. The Praetorian Guard, the Senate, they have both declared for Galba." She glanced upward at the length of the statue. "We no longer wish to have a madman controlling our empire. But your daughter seems to feel otherwise. No doubt aligned with the same enemy as her family." She rubbed at the jewels in the hollow of her throat. "And so you will suffer the same fate as she has. If we cannot have an emperor to execute in the Forum, at least we will have his supporters."

At this, the soldier she'd brought stepped forward, spear held at Alex's midsection, and inclined his head toward the palace.

Decima walked ahead, like a queen with trailing courtiers.

Renae stumbled in the wake of her husband, eyes on the grass.

She was here. Sahara was here. But... executed?

The wine she'd swallowed in the seats of the Circus Maximus threatened to make its way out of her stomach.

Persia followed, the soldier and his spear bringing up the rear.

Renae didn't need to hear her daughter's muffled crying to understand her feelings. It was Persia, not Sahara, who helped Nero escape. Had Sahara suffered for her actions?

And what were they to do? If they left this place, without Sahara, without allowing their actions here to persist, would everything terrible be undone? Or would they leave their older daughter irrecoverably dead in the ancient past?

Her thoughts tangled back on themselves, a tightening knot she could not untie.

"Have you—have you killed her already?" Persia's voice was tight, controlled.

Renae eyed the back of Decima's head.

The woman half-turned and sneered toward Persia. "By now? No doubt. But it's little of my concern."

"Because it wasn't her. It was me. I'm the one who—"

Alex cut Persia's would-be confession short with a quick spin and a furious expression.

Renae's thoughts raced through possibilities. She gripped Alex's hand.

He nodded, as though reading her thoughts.

They must erase this entire day. But they'd need to be in the corridor where they arrived to do it.

She turned to whisper to Persia. "The grotto. As soon as we're able."

"Keep moving!" The soldier behind Persia jabbed his spear into the air beside Persia's shoulder.

Persia's face contorted into a mix of grief and… rage?

The same rage Renae saw on her face earlier, just before the unthinkable.

She plodded forward, thoughts tumbling. Could Persia… could she do it again? Help them all somehow, with her newfound ability? Renae was still unsure what had even happened.

Their little group of five, bookended by an odious woman ahead and her dutiful soldier behind them, crossed the dusky courtyard, into the covered portico at the edge of the palace.

All around them, the perimeter of the courtyard flared to life as dozens of torches blazed in accord as if choreographed. Did slaves carefully time this ritual every evening? It would have been beautiful and fascinating, if they had not been marching to their apparent deaths.

"What do you want with us?" She shot the words at Decima's back. "We've done nothing to you."

"Keep your voice down." Decima continued forward without turning. "It's a new day. Those who opposed us must be eliminated. Your family has proven where your loyalties lie."

"So you're going to walk us into the palace and... what? Leave our bodies on the floor?"

Decima stopped, glanced left and right, then turned on Renae, eyes glittering in the torchlight. "I will leave your bodies right here if you do not stop talking."

Renae lifted her chin and said nothing. But clearly, the woman was not as confident of her position, or her intention, as she wanted them to believe.

Perhaps she and Alex, once upon a time, would have been reckless enough to bolt. But the spear-point wavering mere inches from their daughter's back kept Renae moving, following the odious woman.

Within minutes Decima walked them into the heart of the palace and down an unfamiliar hall.

How far away was the corridor they needed?

Where did Decima say they were headed? The *Sala Ocula*?

Ahead of Alex, Decima drew to a stop outside a chamber door. "In here."

She and Alex slowed at the entrance.

The floor—was it *moving*?

Persia prodded them forward, no doubt pushed inward by the soldier behind her.

Inside, another soldier stood, wide-stance and spear ready.

Decima followed them in. "Kill all three. Take their bodies below, to the wheel. Easiest place to get them out unseen."

How to get out of this?

But then a moment of dizziness swept her.

And a single word, shouted by Persia.

"Run!"

Renae spun to her daughter.

Impossibly, the girl held a spear in each hand, pointed outward.

The two soldiers were on the ground.

She had done it again.

"Run!"

Renae reacted first.

Grabbed Alex's hand where he stood, mouth dropped open.

Hurtled them both into the hall, behind the fleeing Persia.

Persia slowed for an instant, tossed one of the spears to Alex, then pulled her robes to her knees with her free hand and raced forward.

Renae didn't dare look back.

They had only a few moments ahead of the soldiers, who must be pursuing by now.

Did Persia know where she was running?

Shouts at their backs.

The slap of sandals. A woman's shriek of anger.

They rounded a corner, and suddenly all was familiar.

They were back where this day began.

CHAPTER TWENTY-FIVE

"Stop!"

I leapt toward Nero and Jack, locked in an unthinkable dance as the emperor tried to force Jack to inspire his own suicide.

But Jack needed no help. With a quick twist of one arm and a shove to Nero's shoulder, he thrust the desperate emperor backward.

Nero stumbled, righted himself, and snarled at Jack, dagger still in his hand.

A low rumble, like the sound of far-off thunder, arrested our attention.

As one, we looked to the front doors, still flung wide.

Phaon's face flamed red, and he ran to scan the road leading to the estate. "Horsemen! At least a dozen." He whirled on the emperor. "You are undone, your majesty!"

Nero reached a blind hand outward, as though he would grasp at his so-called wife. "Poppea, you must stand beside me!"

But the young person he'd called Poppaea retreated deeper into shadows.

History would record the story of Nero's second wife, Poppaea. But she was not here today.

No, Nero had purportedly kicked his pregnant wife to death more than three years ago.

The figure in the shadows was not Poppaea, but a young man by the name of Sporus. A slave Nero spotted in the year after Poppaea's death. After noting Sporus's resemblance to his dead wife, and in an ongoing delusion, Nero castrated the boy, then forced him into a sham marriage, complete with bridal veil and dowry. He was said to have paraded Sporus through the streets of Rome, showering his "Empress" with public affection.

History said little of the feelings of Sporus, other than he would be dead by his own hand in another year. But the young man's face told me all I needed to know.

I recoiled from the abusive emperor. Despite the clean *palla* I'd donned, my skin crawled. Was there a way to distract Nero, and let the boy escape?

Epaphroditus reached out to clasp Nero's searching, outstretched hand.

The emperor drew him close, dagger still clenched in whitened fingers.

"Help me, Epaphroditus. Have mercy on me."

Epaphroditus wrapped a hand around Nero's hand, steadying the shaking arm.

This was truly happening. I was about to witness the suicide of one of Rome's most notorious emperors. And a second gory death in as many hours.

Jack pulled me across the stones. Away from the two men.

The pounding of hooves increased.

I stumbled backward, unable to take my eyes from Nero and that glinting dagger.

With a sharp cry, Nero thrust the dagger upward.

Jack stepped between me and the sight, pulled my head to his shoulder. "Don't look."

Shouts at the doors, and a glut of soldiers poured into the courtyard.

One of them bolted to where Epaphroditus was even now lowering the bloody emperor to the stones.

The soldier, a centurion by the look of the crest and plume on his helmet, shouted a curse and unwound a white cloak from his shoulders. He knelt in the widening circle of blood and shoved the cloak against Nero's neck.

"Too late," Nero cried, sagging in Epaphroditus's arms. He scrabbled at the cloak at his throat, the red stain widening, and his eyes fixed on the centurion's hand. "Oh, this is faithfulness!"

And then his eyes stilled, his hand dropped.

Dead.

"God's blood!" The centurion wadded the cloak and threw it to the ground. "He was to be executed. Instead—a coward's way out."

Phaon stepped forward. "It is a brave man who sees his end and controls his own fate—"

"Enough." The soldier waved Phaon's words away and turned to his fellow soldiers, wiping his bloody hands against his red tunic.

I tore away from Jack's hold on me. "Listen, we are not part of this—not loyal to Nero. We aren't even Roman—simply a mistake that we were brought here—"

Jack grabbed my arm again and spoke in my ear. "Tell them nothing, Sahara."

"No! I am sick of this!" I squared off against the centurion. "We are meeting my family at Nero's statue at sunset, then leaving Rome. We have nothing to do with any of this!"

The centurion eyed me from sandals to hair. "Ah, then you are Decima's captive?" He sized up Jack as well.

What? Had that woman somehow tracked me here? Did her influence stretch into every villa in the empire?

Jack stepped between us, glaring at me. "Curse it all, Sahara! I just wanted a simple holiday in Egypt! Can you never stay out of trouble?"

The words cut, but I set them aside for the moment and spoke to the soldier. "If you're asking if that woman abducted me against my will—"

"Take her." The centurion flicked a hand at his retinue of soldiers. "Bind her well."

"What—" But I had little time to react.

Two soldiers grabbed my upper arms, pulled them backward and began lashing a rope around my wrists.

Jack lunged for me, but another two men restrained him, and a third drove a fist into his abdomen. He doubled over, his eyes still on me, nothing but anger in his expression.

"Should we bring this one, *Primus*?"

"Leave him. But this one—" he jutted a chin toward Epaphroditus—"with blood all over his hands. Bring him as well."

Outside, in the soft breeze and warm glow of an Italian sunset, the soldiers thrust me to the ground. My knees scraped into the pea-sized gravel.

The sound of Jack yelling from the atrium, and no doubt throwing punches, did little to soften the last words he'd spoken to me.

Rough hands pinned my shoulders, and the smell of leather and sweat floated above the warm scents of summer. More soldiers loitered, among a dozen snorting horses.

"This is madness! I haven't done anything wrong!"

The centurion's voice rumbled behind me. "You've crossed a powerful woman, and that's enough."

I twisted my head to better see him. "How have I—"

"You murdered her husband."

My pulse raced. Already? They knew already?

"And I don't know what you are doing here, but she will not be happy to hear the emperor is dead by his own hand, rather than the public execution planned."

I dropped my head to my chest, gulped a breath to still my shaking limbs. I still had the coin, pressed in the pouch against my skin. But what good would it do me now?

Time travel still seemed so impossible, like play-acting on a stage, with astonishing props.

But the gush and gurgle of blood in the villa courtyard

behind me, and in the back alley where Florin attacked me, were all too real.

Someone yanked my arms behind my back. A coarse rope knifed the skin of my forearms, pulled them tight until my shoulders ached.

The soldier circled me, wordless, and cinched another rope around my waist, playing out the length of it in his hand.

"Haul them both to the Forum."

Epaphroditus appeared beside me, similarly bound.

"*Primus*, what is to be done with the emperor's body?"

The centurion glanced backward to the villa's open doors. "Let his people have him for now. Galba will decide."

A soldier grabbed at the lead ropes attached to Epaphroditus and me, then mounted and turned his horse toward the city.

The horse jerked me forward, nearly off my feet. I trotted forward to regain my footing and keep up with the animal.

Around us, the remainder of the contingent mounted. The sun cast long shadows ahead of us all, distorted and grotesque.

We half-walked, half-ran to keep pace, but our soldier soon fell behind, the rest of the men disappearing into the twilight, behind puffs of dust kicked up by their horses.

The sun was nearly gone now.

I fixed my eyes on the distant statue of Nero across the Tiber River, lit aflame by the setting sun, and more alive than the broken man behind us.

Did my family wait in its shadow? Wait for a daughter who would never come?

CHAPTER TWENTY-SIX

"*K*eep your head down and don't argue with him."
Epaphroditus trotted beside me, eyes fixed on the dust. His words were a mere breath.

"Trust me, I know how he thinks. He's looking for a reason to say we were killed trying to escape. Easier than bringing us in."

"You were a soldier." Something in his voice, and the way he carried himself. I should have noticed it before—the clipped sentences and erect carriage reminded me of Colonel Niger, a friend of my father's, whom I'd seen once or twice since the Great War, or even Ned Lawrence, one of his favorite students at Oxford, who made a name for himself in Arabia.

"Praetorian Guard, twenty-six years. That's all behind me now. My loyalty lies elsewhere."

"I'm sorry about his death."

Epaphroditus lifted his head and smiled sadly. "I wasn't referring to the Emperor. I serve a different lord."

"Enough talking, prisoners."

My guide rope jerked in the hands of the soldier. I stumbled and fell silent as I picked my way across the landscape. We passed from the estate of Phaon and into stony fields.

What now? With Jack in unknown condition behind me, and

nothing certain ahead besides the unlikely chance of meeting my family in time, I was out of options. If I managed to escape whatever fate the soldier dragged us toward, would my parents wait long enough by the statue for me to find them in the dark? Would Jack somehow get free and meet me at the Senate House as we arranged?

All of this trouble, the potential failure to find my family, all of it was due to one woman. Decima's cruel, twisted smile loomed in my thoughts. My chest burned and I tried to fight the dark longing to wipe that smile from her face. Was I, in one day, becoming as bloodthirsty as this society?

The river loomed ahead, with its three-arched stone bridge spanning the water. At the head of the bridge, a small group loitered, an extended family perhaps, out for a sunset picnic beside the Tiber. Several horses nibbled at grasses and two young children gathered flowers into the twilight near the water's edge.

The soldier leading us by ropes nudged his horse toward the bridge with a nod of acknowledgment to one of the men who eyed our approach.

The man's gaze flicked toward me, then Epaphroditus.

Was that recognition in his eyes? A message, even?

Before I had time to process the implication, the peaceful family picnic erupted in chaos.

One man hurled himself toward us. Two short daggers appeared from inside his tunic.

He used one to slash the rope tied to Epaphroditus's wrists. He thrust the other into my fellow prisoner's hand.

Another man charged our captor from his left.

The soldier's sword glinted in sunlight and sliced air.

From the other side of his horse, a third man barreled across the dirt path. With a yell and a shove, he knocked the soldier from his mount.

A moment later, one assailant's sandaled foot pinned the soldier's wrist, his sword useless.

The other two drew daggers on the grounded man.

Epaphroditus kicked the sword far from the soldier's reach and tossed his bindings into the dirt.

"The girl, too." He nodded in my direction.

"Are you certain?" A young man, barely old enough to shave, squinted at me. "She looks like—"

"Cut her loose."

The young man shrugged, then cut my lead rope.

A woman ran from the little group by the river, grabbed the soldier's horse by the reins and pulled it to the other horses that now pawed the ground, alert and snorting.

The soldier squirmed and kicked. "You'll burn for this—every last one of you!"

The man pinning the soldier laughed. "We wouldn't be the first."

The young man who freed me drew his shoulders back. "So, what now, Epaphroditus?"

As much as Epaphroditus had seemed to command both Decima and Florin, the deference paid him by this little group was no slighter.

"We ride out."

What had seemed an extended family now sprang into action like a military contingent.

Children ran to the women, who thrust them onto horseback and mounted behind.

Each man mounted as well, save Epaphroditus and one other who still held the soldier at sword-point in the dirt.

"Sahara, onto the soldier's horse."

Not so fast. I shook my head. "What is happening? Who are these—"

Epaphroditus glared. "Do you want to argue or do you want to escape?"

Good point.

I struggled to mount the soldier's horse, to the amused snickers of the woman closest to me, a rail-thin woman of middle-age, with striking green eyes. The four horns of the saddle were just out of my reach, and the thing had no stirrups, nothing like the rigging on the horses of my equestrian lessons at Highclere.

Could I direct this horse where he needed to go?

But a moment later, Epaphroditus was pushing me backward and mounting to sit in front of me.

We left the soldier, disarmed and screaming curses with an upraised fist, and rode out to cross the bridge.

The horses assumed a fast trot, staying together as we flew across the bridge, the *Ponte Emilio*, I remembered from my studies. The oldest stone bridge in Rome. A visit in 1922 would find only a single massive arch of the three remaining, jutting from the middle of the river, an echo of a millennia long past.

I leaned into Epaphroditus's shoulder and called into the wind. "Where are you taking me? Who are these people?"

He turned his head slightly, his voice nearly lost. "These are friends. Who serve that same lord I spoke of."

"What lord? Were you loyal to Nero, or not?" His association with Decima and Florin, followed by his connection to Nero, and now all of this—my head spun with the alliances and betrayals commonplace to ancient politics.

The younger of the two women, riding beside us, laughed. "You have not told her what pagans and outlaws she has taken up with, Epaphroditus?"

"We are followers of The Way, Sahara."

"What way? I don't under—"

"The way of Jesus the Christ."

Oh, good golly. As if falling into political upheaval on the day of Nero's suicide weren't enough, now my fate rested in the hands of what was still a fringe religion, at the start of a vicious persecution to come.

I scanned my memory banks. It was 68 AD now, four years after the fire that burned seventy percent of Rome, conveniently wiping out tenement housing to make way for Nero's sprawling pleasure palace, the Domus Aurea. The sect of Christians was making themselves enough of a nuisance to have Nero choose them as scapegoats, blaming the fire on them and executing thousands in all sorts of torturous ways, including strapping them onto burning pyres to light his evening garden parties. By now, Saints Peter and Paul had likely been dead four years as well.

But it was not only the new Jewish sect of Christians here in Rome who were endangered. In two years' time, Titus, son of the new emperor Vespasian, would raze Jerusalem, destroy its temple, kill perhaps a million Jews, and enslave those that remained.

"Why would you support an emperor who kills your people?"

He was silent a moment, the only sound the hoofbeats of our party, and I wondered if he would answer.

"I believe we have a duty to do what we can, to influence rulers for good, to use the position we are given, in whatever way we are able."

"Did Nero know—"

"No. I would have been executed."

"The fire, though? It wasn't started by... Christians?" Was that what they were calling themselves yet? My history was a bit rusty there.

"A convenience, nothing more. A place to lay blame on people already hated."

"Hated for what?" My memories of the church we'd attended on Sundays were filled with admonishments to do good, take care of the poor, love your enemies. How had Christianity started out being hated by a people who were so bloodthirsty themselves?

"Rome believes the life and health of the empire rest in the hands of the gods, and by extension, the fervency of the people's worship and placation of those gods. Since we refuse to sacrifice or bend the knee to both their gods and their so-called divine emperors, we are considered pagans. And so we are dangerous. You understand?"

Yes, I understood. What Americans felt for the Stars and Stripes, what British felt for King and Country, this passion burned in the chest of every Roman citizen, and anything less than full compliance to their system of worship would be seen as traitorous.

I nodded. "They hate anyone who would live within Rome's borders, enjoy Rome's bounty and protection, and yet scorn Rome's gods and risk the gods' wrath falling on the Empire itself."

"Exactly."

"And now that he is dead? What is next for you?"

Again, a few moments of silence, then a quick shake of his head. "That is for God to tell me. I only know he has made me for his purposes, and has a future for me."

I sighed into the twilight. "I wish I could be as certain. I seem unable to press into the future, until I fix the past."

"Then you fight a losing battle, I fear. The past cannot be repaired. Only redeemed."

I let the statement float in the dusk for some minutes. Was it true?

Epaphroditus broke the silence, his head turned toward me. "You and your friend. I assumed, from the coin you carried, you were loyal to Nero. But now, I am unsure. What is your purpose here?"

He spoke of current events, but the question seemed to probe deeper. "To fulfill my destiny," I answered, smiling to soften the grandness of the statement.

"Ah." He returned the smile. "And this destiny? It will make you happy?"

"It will make me... valuable."

"Hmm."

"You don't agree?"

He shrugged, facing forward once more. "You speak like Nero. Like Decima, even. As though your worth comes from the things you build, the history you make."

Like Nero? Like Decima?

But it was true, in some sense, was it not? Everything Nero had worked for—his Golden House, his grand statue—what had it meant to him in the end? The glorious kingdom of ancient

Egypt I'd so recently visited was now under the thumb of this Roman Empire, but even Rome itself would soon be in ruins.

So what was man, or any of his accomplishments? A breath. Nothing.

And even the accomplishments that would be remembered— these could be lost to future generations, or mis-remembered, misinterpreted, as I well knew.

Futility, all of it.

I shook off the dark thoughts.

"So, where are you taking me? I need to reach the Domus Aurea." The coin seemed to burn under my clothing, urging me toward the Senate House in the Forum, back to 1922 and away from Roman madness, but I would not leave until I found my family.

"You will be hunted. Decima will not give up so easily."

The woman riding beside us gave a low whistle. "Decima? The girl is more of an outlaw than we are!"

"Give me one of those daggers, and I'll be ready for her next time."

Epaphroditus half-turned his head, his frown visible in the twilight. "I will take you to the Domus Aurea, if that is what you wish."

I lapsed into self-recrimination as we rode.

I truly did feel as though I could drive a dagger into Decima, as I had her husband. What was this place doing to me? Or was it only revealing what was already hidden—years of bitterness, erupting into violence?

But nothing I might do here in Rome would *happen*, as long as I was careful to return to the moment before I'd vanished in 1922, and undo my actions here.

Florin's red-cheeked leering grin floated before me. I had been unwilling to be his victim, despite my ability to erase his actions, because I knew the memory of being victimized would remain, even if my time here were undone. But what would the memory of violence I inflicted on others do to *me*?

Memory flared, of reading Oscar Wilde's scandalous novel,

The Picture of Dorian Gray, years ago. Dorian Gray saw his secret wish fulfilled—that his portrait would bear the marks of all his guilt rather than his own self. After decades of debauchery, the man in the portrait was grotesque and withered, while Gray remained youthful and handsome. But the guilt of his corruption and selfishness twisted his soul, turned him into a beautiful monster.

Once again, a chasm opened between the true past and the fragments *believed* to be true. Would I return to my own time, erasing the history of my actions here, yet somehow retain the violence upon my own soul? Do memory and perception outweigh the reality of what has truly taken place in our past? And if I made some sort of Faustian deal with the devil, to commit violence with impunity here, what would I be giving up in return?

The many-fingered branching of streets drew us in, past the lofty palace of Caesar Augustus on the Palatine Hill, toward Nero's statue.

Despite the growing darkness, the city teemed with people, clotted at street corners, pouring through alleys.

News of the emperor's death had clearly preceded us.

Rome was a city in turmoil.

CHAPTER TWENTY-SEVEN

1155 BC
Theban Necropolis, Egypt

"Slow down, you blasted infidels!"

Giada's chest heaved in the dry Egyptian air. She stumbled and hit the sand with one knee. Scrambled to her feet and resumed her frantic retreat behind Alexander and Renae, who had managed to outpace her after they all fled the Theban palace.

On the sand dune above, Alexander pulled to a stop and shaded his hand to peer down on her. "What did you do? Hurry!"

She huffed up the mound and reached to grab Alexander's outstretched hand. "I—I went back for this." She held up a broad ornamental collar, its rows of stone beads, turquoise, and lapis glinting in the sun.

Renae laughed. "Why?" She glanced over Giada's head to the dark spots moving like scorpions across the desert. "They are right on our tail."

Why had she done it? Why did she go back and grab the piece Alexander had admired, when it was wrapped around the neck of Pharaoh's wife? True, the woman had been rude to her, but was it Alexander's comment about how the necklace would look so lovely with Renae's eyes that drove her to grab it?

She couldn't take it home with her, of course. Nothing done here in the past remained behind, and nothing could go forward with them. Snatching the necklace from Tiye was a non-sensical impulse, and now she'd slowed their escape, and maybe gotten them killed.

"I thought it would look great with that sapphire silk gown I have back home."

Alexander watched the oncoming pursuers. "They're on horseback. They won't be long." He took the luxurious collar from Giada's hand and waggled it in front of her. "And you've only given them more reason to believe us looters!" His grin softened the accusation.

In the three adventures they'd shared, first in Rome on the day of Julius Caesar's assassination, and now this, their second jump back to ancient Egypt, Alexander's opinion of what he called her "recklessness" always had the tinge of admiration about it. Her recklessness was what he liked best about her.

She winked and shrugged. "Then we'd better get out of here."

The three crested the dune and fled down the other side, sandals sinking deep into hot sand.

Alexander still held the necklace in one hand. Perhaps he wished it didn't need to be left behind as well.

"I don't see the entrance! Do you see it?" Renae slowed her descent and scanned the desolate miles ahead. "I think we ran the wrong way!"

Alexander and Giada shared a bemused look. Renae's sense of direction was legendary by now.

"If you think we went the wrong way, we must be right on track," Giada said.

Renae squinted and stuck her tongue out at Giada. "Very funny."

"It's there." Alexander pointed to the narrow slot where they entered 1155 BC last night from the university's digsite.

When Giada had said goodbye to Alexander and Renae

outside the Roman Forum last year, with the blood of Julius Caesar still spattered across her *palla*, she had felt part of something so much larger than herself. Her acceptance into Tempus Vigilia was swift, but through the rest of the semester in Italy she never found the connection with anyone, even in their secret society, that she experienced during that day spent with Alexander and Renae.

When she returned to Philadelphia, the temptation to break their pact and search through history for them pressed on her through every lecture she attended, every late night spent poring over her books and her newfound love for history.

And then, one day, there he was.

Alexander. Standing on the grassy square outside College Hall. Staring across the open space at her, jaw dropped. Wearing striped trousers and a brown jacket that matched his bowler hat. A single hand, lifted in silent, stunned greeting.

They walked toward each other, slowly, without breaking eye contact. As if each pinned the other in place, in time, with only the strength of a shared look.

When only an arm's length of space separated them, they each stopped, suddenly awkward and hesitant.

"You—are you—" Alexander rubbed a hand over his face, his eyes. "Are you here from—" he glanced sideways and leaned forward, his voice low, "—the *future?*"

"Yes," she whispered back. "In my time we have machine parts for arms and legs, but I have assumed human form to find you."

His eyebrows lifted. But only briefly. Then, there was the smile she well-remembered.

"You are joking. You are a student here. Now."

She grinned and hugged her books to her chest, feeling a warmth spread through her. She had missed him, so much more than she even realized.

"I can't believe it." He stepped closer, took one of her hands in his.

She squeezed his fingers, and could only smile.

"Renae will never believe it, either."

Her smile slipped. She pulled her hand from his grasp. "Renae? She's here, too? Now?"

His head bobbed. "We ran into each other the week after I returned from Italy. She had already been back for a semester. You?"

"December."

"Unbelievable."

But it was true, they had found each other again, and the agreement to repeat their Rome adventure was not far behind. It took Alexander and Renae a bit of cajoling to get Giada accepted as part of their dig team this semester in Egypt. She was no historian, and still felt like a fraud. But they'd gotten here together. Once here, their next plan quickly coalesced.

And now they were on the dunes, chased by Medjay, sprinting headlong toward the tomb of Seti I, in hopes they could return to their own time before the military guardians of the palace of Ramesses III hunted them down as looters and left them dead in the desert.

"Faster!" Alexander prodded Giada's lower back, forcing her down the sandbank in more of a freefall than a run. "If we can get into the tomb before they come over the dune, they may not see where we're hiding!"

Moments later they were sliding down sand-swamped steps, nearly obscured if one didn't know where to look, then crawling into darkness through a narrow slot.

Alexander brought up the rear, pushing the two girls deeper into the antechamber of the tomb of Seti I. Here, in this time, it was only a small opening, frequented by tomb-robbers. Alexander's large frame blocked most of the square opening they'd entered, and left him outlined by a narrow band of sunlight, like the bright line of a dark cloud. He puffed with exertion and flopped against the wall.

"Do you think they saw us?" Renae's voice was thin and high, a reedy echo in the vault.

"Can't be certain." He held the gold-clasped collar against the light and rattled its half-circle of polished stones gently. "They'll be looking for this, though."

Giada grabbed the piece from his upraised hand and laid the central section across her palm.

"Giada, why take such a risk?"

She shrugged. "Wishful thinking, I guess. One of these days maybe we'll figure out how to bring souvenirs back with us."

Alexander leaned toward the opening, positioning his left eye so he could see the steps.

"I've heard some people can." Renae's voice held a reverence unlike her usual playfulness.

Giada would give about anything to bring artifacts back, just souvenirs she would keep hidden, of course, to remember their adventures. "Who can? How?"

"I don't know. But I've heard some people are able to… make changes."

Alexander's head swiveled back toward them.

Giada squinted at Renae "Changes—to the past?"

Renae's nod in the darkness was nearly imperceptible. "And they can also bring things back home with them when they return."

"Ha!" Giada waved a hand. "Sounds like bedtime stories Tempus Vigilia parents tell their children."

"Maybe. Maybe not."

"I don't think—" Alexander hesitated "—I don't think we're supposed to speak about it."

Giada crossed her arms. "Who says we can't?"

"I don't know." He went back to peering up the stairway, as though the subject were closed.

Giada squinted past him. "How much longer, do you think? I don't want to stay here all night."

"At some point they'll give up. Then we can go back to the surface and get out of here."

They waited perhaps another half hour, using the time to argue about their next destination. They had only four more weeks of the semester in Egypt, and while Giada and Alexander wanted to visit Tutankhamun, Renae had her heart set on meeting Hatshepsut.

Finally, Alexander slipped back through their notched opening and crawled, quiet and slow, up the steps.

Giada's heart bounced against her ribcage, waiting to see if Alexander would be spotted by their pursuers on the surface.

Seeing the history was magnificent—wandering the tombs in their original splendor—but for her it was the chase, and only the chase, that made traveling through time worthwhile.

CHAPTER TWENTY-EIGHT

June 9, 68 AD
Rome, Italy

From my precarious position behind Epaphroditus on the conscripted horse, I watched the members of our rebel band peel away into the city one by one. Unspoken nods and glances between them conveyed more than I understood.

I grasped Epaphroditus's sleeve and pulled back on the arm that held the reins.

"Thank you for getting me this far." I pointed to the statue, still in the distance. "I can make my way from here."

He flicked the reins to speed the horse through the mobbed street. "You'll never make it inside the palace grounds alone. I have many friends there."

"I don't understand—why are you helping me?"

He guided the horse around a three-man brawl in the street, then turned a sharp right into a darkened alley.

He shook his head, barely distinguishable in the dying light. "You are about the same age as my daughter." His voice thickened. "What she did to you—Decima—in her *triclinium*—it was not right."

We rode with silence through the cacophony of the city.

I kept my eyes trained on every passerby, willing each of them to be Jack.

Where was he? And was he still as angry as I'd left him, at the way I'd pulled him into trouble yet again?

With Nero's death, the infamous "Year of the Four Emperors" was about to ensue. The general Galba was on his way to Rome to be declared emperor, but he'd be dead by January, replaced by Otho, who in turn would sacrifice himself to suicide within three months to save the empire from civil war. Vitellius would replace Otho, and then himself be executed eight months later. Only Vespasian, declared emperor eighteen months from now, would be able to hang onto power for good, founding the new Flavian dynasty which would rule the Roman Empire for nearly thirty years.

But tonight, people either rejoiced that the madman Nero was dead or rioted over the indignity of an emperor chosen by the gods being rousted from power.

We approached the Domus Aurea from the west, crossing a vast courtyard of lush gardens flanked by fields and vineyards, pastures and manufactured forests. Ahead, torches flickered to life in the arches of a three-sided stone colonnade that enclosed a man-made lake fronting the main section of the palace. Only the top half of Nero's statue was visible from here, reaching for the heavens beyond the palace itself.

What would Epaphroditus say if I whispered that in less than fifteen years this lake would be filled in with dirt and replaced with the Flavian Amphitheater, better known as the Colosseum?

What would any of us say if we could look into our own futures? Hard enough to look into our past.

We dismounted at the edge of the colonnade, and Epaphroditus handed the reins to a servant who materialized from the darkness.

"Come," he said, and hurried down the edge of the portico, along the length of the lake.

This close to the statue, my head began to pound. I leaned

forward, as though falling toward the end of the long corridor rather than walking.

I was so close. So close to seeing my parents again, to meeting my sister.

My companion laid a hand on my arm, slowing my race toward the statue.

I jerked my arm from his grasp.

But he pulled me into a darkened doorway with a finger to his lips.

We waited a moment, then two.

Three soldiers ran past, hands on their sheathed daggers.

Epaphroditus pulled me from the doorway and we continued.

"I'm sorry." I kept my voice at a whisper. "I—I am very eager to see my family. And afraid I may be too late. I may have already missed them."

"You won't see them at all if you draw too much attention."

I nodded, tight and tense in the shoulders.

We reached the main palace building, crossed into a torchlit chamber, and kept moving.

My gaze jumped from paint-splashed fresco to marble statue, from tinkling fountains to ceilings fretted with ivory and inset with gems.

Howard Carter would kill to see this.

Out the other side, then, into the open courtyard that enclosed the statue. The grass tickled my ankles.

We ran past a fountain, and I paused to scoop water with my fingers, then splashed the grime and sweat from my face. Fish with gold and silver scales reflecting in torchlight skidded away from my fingertips.

Epaphroditus slowed and turned, his expression incredulous. "What are you—"

"I haven't seen them in years. I don't want to look like —like—"

He grabbed my dripping hand and pulled me forward. "You look fine. Come!"

We reached the base of the statue in moments. The silhouette of Nero's head carved a dark line against the night sky, but the lower half of his naked, bronzed body glowed in the light of a dozen torches.

I drew up short at the base, a powerful wave of nostalgia sweeping me. Of memory...

The Statue of Liberty. On Ellis Island. Standing at its base.

When had I been there? With my parents? Perhaps we had family members come through. Part of the swell of ten million immigrants that inundated New York City in the past few decades, chasing a better life. A deep ache accompanied the memory, an ache for something that seemed to belong to another life, another me.

I scanned the enclosed base of the statue. Would they look the same? Would seventeen years seem like nothing, once I spotted them?

Or had they given up when the sun disappeared beneath the horizon, and I was not here?

"Mama?" I ran left, toward the corner of the rectangular enclosure. "Papa?"

Around the left side, then the back. A tray of artichokes and clay jug lay oddly abandoned in the grass, but no family waited.

I turned and headed toward the front of the statue. The base of my neck buzzed with anxiety and my mouth felt like dust.

At the front again. Still nothing.

Epaphroditus spotted me and waved me over. He was in a low conversation with a slightly-built, young soldier.

"They're not here!" My voice sounded thick and half-strangled.

"This is Sergius. He's one of ours, loyal to the dynasty but also working inside the cohort of dissenters. Tell her what you told me, Sergius."

The soldier shrugged shoulders too bony to be strong. "She sent word to have me wait here, in case they put up a fight."

I shook my head, squinted at Epaphroditus. "Who? I don't—"

"Decima." Epaphroditus's lips tightened and he nodded to Sergius to continue.

"She had me positioned here, and Pius inside. She wanted to get them in there," he nodded toward the palace, "rather than do it here."

"Do—it?"

"Kill them, I think. She said they were traitors to Nero."

"She is the one—"

Epaphroditus held up his hand to stop my frantic but useless protest.

"I don't understand." I searched the soldier's eyes for answers, then turned a pleading look on Epaphroditus. "How did she even know they would be here?"

But it was Sergius who answered. "The centurion Pius gave her news. He said the woman who killed her husband, who helped Nero evade arrest, was to meet her family here."

Epaphroditus scanned the courtyard, alert for enemies. "She sees you as a threat, still. As somehow involved with helping Nero, but also knowledgeable about her own betrayals. And then of course there is Florin. She can't leave you alive." He glanced toward the statue and grimaced. "Or your family, apparently."

"What about Jack?"

"What is Jack?"

I closed my eyes and leaned my head back to take a breath. "My—companion. The man with me, left behind at Phaon's estate."

Epaphroditus looked to Sergius.

The soldier shrugged and shook his head. "She told them to follow her, that she would take them to their daughter's body."

I clutched my stomach. "Something happened to my sister?"

Sergius frowned. "No, I think she meant you. She said you'd been arrested and executed in the Forum for helping the emperor escape justice, and that your body was brought here. She offered to take the three of them to you."

This woman.

"But she is planning to kill them?"

He shrugged apologetically in the direction of Epaphroditus. "I didn't know they were friends of yours."

"Where? Where did she take them?"

"The *Sala Ocula*. That's where she told Pius to wait for her."

The Eye Room? I studied the grass at my feet and flew through remembered facts in the catalog of my mind.

"It's a dining hall," Epaphroditus said. "An amazing feat, truly. Rotates all day, with an—"

"—opening to the sky in the center, an *ocula*." I finished his sentence in triumph. Of course! Suetonius had spoken of it in his biographical work, *De Vita Caesarum*. The Life of the Caesars. Historians had debated for years whether it was real.

I turned on the soldier. "Take me there."

"He cannot, Sahara. He's on duty here. But I will take you."

A muffled shout at the edge of the palace drew our attention. The chaos of the city seemed to be intruding into Nero's secure palace complex.

Sergius grabbed Epaphroditus's shoulder. "You should return home, my friend. Your wife, your daughter—Decima knows where you live."

Concern, uncertainty, and then fear flickered in my new friend's eyes.

He'd done so much for me. I couldn't hold him longer.

"Go." I nodded. "Just tell me where to find the hall, and then go. With my thanks."

They turned me toward the east, to a large dome that blistered above the palace roofline, and then I was running. Running across the courtyard to find the fabled spinning dining chamber, before Decima took her revenge.

CHAPTER TWENTY-NINE

*W*ould they believe Decima? Believe I was dead, after all this time spent trying to reconnect? Would they give up on me?

I raced along the dark corridor. Was I on course toward the dome I could no longer see? My headlong rush took me past servants, soldiers, and bewildered nobility, all wandering in confusion or clustering in tight, suspicious-eyed groups beside pillars or fountains.

Through dimly lit palace halls, fingers trailing the walls. Everything seemed coated in gold, encrusted with gems, slathered with mother-of-pearl, or painted with fanciful murals.

A low thrumming beneath my feet pulled me into a long chamber. A wide doorway at its apex opened to another, inter-connected chamber.

Torchlight blazed to my right, through a stone arch opening into a larger hall.

I darted through the opening but stumbled at the threshold.

The floor rotated beneath my feet.

I swayed and gripped the doorframe to regain equilibrium.

Of course. The description in Seutonius's work implied the entire building spun, a feat scholars claimed as a historian's flight of fancy. But it was the *floor* of the octagonal chamber that somehow rotated slowly, no doubt by generated power that caused the underground rumbling now reverberating through my feet.

Above me, through the open dome of the *ocula*, the stars pricked the night sky, grounding me. Marble panels rested on sliding tracks, perhaps to change the view as the evening progressed.

It was like stepping into Tut-ankh-amun's tomb with all its wonders.

Would I ever get back to my life's work?

Purportedly, Nero had showered perfumed mists and rose petals onto his guests from this dome. Was there no end to the man's excessive indulgence? No wonder he was hated by so many.

I scanned the room in an instant.

The remains of a feast, still spread on low tables.

Servants clearing the mess.

A soldier, scowling at me from across the room.

No parents. No sister.

No Decima.

The rumbling under my feet worked its way up into my chest like an expanding premonition of disaster.

The soldier guarding the opposite side of the chamber stalked across the center, avoiding tipped cups of spilled wine and the detritus of the vacated partygoers. A puckered scar ran the length of his left cheek, from eye to mouth.

"Are you Pius?"

He touched a hand to his dagger, perhaps in reaction to my aggressive tone.

"Are you Pius? Sergius sent me. Said you were waiting here for Decima."

"Who are you?"

"Where are they? Decima? The other three?"

I couldn't bring myself to ask if he had done her bidding. Killed my family.

"There was nothing I could've done! They were aided by the gods, or perhaps they are demons!"

"What happened? Where have they gone?"

"She followed them. But they slipped through… Somehow… I don't understand."

"Speak clearly, man! Tell me what happened!"

"I had them! Had the man in my grasp, his wife at sword point."

My stomach lurched.

"And then, somehow, somehow, they were fleeing the room—with our spears in *their* hands! I saw only their backs!"

His face was a mask of fear and confusion.

I felt no less confused. If my family traveled to a new time from this place, wouldn't they have simply disappeared? How could they be seen again, running through a doorway?

"Where did they go?"

He shook his head. "I don't chase after gods or demons."

I slammed a fist against the doorframe with a muttered curse.

He lifted his eyebrows. "Are you one of them?" He lifted his sword, no less threatening because the hand shook.

I took advantage of his hesitation and fled the room. Outside the dining hall, I relied on my gut to choose a direction. If I were fleeing this place, which way would I go?

A darkened doorway beckoned. I dashed through it, and stumbled down a flight of stone steps. Catching myself in time to brace my hands against stone walls, I picked my way downward into darkness.

The rumble increased as I descended, and the walls grew slick with humidity.

Somewhere in this palace Nero supposedly installed two magnificent baths, one with sea water and one with sulfurous mineral water.

Was I headed into those baths?

I should've grabbed a torch from a wall socket. I could barely see my own feet. But a dim light far below pulled me forward.

"Mama? Papa?"

I kept my voice to a whisper but it still echoed back at me, too loud.

I reached the bottom, proceeded along a narrow tunnel toward the slight amount of light. The source of the noise was close now.

The tunnel opened at last into a subterranean vault. I paused at the entrance, and lifted my eyes to the mechanism in front of me.

A water wheel, like one to power a riverside grain mill. But instead of turning a stone to grind wheat, the wheel's motion must turn the revolving floor of Nero's dining hall above. Ingenious.

But the vault was empty of people.

I dragged my fingers through my hair and inhaled a deep, salty breath.

Where are you? Where would you run?

To the location where they could escape.

If my family thought me dead, if they gave up hope of intersecting with me here, with Decima chasing them, the only logical place for them to flee would be the place where they could travel forward in time. The place where they had entered ancient Rome.

Think, Sahara.

Living in the early 19th century, where would they have chosen? The Roman Forum had barely been re-discovered, and excavations were still in early stages.

The grotto.

The frescoed hall that sparked the Renaissance. All of those artists and adventurers, many living in, or passing through, Venice. Had my parents ever met any of them? Casanova? The Marquis de Sade? They all lowered themselves by ropes into a hole, to feast their eyes on art lost for a thousand years. If my parents arrived here from the early 1800s, they would have come through to 68 AD in that grotto.

I spun in place. Which way from here? Back up the steps, and risk encountering the soldier I fled?

Or through this chamber, toward an unknown section of the palace?

I opted for the unknown. Sprinted across the chamber, toward the shadowy outline of a staircase on the other side.

And then suddenly I was on the ground. A jolt of hard stone slammed my hip. Ankle and foot twisted under me. Arms splayed across wet stone.

A stupid fall on a slippery floor.

I paused for a moment to suck in a breath of pain, then pushed upward and stumbled forward.

The ankle was bad, and nearly gave out under me.

I staggered across the chamber, throwing weight on my good leg, half-dragging the other. Angry tears stung my eyes, but I didn't bother to swipe them away. Blood pounded in my ears, but I was not going to abandon this chase yet.

Up the steps, into yet another palace hall. I paused and listened.

Despite the term *grotto*, the chamber that so inspired a generation of artists wasn't subterranean in the first century. Right now, in this time, it would likely be one of the main halls of the palace.

I limped along the corridor, one hand braced against the wall.

A woman's voice drifted from a corridor around the corridor.

Decima. From only her voice, I could see the curl of her lip, the snarling hostility in her eyes.

I rushed forward, then slowed at the corner and pressed myself against the edge, trying to remain unseen. Stood on one leg that trembled with exhaustion and fury and desperation.

"I don't know who you are, or what you are, but abominations like you cannot be allowed to pollute the empire."

Decima's strident tone carried a hint of fear.

"It is you who is the abomination! Sending an innocent girl to her death!"

At the voice, I nearly fell to my knees. Even after all these years, a girl knew her mother's voice.

I clutched at the corner of the wall, willing myself to remain unseen. I could take no chances on Decima spotting me, or doing something hasty. But I leaned my forehead a fraction past the corner.

And then, there they were.

All three of them, backs against the wall at the end of the corridor, holding hands, with my sister in the center.

Each of my parents had a free hand braced against the wall.

They glanced at each other. My father nodded.

The signal to my mother. The same way Jack and I would nod to each other, just before we traveled.

Everything seemed to happen at once.

Decima flicked a hand.

A soldier thrust a short dagger toward Persia's chest.

I threw myself into the hall with a throaty scream.

The girl between my parents lifted her head from the knife rushing at her heart.

My parents' attention was on that dagger, but my sister was looking at me.

And then everything stopped.

Just for a moment. For one long, mind-bending moment, everything stopped.

The dagger in mid-thrust.

Decima, frozen in place.

The dancing torches, stilled to carved tongues of flame.

Even the air seemed to thicken and solidify around me.

My family, however, lost its solidity. Caught between here and the future to which they would return, each of them was a gossamer thread, a shadowy white outline.

The only thing moving in the entire corridor was my own run toward my family, and my sister's lifted head.

Her lips parted, eyes widened. She gasped, leaned forward, away from the wall, still clutching my parents' near-translucent hands.

I drew to a stop, eyes locked onto hers.

She whispered one single word.

"Sahara!"

I reached for her like a drowning woman reaching for a rope.

And then they were gone. My lifeline jerked away, leaving me to plunge to the depths once more.

In their absence the hallway flared to life.

But something in me died.

The soldier's knife-thrust rushed forward, but its point rammed empty stone.

Decima whirled. "They've done it again! The demons!"

Her eyes landed on me and she shrieked a curse and lifted a bony finger.

A rush of footsteps sounded behind me.

Two men flew around the corner. One bumped my shoulder and nearly sent me sprawling.

"My lady, citizens loyal to the emperor are storming the palace."

The other extended a hand to Decima. "We must get to the Forum where we can be protected. Galba is sending troops."

Decima threw a frantic glance at me, then back at her guard. "Take the girl. She is as evil as they."

And then she was gone, escorted by the men who came to warn her.

I barely noticed the soldier's grip on my arm.

Once again I was separated from my family by an impossible chasm, with no idea where to search. No idea of Jack's location. An injured ankle. And a crazy woman who wanted me dead.

A bubble of manic laughter rose in my chest.

I breathed it out, then sagged to the floor.

CHAPTER THIRTY

"Get up."

I kept my eyes closed against the sharp prod of the soldier's toe into my side. The cold floor of the corridor caressed my cheek, cooled the hot flush of my skin. How could I be so hot, when I was drowning?

"I said, get up!"

What would he do if I simply continued to lie here? Run me through with a sword?

Perhaps.

The unpleasant thought curled me into a ball. I struggled to pull myself upright, to brace my back against the nearby wall.

"Will you curse me, too, woman?" The soldier's sword was held at arm's length, its point only a breath away from my throat.

"Perhaps."

I could curse everyone and everything today.

How did this nightmare happen again? I tried once more to meet my parents, to learn how to stop them from leaving me as a girl. But it was all a repeat of Egypt. Nothing ever worked.

Was Jack wrong? Was it possible for me to change history? Or was everything destined to happen the way it always happened?

The questions of time travel philosophy mattered little. I had lost my chance.

Or rather, Decima took my chance from me.

"Are you a demon, as she says?"

"She is the demon." The words hissed out between clenched teeth, hot and sizzling.

The soldier took a step back. "You speak lies. Just like the others."

My head sagged against the wall. Above me the frescoes sprawled across the ceiling and upper register of the corridor, reminding me of Raphael's "Transfiguration" in the Vatican Museums.

"This will all be gone one day, you know." I waved a vague hand at the ceiling and walls. "All of it will crumble to dust or be buried by the soil of centuries."

"So now you will curse Nero's Golden House as well?" He advanced on me another step.

I lifted my head to look into his eyes.

"*You* will crumble to dust. I will crumble to dust."

His face drained of color, and the bony protrusion of his throat spasmed.

"You speak more like a priest of Apollo than a demon."

Is there a difference? Gods or demons, was any of it real?

All we truly had were the actions we took, the work we accomplished, with the time we were given. And what had I done? Squandered my time digging in the dirt and uselessly chasing my family through time.

The Forum and the Senate House seemed like the other side of the world. Despite the coin still secreted beneath the folds of my *palla*, I had a little chance to escape, and no chance to accomplish the only important thing.

A low murmur of voices in the corridor drew the attention of my soldier. The point of his sword dipped.

If I had an ounce of strength left, I would use his distraction to at least attempt to get away.

Instead, I leaned my head against the wall and closed my eyes.

The conversation, and the steps accompanying it, stopped outside our chamber.

My soldier peered through the doorway behind me.

"What goes on here?" A smooth voice, feminine yet authoritative, filtered into the chamber.

"A traitor to the emperor, my lady. Caught assisting others who infiltrated the palace."

Traitor to the emperor? The factions of these power plays blurred. Epaphroditus seemed loyal to Decima, but then loyal to Nero. The soldiers helping Decima here at the palace—they were friends of his, so I assumed they were traitorous double agents, like Epaphroditus. But now we were back to another soldier holding me at sword point, following Decima's orders, accusing *me* of being traitorous to the dead emperor. I shrugged against the muddle of my thoughts.

A shuffling of sandals in the hall, a swish of robes. "Let us see what sort of enemy is able to slip past even an emperor's palace guard."

I turned my head, slow and heavy, toward the door. Lifted my chin to meet my newest enemy.

"Only a woman, Empress. I have her well in hand."

The figure of the young man, Sporus, still dressed in all the finery of an emperor's wife, filled the doorway.

He gazed down on me, eyes widening with surprised recognition.

A slow evolution of emotion played across his face. Confusion, then a wary glance at the soldier, as though deliberating the wisest next step.

"This is no traitor. She has been of great help to me, and to the emperor himself."

He slapped the soldier's sword-hand downward. "It is that snake of a woman Decima and her horrible husband, Florin, whom you should be holding at the point of a sword."

Sporus held a hand out, to lift me from my huddled position on the floor.

I stared at the hand, unmoving.

"Come," he bent and gripped my elbow. "Come, my lady, let us get you somewhere safe."

I struggled to my feet, tested my weight on my ankle, and fell.

Sporus snapped his fingers in the direction of the hall.

"She is injured." He turned on the soldier. "What have you done to her, fool?"

The soldier stepped backward. "Nothing, my lady. She was injured before I saw her."

Two others appeared from the hall at Sporus's bidding.

"Carry her to the courtyard."

The cowering "wife" of Nero whom I met at Phaon's villa was gone. Sporus seemed confident in his position and in his demands.

A moment later I was swept into strong arms. I leaned my face against the shoulder, uncaring about my rescuer's identity.

The cool night breeze was soon on my face, the smell of Nero's abundant flower gardens caressing my skin.

Sporus spoke near my ear as we walked.

"It is unsafe for either of us to be about." His voice was gentle. "It is much too soon to know which way the political winds blow. Whether you and I will be enemies of the state, or heralded as the few left who dared to challenge a rebellious faction."

We shifted directions abruptly. Turned out of the courtyard, toward the engineered forest at the edge of the palace complex.

"You said you had family here. Where shall I have my men take you?"

I shook my head, likely unseen against the shoulder of my rescuer. "They are gone. I only want to go home."

"Very well. I will arrange transportation. Where is your home? Pompeii? Stabiae?"

"Far from here." *You've no idea.* "Can you take me to the Senate House? In the Forum?" I lifted my head to look at him.

Sporus's eyes were drawn down in suspicion. "What business do you have with the Senate?"

"None. I assure you. I'm to meet my friend there."

"Your friend, Moretti?"

I laughed—that half-mad laugh which seemed to follow me. "Yes, Moretti. Have you seen him? Where is he?"

But Sporus only nodded. "We will both go to the Forum." He spoke to his second companion. "Fetch a litter. Not my own. Too recognizable."

Self-respect dictated I insist on being set down, to walk myself, but we were moving quickly and my ankle still throbbed. I rotated it slowly against the swelling. Probably not broken, but I wasn't running anywhere. A dull pain was creeping up my leg.

Did I black out? It seemed only moments later I was hoisted into a curtained litter held by two long poles borne on the shoulders of slaves. I tumbled forward into a mass of white cushions, righted myself, and retreated to the back of the litter, where I slumped against the support of a canvas-like fabric stretched taut. Scarlet curtains hung on either side, to keep us secreted from the world.

The other man placed a step for Sporus, who climbed elegantly into the litter beside me, arranged his sumptuous purple robes around his legs, and nodded to the two waiting men.

"The Forum."

And we were off.

The bucking of the litter on the shoulders of slaves eased into a rhythm. Hypnotic and steady.

Could I curl into these cushions and drown the truth in blessed sleep?

This moment of respite was far from guaranteed. The Senate had been calling for Nero's head. Sporus was not a safe escort. And Decima still expected me to be delivered to her feet, no doubt.

I should be running in the opposite direction, not headed for the very place she'd ordered my execution.

What would it be, if she caught me? A stake and a pyre? A quick and merciful beheading? Perhaps dangled before lions in a gladiator's arena? There was always the Roman favorite, crucifixion.

I shuddered and shrank further into the dark recess of the litter.

Not only had I accomplished nothing of value with my life, but I was now likely to die an ignominious death, far from anyone who knew or cared about me.

Sporus fingered the edge of the curtain, opened it to only a slit, to watch the city tumble past.

"The mob grows larger. And angry."

"Angry that he is dead? Or that they didn't have the chance to see him suffer?"

"Yes." Sporus sniffed and shook his head. "All of it. Any of it. They rarely know what they want. We keep them busy and spoiled and entertained so they won't ask questions."

He turned to me and pulled a jeweled headpiece into his lap. "Or at least, that's what we did. That is all over now."

Did he mourn Nero or rejoice? Perhaps he didn't know what he wanted, either.

The buzz of voices outside the litter heightened. I could almost feel the press of the people outside the curtains. Would they investigate its inhabitants? Would curiosity about what nobleman or his wife traveled through the Forum in style bring our transport to a halt, see us yanked into the street?

But we continued on, jolting and bumping through the Forum's crowds. The occasional flare of a torch lit Sporus's face, outlined our shadows against the fabrics.

I chanced a glimpse through the curtains myself as we passed the Temple of Vesta. A set of wide braziers blazed on its white marble portico, its steps scattered with people celebrating. Or protesting. Impossible to say.

Perhaps I would make it to the Senate House.

How long would I wait for Jack, before using the coin to travel home? The question was unanswerable. If I left him here, without the coin he'd used to get here, the only way he could ever return to 1922 would be for me to send another time traveler to find him in ancient Rome with the same coin. The chance of accomplishing such a thing was infinitesimal. I could not leave unless I knew he was... dead.

No. Stop, Sahara.

"Please, Sporus, tell me what you know of my friend."

His eyes narrowed. "How do you know my true name?"

I bit my lip, searched for any reply that would make sense to the young man.

The litter stopped abruptly.

I turned to Sporus. "Is this it? Have we reached the Senate House?"

"I do not—"

A rough jolt to front of the litter cut his answer short.

Then a frenzied shout, like a hundred upraised voices.

The litter slammed to the ground.

My teeth caught my lip. I tasted blood.

The mob was upon us.

CHAPTER THIRTY-ONE

*T*he air outside our abandoned litter pulsed with the chants of a hundred, perhaps a thousand.

I floundered among the white cushions, scrabbling for a solid thing to grab. I searched Sporus's eyes for reassurance. Would they tear us to pieces, or have mercy on the boy whose life had already been so difficult?

In the darkness, the whites of his eyes glowed like bright orbs, his lips a matching O of horror.

The litter tipped.

I stumbled through the blood-red curtains, already shredded by a dozen ripping hands.

A fragment of fabric twisted between my fingers. Would it hold? Would it keep me anchored to the iron frame of our transport?

Already our cushions were trampled into dust, and pebbly stones ground into the bare skin of my thighs where my *palla* bunched at my waist.

Someone dragged me to my feet, and I leaned, too heavy, on my twisted ankle.

A shot of agony crippled me, bent me forward.

Rough hands grabbed my hair and yanked me upright.

A fist to the ribs.

I tasted bile, and an assault of odor—the smell of ancient stones and mob sweat.

Ahead, the small, inset windows of the Senate House glowed with torches inside. The huddled silhouettes of conspirators passed before the flames.

How would we get past all these people, to find the place we could travel home?

But why should I even think that far? Where was Jack?

How close, how close I had come to going home to 1922. And yet how far I still was, and how likely I would never make it.

The despair of never being able to find my family, the hopelessness I felt since that fleeting, frozen moment when Persia and I met for the first time, all blended with the certainty I would die here in ancient Rome.

A sharp cry behind me turned me to Sporus. I clutched at my midsection, bracing tight fingers against my bruised ribs.

"Let him go! Leave him alone!"

The mob tossed the boy between them like a plaything. Like the plaything he had always been to powerful people.

"Oh, is this your mother, Empress?" Rude laughter, kicks and jabs.

Sporus flung an arm over his face.

"See how he guards his eyes, men?" This from a man in a tunic stained like a butcher's apron. "That's because there's nothing left to guard down below, eh?"

The men in his company roared with laughter at the joke.

I reached for Sporus, wrapped fingers into his robes, and pulled him toward me. My muscles rebelled and my head spun.

A woman's voice, pealing and high, coming from behind and above, turned the men. Their chins lifted, a rapt audience.

"Countrymen, this is the day of your liberation! The madman is no longer with us. We are free! Free to be ruled by one far more respected by his soldiers!"

Decima. The woman was everywhere. Everywhere I needed to be, blocking my every move.

As if she sensed my thoughts, her eyes skimmed the heads in front of her, slowed, and stopped to lock onto me.

A shove from behind knocked me forward. I fell under the heels of a dozen stomping Roman citizens.

Flat on my belly, I propped elbows in the gravel, and lifted my head.

Decima stared down at me with a hostility that could have ignited the air between us.

The crowd must have sensed her rage, for it parted like a churning, heavy curtain to allow a channel of heat to flow from where she stood, down to where I lay on the ground.

The stone rostrum, the platform at the end of the Forum where luminaries such as Cicero had delivered oratories to inspire an empire, now held one spiteful woman, out for blood.

Through my haze of pain and terror, one of my persistent and ridiculous questions arose. Did archaeologists know the original stone rostrum held a wooden platform, extended beyond its lip?

I pulled my gaze from the splintered wooden slats under her feet, up the outrageous gold and purple threaded robes she wore, past the heavy jewels at her throat, to her red-painted lips and then her fiery eyes. My breath came in short gasps, chest expanding against the stone beneath me.

"Here!" Her arm raised and finger pointed. "Here is one who has betrayed us all! We should have seen the madman brought to us, executed before our eyes, where we could know the gods had meted out justice. But the traitors among us spirited him away, allowed him a coward's escape. And here is one of them, in our midst!"

I dragged myself to standing.

Oddly, those around me backed away, as if the taint of my betrayal would spread to them. A vacant circle widened, until I stood in the bullseye of Decima's wrath.

"Perhaps we do not have the madman, but at least we have his friends. Bring her!"

At this directive, the crowd rippled, and rough hands seized me from behind.

I tried to pull away, a useless effort.

They dragged me, limping, to the side of the rostrum, up a half dozen marble steps, and onto the raised dais to stand beside Decima.

The orator Cicero came to mind again. His head and hand nailed to this very rostrum for speaking against Marc Antony, in the chaotic aftermath of Julius Caesar's assassination.

I searched the crowd for a friendly face. Even a *familiar* face would be welcome. Sporus was gone, hopefully safe. Epaphroditus and the others—Phaon and Neophytus—most certainly huddled in their homes, keeping their families safe. I was alone. Once again.

"Sahara!"

My name—bellowed across the top of the mob—from my left.

There, on the steps of the Senate House.

Jack.

Decima's accusations had backfired, drawing attention to me and bringing Jack to my rescue.

He disappeared down the steps and into the crowd.

The crowd puckered and creased as he shoved his shoulders into one rioter after another, driving toward the rostrum like a scythe through a field of wheat.

My relief was physical, as though the waves that pinned me underwater for so long could finally recede.

But the relief was short-lived. Only meters from the platform, the crowd jumped him.

Nearly close enough to touch. Close enough to see the purpling bruise around his eye, the torn and bloody fabric at his shoulder.

He strained forward against the grip of his captors. His eyes never left my face.

Beside me, Decima screamed in my ear.

"Traitor!"

Could I throw myself from the rostrum? Would the crowd catch me, drag me away? Somehow, even an angry mob seemed preferable to Decima's flaming hatred.

I focused on Jack's face. It took three men to hold him back, and still he struggled and fought to reach me.

Why had he come here? My own spark of anger surged in my chest. Unreasonable, perhaps. But he knew what it meant to me to find my parents.

Why did he not go to the statue, and warn them away before Decima found them?

His angry words at Phaon's villa echoed. He didn't ask for any of this. I would never forgive myself if he were hurt because of me.

Decima clutched at my arm and yanked me toward herself. "What should be done with Nero's friends, citizens?"

I locked my eyes onto Jack once more, drew strength, then lifted my chin to yell above the crowd.

"Ask yourselves!"

Those closest to the rostrum quieted, as though shocked I could speak.

"Ask yourselves, if you are certain who the traitors are among you. She tells you the emperor is dead. But what proof do you have?"

A murmur of confusion spread through the crowd.

I knew my history. In the twenty years to come, no fewer than three men would come forward, claiming to be Nero. Without a public execution, and denied burial in the family's Julio-Claudian mausoleum, rumors persisted for years that Nero was in hiding, and not dead at all.

"Perhaps it is Decima who is the traitor! She has secreted him away, to bring him back when you least expect! You know the emperor escaped with his secretary, Epaphroditus. And who among you does not know that Decima and Florin have been that man's close allies for many years?"

Perhaps I would never figure out the machinations of Roman politics, but I could use the mess to my benefit.

Decima howled. "Foolishness! It is Epaphroditus who betrayed us! And this woman, who murdered my husband!"

The crowd seemed unable to follow the exchange.

From the center of the mob a familiar voice called. "Where is his body, then? Show us the emperor's body!"

Jack. Giving credence to the tale I was spinning.

A lightheaded feeling of déjà vu swept me. Did the rumors begin here? The years of suspicion that Nero was hiding, the "false Neros" coming forward—did all of it begin with one foreign woman screaming impossible scenarios into the night air?

No. No, I would not make any of this reality when I left this place. I would leave ancient Rome untouched by my footprints.

Unless I never left.

Unless I died here tonight.

CHAPTER THIRTY-TWO

"She speaks the truth!"

Another voice, coming out of the darkness.

From my position on the rostrum beside Decima, I tried to follow the voice, to see where it came from, but the flickering torches were spots of heat in my vision, and everything blurred.

"This woman had nothing to do with the death of the emperor!"

From out of the crowd, Epaphroditus emerged. But did he speak of Decima, or of me?

The crowd was as confused as I.

It was true I had nothing to do with Nero's death. The crowd believed Decima and Florin came against the emperor, to free them from his insane, tyrannical rule. I was trying to convince them she secretly supported him and even now had him in hiding.

If Epaphroditus spoke in my defense, and it was well known he was both an ally of Decima, and loyal to Nero, then what would his defense of me prove to anyone?

My head spun.

"It is Decima, and her husband Florin, who have whispered treasonous secrets into the ears of the Senate."

Still so vague.

Epaphroditus shouldered through the crowd, toward the platform.

Decima took a step back.

I felt the energy shift, anger and resentment flowing away from me, toward her. I stepped to the side of the platform.

Around us the crowd seemed to multiply in number and volume.

Jack still struggled against his captors.

But attention centered on Epaphroditus, reasoning with the crowd.

Decima turned on me, hands curled into claws.

"Where do you think you are going?" She lunged for me, grabbed at my robes.

I tried to twist away.

She hissed into my ear. "I don't care what lies you tell, I know you murdered my husband!"

I pulled from her grip, stumbled backwards over the splintered boards of the platform.

A great cracking sound shot through the air, followed by the roar of flames at our back.

We both turned to see fire lick the platform, even as the support fell away under the hacking of a dozen improvised hatchets.

The citizens of Rome were done listening to two women above their heads.

The floor beneath us canted.

I try to hold my balance on the shifting boards.

Decima rammed me and knocked me forward.

The supports on the other side of the platform gave way. The entire wooden structure pitched forward.

The faces of the crowd and the stone pavers rushed to meet me, but my grip held between two slats of wood, feet flailing.

The chants of the mob and the crack of the flames fused with Decima's screams as her voluminous robes billowed into the fire and caught.

She slid from the platform to the ground, then rolled and slapped at her flaming clothes.

Around her, men bent to grab her arms, her shoulders, and drag her into the mob.

I turned away. Refused to feel responsible.

I adjusted my finger-grip into the slats, but it was useless. I was going down.

And then there was Jack. Arms under me, bearing me up, carrying me away, as though I were some Victorian maiden, fainting in the arms of her lover.

We pushed through the crowd, Jack using my crossed ankles as a battering ram.

I pulled my injured foot under me and winced at each jolting step.

We were on the steps of the Senate House a moment later.

Jack set me down, then cupped my face in his hands. "Are you hurt?"

"I saw them, Jack. I saw my family."

His eyes widened. "They are here?" He turned his head to scan the Forum below us. "Where are they?"

"They're gone." I choked back a sob. "I missed them." I burrowed a fist into his shoulder. "Why didn't you go to the statue? Meet them and tell them I was coming?"

Jack's lips parted. "Are you serious? Phaon told me they dragged you away bound with ropes, to hand you over to Decima for execution. Did you actually think I would do anything but search for you?"

"None of that matters! The only thing that matters is completing what I came here to do. Saving my parents, my sister."

But even as I said the words, I knew them to be untrue.

There must be more to me than my ability to undo my past mistakes. More, even, than the work I found so important. Epaphroditus was right. Trying to fix the past was a losing battle.

Jack still held my face in his hands, but he released one to wrap an arm around my waist and pull me toward him.

"I will always choose you first, Sahara. Even without them, you will never be alone."

The ocean drowning me for hours—the one I finally dragged myself from in my defense to the crowd—now it seemed there was a warm fire blazing on the beach. A fire lighting something deep within, a feeling burning hotter than any emotion I'd ever known.

But with the heat came fear, the old fear that Jack was not to be trusted. That he had family connections dangerous to me. That it was unsafe to trust anyone, with my life, with my future, with my heart.

"But you said you only wanted a holiday in Egypt—"

"Yes." He gripped me tighter, as if to cut off my repetition of his hurtful words in Phaon's villa. "Yes, I wanted to roam the world, roam through time to whatever destination lured me. But that was before I met you. Now all I want is *you*, Sahara. And it terrifies me."

I blinked a smile through a wave of warmth.

"Sahara, I am so sorry you weren't able to find out how to warn your parents in Venice about whatever took them from you. We will find another way. But now, it's time to leave."

He swept the hair from my eyes and tipped my chin back. "You have the coin?"

"The one thing I didn't lose."

We pushed through the doorway of the Senate House.

Inside, we found ourselves in the midst of a shouting match. On either side of the wide chamber, men sat and stood on the tiered marble seats, shouting, gesturing, fists raised. An odd replica of stories I'd heard of Parliamentary debates.

Some things never change.

And yet... some things did change. I had changed. I'd begun to lean toward letting go of the past, rather than insisting on fixing it.

Jack held my elbow and steered me from behind, as we wound our way through senators and their adversaries.

Would we remain anonymous until we reached the back of

the Senate House? What would happen if we simply disappeared from their midst?

But no, the rules of time travel asserted themselves from the jumble of things Jack taught me. We would not retain our time here, so the moment we left, our presence was erased. There would be no disappearing couple, leaving people scratching their heads... suspecting we were demons.

Wait...

What did it mean? My parents, my sister, they disappeared, and yet they were remembered.

Did they leave here revising history again, as they had in Egypt when they left me a clue in the tomb of Tut-ankh-amun?

The larger question was one I had not given myself time to ponder. The bizarre, frozen moment when my sister and I recognized each other. The moment when time stopped. For everyone but the two of us.

We reached the column where it all started, at last.

Jack turned my body to his, blocked my view of the churning crowd of senators, and nodded.

I pulled away the folds of my robes until I reached the tiny purse hanging from a rope tied at my waist, and fumbled at the knotted string with shaking fingers.

All the trauma, all the emotion of the past twelve hours seemed pent-up in my useless fingers.

"Let me." Jack loosened my hands from the string and reached for the pouch that lay against my thigh. The touch of his fingers was cool on my fevered skin as he worked at the knot, sending a shiver through me.

"Who is this? Is this one of them?"

A shout behind Jack.

The coin, free in his hand.

We turned to face yet another angry enemy.

"Isn't that Decima's traitor?"

Jack held the coin with his fingertips and nodded to me, grabbed my hand and brought it to the coin.

I pinched the other side of it.

We bent our heads.

I fixed my mind on the return. Careful to think only of the moment I left 1922, the chilly December morning in a Forum gray with drizzle.

Nothing.

No vertigo, no nausea, no headache.

I lifted my head with a stab of fear that Jack would be gone.

But he faced me still, a question in his eyes.

"It's not working." The words rushed out in a frantic whisper. "What are we doing wrong?"

Two senators squared off in front of us, though neither seemed willing to accost us.

One of them called over his shoulder. "Quintus, bring guards from outside to take these two."

Jack pulled the coin from my fingertips, turned my hand, palm facing up. Placed the coin in my palm, then laid his own hand over mine, and tangled our fingers together to warm the coin between us.

He looked into my eyes, wrapped his other hand around the back of my head, and pulled my mouth to his.

This kiss was different than the one we shared under the coverlet in Phaon's villa. Our first had been slow, tentative. Secretive, even.

This kiss was desperate. The frantic connection of two people who feared being ripped apart.

He released me, smiled, and bent his head.

Lips still stinging with the passion of his kiss, I joined him in the forward bend, our hands still clasped together with the coin between.

Apparently there was another rule of time travel, one even Jack had not known.

The handclasp we'd used to travel here worked.

The spinning began. The darkness fled.

CHAPTER THIRTY-THREE

1155 BC
Theban Necropolis, Egypt

From her position on the steps of Seti's tomb, Giada watched Alexander climb to the top, to check if their pursuers had given up.

"Pssst." Alexander's obvious signal brought Giada and Renae to their hands and knees, to crawl through the opening and join him on the steps. His head was still a few inches below the surface level.

"I don't see anyone," he whispered down over his shoulder. "We should have enough time." He squeezed to his left, making a sliver of room beside him.

Renae clamored up to join him, and Giada pushed between Renae and the hard-packed wall.

They could barely reach the top step, each with a hand splayed across it. The step they'd used to travel here.

Giada laid the necklace on the second step, feeling a reluctance to leave. "Guess I'll leave this here as a peace offering."

If she were honest with herself, she loved the danger of it all, and it was the danger which prompted her to grab the necklace in the first place. She could not be content to be a mere tourist, stopping by to gawk at freshly-painted frescoes and newly-carved columns and then returning back to her own time with nothing more than the knowledge of a few more facts than her non-time-traveling fellow students would ever have. What was the point in that? No, it was the danger, the adventure, that drew her. The possibility of being caught, of being stranded, of living one's entire life out-of-time.

And this latest lark in 1155 BC had been no different. They had taken on militant priests and Medjay police, escaped certain death, even made some fascinating friends in the ancient past.

Alexander lifted the jeweled collar up to the light, where the turquoise caught the sun and cast a thousand green-tinged shards of color against their bare arms. "Those idiots don't deserve it." He pushed upward until his head was above the surface and used his free hand to start digging a trench in the sand.

Renae pulled on his tunic. "What are you doing?" Her voice was a hiss. "Get back down here!"

"One more minute." He finished his trench, laid the gemstoned collar in it, then scooped sand back over the piece. "There, Giada." He smiled down at her. "I'll leave it right here, for you to find it when you need it."

She grinned at the gesture—useless, since it would revert to its place in Tiye's bedchamber once they left—but nice, all the same.

"Ready?" Alexander's warm eyes were on both of them, a smile that encompassed them both in equal measure.

They each placed a hand on the step once more, took a collective deep breath, and bent their heads as if in prayer.

But if Giada were one to pray, the only words on her lips as they spun through time would have been a request, to whatever gods might answer, to have Alexander's smile take in her alone.

The return to their university digsite from the top step of Seti's desert tomb knocked the wind from Giada's lungs. She lost the strength of her arms and hit the steps with her chest.

Beside her, Renae was laughing, shaking sand from her hair, pushing herself upward. "That never gets old, does it?"

Giada rubbed her bruised sternum. "Right." A surge of panic pulsed there. "Where's Alexander?"

Renae swiveled left, but there was nowhere to hide on the narrow steps. Above them, the night air had sharpened into cold pinpricks, in stark contrast to the heat-stifled afternoon they left behind. Their fellow interns would be asleep in their dig tents, just as she, Alexander, and Renae left them.

Renae was already scrambling from the stairwell. "Alex?" Her harsh whisper carried across the open air.

Giada didn't try to silence her. The rising dread coursing through her veins made her want to scream his name into the dark.

The lantern they brought still sat at the lip of the stairs. Renae snatched it up, extended it to the length of her arm, turned a tight circle in the sand.

"Where is he?" Her voice trembled. "Where did he go?"

Giada voiced what they both knew to be true. "He couldn't have gone anywhere, Renae. There wasn't time."

"But why would he stay there? Without us?"

In the wavering lantern light, Renae's ghostly face seemed to hover in the darkness.

"But even if he stayed weeks, years—"

"—he would have returned to the same moment we did."

They both exhaled as one, still turning circles.

Renae lifted the lantern to Giada's face. "Have you ever heard of someone being—lost?"

"During a return?" Giada was still combing the desert, willing Alexander's silhouette to appear against the violet sky. "No. But then, you know I haven't had the typical traveler experience."

No, not typical at all. Her mother and sister barely spoke of their travels, refused to train her, and wanted to hear nothing of her experiences. What knowledge she'd cobbled together came primarily from Tempus Vigilia, or from Alexander's and Renae's collected training.

"What about you?" She stepped close enough to Renae to study her eyes. "You're the one who knew about travelers who could make changes. Is that—could that be what's happened to him?"

Renae's arm lowered, as though the lantern grew too heavy. "I don't know. I've only heard fragments. Nothing that explains... this." Tears glimmered on her lashes.

Giada's didn't want to cry. She wanted to hit something. Hard.

A discreet throat-clearing near one of the dig tents turned both girls toward the sound.

"A bit late, isn't it, ladies?"

Donald Dorman, the site director. Built slight, with a wispy cloud of white hair and mustache to match, he looked more Einstein than archaeologist.

Giada lifted a hand. "Just couldn't sleep, Professor Dorman."

"Yes, well. Perhaps if you were lying on your cots, you'd have more success."

Renae exhaled, a sound that mirrored Giada's rough landing moments ago.

Giada felt the girl's hand find hers and squeeze.

Renae's eyes were large and intense. "If you see him before morning, come and get me."

Giada returned the grip. "You, too."

Renae nodded.

They parted, each to their own tents.

Giada flopped to her cot, with its paper-thin sheets and meager blanket, without bothering to remove her boots or jacket. She didn't want to risk waking her tent-mates and enduring their questions about where she'd been.

Despite Professor Dorman's suggestion, lying prone on her cot did nothing to bring on sleep. Instead, Giada lay studying the dim outline of the stretched canvas above her, listening to the quiet snores of the two girls who shared her tent. She reviewed every moment of their time in 1155 BC, searching for a reason, an answer, even a tiny clue, as to how Alexander might have vanished.

Inexorably, her thoughts circled to Renae's whisper of time travelers who could change the past, even bring items back with them. How did that fit with his disappearance?

If Alexander *had* somehow changed the past, where would he be now?

The whole system for those gifted with the time traveling gene depended on a single fact from its immutable Codex: travelers always returned to a fraction of time before they left, then passed through the moment of their original travel, thereby erasing the time they spent in the past.

Could Alexander have circumvented that principle somehow?

Giada jolted upright in the dark, braced on her elbows.

The only way he could change the past would be to *not* erase his time there. And the only way to leave his actions intact would be to return here *after he left.*

What did it mean? She struggled to fit the mental pieces together.

If her hypothesis was true, only two possibilities made sense. He would return to a moment *after* their original jump backward, or he would return to some amount of time passed, perhaps the same amount of time as they had been gone. And if the latter, then he wouldn't be returning for a while.

She slumped backward onto the sheets, drew the blanket around her shoulders, and curled in on herself.

Renae would be half-crazed, waiting to see if Giada was right. And how would they explain Alexander's disappearance and sudden reappearance?

Sleep came, finally, stealing over her like a pale moon rising over the desert. Her last thoughts were of Alexander, burying a jeweled collar, just for her.

But when her eyes flicked open a few hours later in the pre-dawn, a single idea lodged in her mind, like a shining gem.

If Alexander was able to change the past, that jewelry piece might still be hidden under the top step of Seti's tomb entrance.

After a silent glare at her two tent-mates to ensure they still slept, she peeled the bedding away and slipped from the tent. She grabbed a pick and hoe from the equipment lean-to and crept toward the tomb, glancing over her shoulder to ensure she was alone.

Alexander dug the trench at the top step with his fingers, in the space of only a minute or two. If the necklace was still there, it could not be too far down, even after being buried by a ton of sand for a few thousand years. Belzoni had done most of her work for her. When he hit that first step, he went downward toward the tomb, leaving the area behind the steps untouched. Archaeology was often more opportunistic than thorough. Relative to the step, the jewelry piece should be no more than a foot below the surface.

Giada used the pick with gentle precision to loosen a few inches of dirt and sand, then switched to the hoe to gently scrape it away. She repeated the process twice more.

Already, she was composing a story in her mind. What explanation would she have, for rising early and choosing to dig here, in the very location of an important find? A hunch? Looking for something else?

But then, did the believability of her story make a difference? Even if some suspected it were false, no one would ever guess the truth.

Some part of her remained detached from the digging, noticing her intention to claim the find publicly, rather than keep the trinket for herself as a memento of their time in the past, as she'd declared to Alexander and Renae.

The hoe clinked against something solid.

Giada exhaled, fell to her knees, lifted her eyes to the rising sun. It might be a stone. A pebble, even. But if it was not... If it was not, then her life could hinge on this moment. She breathed in the dusty air, said a vague prayer toward the pinking horizon, then dragged her fingers through the sand.

And there it was.

A single turquoise poking through. A dull, sand-crusted glow in the watery morning light, but she'd seen how it looked in its original glory.

She scanned the digsite's tents for movement. Still no one.

Now she needed a plan.

Hours later, the team still hunched around the worktable where small finds were placed, under a dirty canopy. Her well-timed "discovery" after a few team members emerged from tents in search of coffee had made her the center of attention ever since. She'd enjoyed backslaps, handshakes, and was even awkwardly embraced by Professor Dorman, who declared the necklace Nineteenth Dynasty and the greatest find of the University's tenure in Egypt thus far.

"You'll be in the history books, my girl." He beamed on her like a proud father.

Only one team member remained less than congratulatory.

Renae stood apart from the excitement, her face pale and tired.

Giada felt Renae's confusion and sadness falling on her like a damp burial shroud all morning. She retreated from the attention when no one was watching and found her friend hunched on her cot, crying softly.

Renae lifted her eyes at Giada's entrance, and they flashed from grief to anger in a heartbeat. She jumped to her feet.

"How can you stand out there—listening to them congratulate you—when you know—"

Giada crossed the tent and gripped Renae's arms, silencing her. "He'll be back soon. Renae, it's going to be fine. He'll come back."

Renae's eyes searched Giada's face, questioning, inviting reassurance.

"I think he's one of them." Giada lowered her voice to a whisper, to contain it within the thin walls of the tent. "One of the people you were talking about, who can bring things back and change the past."

Renae's lips opened, then closed again, and she shook her head.

"No, listen. That's why I was digging there, to see if the necklace might still be buried where he left it. For me." She couldn't resist that last addition.

"But he didn't bring it back. He didn't come back at all!"

"No, but he changed its location. He changed the past."

Renae pulled from Giada's grip and sank to her cot. "But then, where is he?" She lifted tear-stained eyes to Giada.

"I'm not sure. But I think, maybe, he didn't come back to the moment before he left, like we did. Instead, he'll come back to the time that passed while we were gone."

Renae inhaled, a tiny gasp. Her brow furrowed, searching her memory. "But that will be... perhaps soon!"

"Right. I'm telling you, he'll be fine. Although there is one issue I can see."

Renae watched her, wordless.

"If my guess is correct, then instead of coming back late at night when we left here, he'll return to the steps in the middle of this afternoon. In front of anyone working there."

Renae rubbed at her forehead, eyes closed. "I don't care if he reappears on a Broadway stage. I just want him back."

"I know." Giada patted Renae's hand, but the girl yanked it away.

She felt the coldness emanating from her friend.

Despite Giada's reassurances of Alexander's safety, a rift seemed to have opened between them.

Or perhaps it had always been there.

Perhaps it was only Alexander who had ever held them together.

CHAPTER THIRTY-FOUR

December 11, 1922
Rome, Italy

*J*ack gripped my hand with a solid and steady pressure. An anchor, until I found my feet under me in the back of the Curia Julia.

The customary spin through time did not nauseate as much as previous trips. Perhaps I was getting better at all of this craziness.

My first look at 1922 included Jack's face close to mine, his eyes smiling.

"You okay?"

I took a deep breath. "Relieved."

Behind Jack, a young woman in peachy frills and lace called to her traveling companion.

"Watch this, Tony!" She climbed to the first tier of the Senate seating, arm raised in a royal-princess wave to the empty room. "I *say*," she called out in a distinctly fake British accent, "Let them eat cake!"

Jack and I glanced at each other.

"Wow," Jack cocked an eyebrow. "Wrong on so many levels."

A laugh grew in my chest and burst out, a bit of hysteria I couldn't quite control.

Jack hugged me to himself, smiling over my laughter, but perhaps concerned I was losing my mind.

"I'm fine." I breathed out the last of the hilarity, turned my face into his chest, away from the couple who eyed us suspiciously. "I'm fine."

"Let's get out of here." He snatched up the umbrella, right where he'd left it at the base of the column, tugged me toward the double doors of the Senate House, then out into the cloud-laden Forum with its drizzly December rain.

We had missed nothing of 1922, and only been in the Senate House for less than five minutes in this time, but I still felt the effects of twelve hours in ancient Rome. Had it truly only been so little time?

Jack opened the umbrella over our heads, circled my waist with his arm, and we stepped down toward the grassy stones of the Forum.

Directly ahead of us lay the two-thousand-year-old remains of the rostrum, where minutes ago Decima slid into the mob. We slowed, and I shuddered and trained my eyes away.

Jack's hesitation wasn't the distraction of the rostrum. Instead, he scowled across the ruins, toward a thin man in a peaked cap, leaning against a broken stub of a column, watching the Senate House steps.

The man straightened a moment later, as though surprised to see us.

Had he been following us? Perhaps expected us to stay inside long enough to tour the building?

I squinted through the rain. "Jack?"

He growled something I didn't understand. Something like, "enough of this," then started across the Forum toward the stranger, still keeping me close under the umbrella.

It wasn't until we were nearly upon him that I recognized the red-haired man. I stopped short.

Jack kept moving, then reached back to catch my arm.

"Jack—this man—he was in Egypt—"

"Come, Sahara."

We faced the man together.

Jack was still frowning. "What are you doing here, Reuben? I told you, I'm not going back yet."

The man, Reuben apparently, folded his arms across his chest. "You know she won't let me get away with coming back without answers."

"I'm sick of this, Reuben." Jack poked a finger into Reuben's chest. "Tell me what you know."

Reuben grabbed his wrist. "You forget I've been working for your aunt for three years. There's nothing you can do to me that she hasn't already."

"The truth, Reuben. What's her interest in Sahara? In the Aldridges?"

Reuben's eyes flicked to me. He shrugged. "Don't ask me. More of the same, I guess. What she's always done. Don't pretend you don't know how she's made all that money."

"What are you talking about? Her company has contracts for salvage—"

"Ha! Are you really so naive? You believe the cover story she's been telling for decades?"

"Say it straight, Reuben."

Reuben stood taller and pursed his lips, as though deciding if Jack were worthy of the truth. Then a glance at me.

"Say whatever you have to say. I'm sick of secrets."

Reuben shrugged. "Your funeral." He pulled a cigarette from his pocket, then a tiny matchbook. The match flared in the late-morning gloom. "She's not a salvager, Jack. She's a looter. She's had a Revisionist on the payroll for years. At least until recently. Sends him back through history to plant artifacts for her, change locations of items, create passageways for her to tunnel through."

Jack's face drained of color. "She couldn't possibly get away with that. Not with the Society watchdogs—"

"She's got a few of *them* on the payroll, too. You underestimate her." He took a long drag of the cigarette. "She's quite a woman."

"For *years*? She's been doing this for years?"

Reuben laughed, a humorless snort through his nose. "Since college, I think. Got a taste for it back then, somehow."

"So if she already has someone doing her dirty work, what does she want with Sahara?"

The muscles between my shoulder blades tensed. I held my breath for the answer I desperately needed to hear. I didn't dare interrupt, for fear of stopping the flow of the man's confession.

Reuben dragged on the cigarette and funneled the smoke out slowly through his nose. He raised his eyebrows and waited, as though Jack should know the answer already.

"Victor."

"Now you're catching on."

"Did she kill him?"

Reuben snorted. "Hardly. He was her ticket. Not to mention her... shall we say... *companion*."

"So now you're supposed to report back to her. About Sahara."

"Among other things."

"Such as?"

"As I told you in Egypt, about what's happened to you."

Jack pulled me closer and steered me toward the other end of the Forum. "Well, we're going back to Egypt. You can tell her whatever you like."

"You know I've got to follow you there. That's the job, old man."

"Then we'll see you in the desert."

We hurried through the Forum, heads down.

Did Reuben follow us even now?

I squashed the million questions burning in my throat. I wouldn't ask them until we were well away from Reuben. And Jack seemed in no mood to hear them.

Besides, my mind was crammed to overflowing with the events of the past few hours.

The coin, the coded papyrus, left by my father on the painted chest in the corner of Tut-ankh-amun's tomb... none of my guesses had been the wild imaginings of a distraught daughter.

My parents, my sister. They were *there*. They had traveled to the Rome of 68 AD to meet me. Had been at the statue of Nero.

Why didn't they wait for me?

But my sister's face in that moment when the world went silent, the utter shock at seeing me... Something, or someone, convinced them I wasn't coming.

She was so pretty. Persia. My sister. I had no reason to believe the suspended moment was her doing, and yet I believed it with all my heart. My sister could stop time.

Why didn't she stay long enough to tell me where to find them next?

Questions without answers. But at least I had a few clues.

My father's blurred warning on the papyrus.

PS Trust no one, especially G...

...etti

Well, I had trusted someone. A Moretti, even. But I was holding onto that "G." And Jack's angry shock at Reuben's revelations. I had to hold onto that.

Thirty minutes later we were seated in the corner of the quiet Caffè dei Sapori. Other than the two of us, the cafe held only an older couple in the corner, sipping from steaming cups beside a crumbly brick wall, smiles trained toward each other amidst the soft violin playing from a phonograph somewhere.

If Reuben had followed, he was waiting in the rain.

Our clasped hands nearly covered the tiny tabletop, circling two steaming cups of espresso. I studied our intertwined fingers, and began my interrogation.

"Jack, I need to know—"

He squeezed my hands, silencing me. "I will tell you everything, Sahara. It's time."

The way he said it made my stomach seize. There was bad news coming. And although it was barely noon here in this cafe,

I had just lived through the longest and most exhausting day of my life. Could I survive whatever came next?

"First, I told you the truth about being fascinated by you, since my aunt first met you when you were fifteen. But I made you believe it was my curiosity that kept me checking on you, asking Giada if she knew your situation."

I breathed in quietly, forcing air into my lungs.

"In reality, it was Giada who was checking on you, and keeping me informed about you. Keeping me... interested in you." His eyes strayed to the window and the street beyond. "Now I wonder if it was more than indulging my interest. If perhaps she was... playing me."

"Playing?"

He returned his attention to the coffee and our hands. "Yes, stringing me along. Making it seem casual, when really she was grooming me for this moment, when I would come to Egypt to meet you."

"Why?"

"To give her information she couldn't get any other way."

My heart stuttered. "To find out if I was a Revisionist?"

He nodded, still not lifting his head, but I could see the closed eyes. "I'm sorry."

"And have you told her that I am?" I pulled my hands from his grasp. "Actually, I don't even care what you've told her. I want to talk to her myself. Tell her what I think about her shadowing me for years."

"It's not that easy."

"Why not? I'll send a telegraph. I don't care what it costs—I'm going to ask every question I can think of!"

"You can't send a telegraph to where Giada is."

"I thought she lived in Philadelphia, with you—"

"She does. In 2002."

"Two-thousand-and-two what? Is that the street number?"

"No, Sahara." He reached for my hands again, finally meeting my eyes. "In the *year* 2002. That's where I came from."

CHAPTER THIRTY-FIVE

$\mathcal{W}$hatever else I felt in that moment—confusion, anger, even fear—one emotion mastered them all.

Betrayal.

How long had it taken me to trust this man? To convince myself his deceptions were minor, and long behind us?

My numb lips formed a question. "I thought you said it's not possible to travel to the future."

"To your own future. Yes. *You* can't go to 2002. But that's where I came from. For me, 1922 is the past."

Eighty years in the past, to be exact.

My present, even my future, was someone else's history.

A coldness shivered through me. As though I'd walked over my own grave.

"She said it was a birthday gift." Jack's words escaped through clenched teeth. "Had everything ready for me here. Money, clothes, even the press credentials."

"You're not a reporter."

It seemed inconsequential at this point, but I was searching for more lies to add to the growing pile.

"She knew I'd love nothing more than to be here for the discovery."

TRACY HIGLEY

"You knew about the tomb. Before we found it."

"When Reuben showed up at the digsite, that first day I met you, I didn't know what to think. But then later, he was asking questions about your parents, your sister even, and I wondered if there was more. But I couldn't believe she would... *use* me."

"Reuben is from 2002 as well." My list was growing.

Jack reached for me across the table.

I scraped my chair backward, the sound discordant against the soothing strings playing from the phonograph.

"Sahara, you must believe me—"

"Must I?"

I was out of his reach, but that didn't stop him.

He stood, circled the table, lifted me from my chair. Gripped my arms and pulled me to him, his face within a breath of mine.

"Sahara, I only want to help you. To find out the truth, about your parents." His eyes roamed my face as though trying to read my soul.

"Even if the truth is that your aunt is to blame for everything that happened to them? To me?"

He released my arms but did not step away. Still close enough to catch me if I bolted. "I couldn't believe your suspicions were true. I thought, at first, if I helped you find them, I could reunite you with them, and vindicate her, all at once."

"And now?"

"And now." He returned to his chair, slumped into it, and banged a fist on the table. "And now, I believe you. All of it. Nothing else makes sense. Sending me back here to befriend you, then sending Reuben after me, to ask questions about your parents. About *your* abilities."

A new thought rocked me.

"When she visited me at Highclere—she had traveled through time!"

"Yes. She wanted to go back and meet your parents. But she missed them."

"Did she miss them, though? Or did she find them in Venice? And what did she want with them?"

He shook his head, then raked a hand through his hair. "I don't know. Maybe it's only as Reuben said—she's looking for Revisionists to help her grow her empire."

"Well," I snatched up the umbrella and turned for the door. "You can go back to Philadelphia, back to 2002, whatever that looks like. And if you care about me at all, you'll tell her I'm only an ordinary Observer, like all the rest of you."

"Sahara, I'm not leaving. Certainly not until you find your parents. And until I know you're safe... from her."

"And how am I going to do that, Jack? Find my parents? She's made it impossible!"

My chest burned with a fury that seemed to have a thousand destinations. Jack, Giada, the crazy Decima, even my parents who had let themselves somehow be tracked or trapped by Jack's aunt.

But running under all of it was an anger reserved only for myself.

Because I had once again fallen for someone who would use me for his own purposes, then disappear when he was done with me. Only this time, he wouldn't disappear into the halls of academia and an engagement to a girl whose father had a peerage. No, this one would disappear into the future, a future inaccessible to me.

And he had always known it.

Another question pinged, like an arriving elevator in my brain. "You've been to this time, 1922, at least three times. When I first met you last month, then after we returned from Tut-ankh-amun's tomb, and now today, arriving back from ancient Rome. I thought it was impossible—"

"Because I haven't yet gone home. Remember the shaft of the well? I've gone deeper than 1922, several times, then returned back up the well shaft to 1922. As long as I don't return to 2002, my original time, I can keep sliding up and down the well."

He didn't need to say more. Once he returned to 2002, he could never come back here.

"Do you remember what you said once, Sahara, about your parents getting stranded in the nineteenth century?"

I shrugged and shook my head. What did it matter?

"Well, I remember. I remember word-for-word. You said it must have been torturous for them. To be forced to stay in a time not their own, separated from everyone they cared about, for the sake of someone else they loved."

"I get it, Jack. Obviously, you don't want to experience that—"

"No! That's what I knew you would say. It's why I didn't tell you—couldn't tell you—about my time."

"Well, I was right about them. And I'm right about you."

I pronounced the words with finality, and Jack seemed to understand I would refuse more discussion about it.

"Then let's go to Venice." His blue eyes sparked fire, the way they did whenever he got excited over a new idea. "You thought about that idea before. Before you found your father's message. It's a quick train ride from here. Maybe we'll find something about them in Venice."

Despite my anger, the gears in my mind clicked and whirred. "But if they went back to the early 1800s, to meet Belzoni for some reason, and they never came back to 1905 to revise history, then anything they did in that time would be gone."

Jack rubbed his hands together as if chilled. "Not necessarily. It's not really the return that causes history to be revised. The changes are truly happening as they happen, as you act in that time. It's only when you *return*, as an Observer—or as a Revisionist who chooses not to revise history—that you *erase* the changes."

"So until your actions are erased upon your return, they exist."

"Right. If your parents have never returned to a date later than their time in nineteenth century Venice, we could find evidence of them there. It's a small city. If they made any kind of splash there in the past seventeen years, it might be recorded somewhere."

"If I go to Venice, Jack, I am going alone."

He blinked and looked away.

But not before I saw genuine pain there.

"I—I don't blame you, Sahara. I only wish there were some way I could convince you."

"Convince me of what? That you were a pawn, albeit a willing one, in some mysterious game of your greedy, shady aunt? Fine. I believe you. It changes nothing."

"She *raised* me, Sahara. After my mother—" He exhaled, shook his head.

I steeled my heart against his grief.

"You can't stop me." His voice had taken on a harder edge.

"Well, whatever you're planning, I don't actually care enough to try to stop you."

"Good. Because I'm going to Venice." He stood, fished a few bills from the pocket of his trousers, and tossed them onto the table. "I'm going to Venice to find your parents."

I wanted to blurt out, "No, *I'm* going to Venice!" like a child competing for a favorite toy. He could not take away the only good idea remaining, since Decima snatched away my chance to reunite with them.

And so, in the end, we both traveled to Venice, aboard the steam locomotive from Rome, which we boarded an hour before dusk. Jack insisted on paying for two sleeper compartments, then followed close on my heels through the narrow passageway to berths 114 and 115.

"Are you hungry?" He unlocked 114 and pushed the door open, then handed me the key. "We could get some food in the dining car."

I took the key and my bag from him and pushed into the room. "Thank you, no. I believe I will get some rest."

I closed the door on his worried expression and sank to the cot built into the wall, able to take my first deep breath since the words "two-thousand-and-two" dropped into my life, like a bomb from a warplane.

The narrow compartment was little more than the cot, a shelf above, and small wooden chair beside the window. And a door, connecting it with compartment 115.

I curled on my side on the bed and closed my eyes.

The future. What was it like?

I could ask questions for weeks and probably not be satisfied. But did I want to know?

Had Jack already researched my entire life, all the way to its conclusion?

Because unless medical science had greatly extended the average lifespan, by the year 2002, I would be 112 years old, and most assuredly dead.

The train chugged out of the station, picking up speed until the *clack-clack* offered the escape of numbed sleep. I tried to sink into the bedding, to bury myself where I didn't have to think.

A furious pounding on my compartment door jolted me upright.

I lurched for the knob, jerked it open, if only to stop that pounding.

"I couldn't tell you."

"Jack, what is wrong?"

His eyes were wild, frantic. He'd loosened his tie until it hung in a noose around his neck, and his hair looked like he'd thrust his head out the window of the moving train.

"I couldn't tell you when we first met in Egypt, because I didn't even know if you could travel in time."

A sharp-chinned woman in a dressing gown approached from the next car, then waited to squeeze past Jack in the hall.

I grabbed his arm and pulled him into my compartment, then turned and braced my back against the closed door.

The berth was only a couple meters wide, but Jack managed to find a path to pace.

"And then, after, when we were with Ankhe-sen-amun, and helping her, you were still so new to all of it, and I—I—didn't expect—"

He rubbed at his jawline, still pacing.

"Didn't expect what?"

A TIME TO WEEP

"To feel this way!"

My hands flattened against the cool of the door, and I could feel the metallic growl of the train through my body.

Jack was facing me now, his eyes intense with confession.

"You have to understand, Sahara. For more than fifteen years you have been this romantic person from the past to me. Like a folk hero, or a character from an adventure novel. I don't know what I expected, when I traveled back to 1922 to meet you. But in all the trips through time I've ever taken, the people I met were little more than legends and stories."

His words were pouring now, as though he couldn't speak them fast enough.

"Do you understand? All the people I've met in the past, they were like walking, talking museum pieces to me. They weren't real."

He closed the distance between us, wrapped his hands around my waist. "They weren't flesh and blood."

He pulled me to him, forehead touching mine.

"They weren't smiling eyes and a laugh that lights up a room."

He pressed his heated cheek against my own, his voice low and quiet in my ear.

"They weren't a million questions. And such surprising courage."

He paused, and his heart beat against mine, in time with the train's rhythm.

"I never expected to feel this way about you, Sahara. And I didn't know what to do."

I closed my eyes and surrendered to the hopelessness of desire. "Because you can't stay here. And I can't go there."

"I can stay."

Three words, whispered against my hair, words that wrapped me in belonging.

But I shook my head, pulled away. "I can't keep you in this time. Won't keep you, separated from your family. From Giada, no matter what she's done—she's still your family. And your father—"

269

He turned from me and crossed to the window. Grabbed the frame above it and leaned his forehead against his hand. "My father abandoned me, and my aunt lied to me. Now she's trying to use me to increase her profits. What is there to go back to?"

But no. I'd lost my family to the past. I was not going to be responsible for stranding Jack in his past.

"You can't stay here..." I wanted to say *for the rest of your life*, but we hadn't even spoken such feelings. How could I presume that was what he wanted, even as I tried to talk him out of it?

I was still pressed against the compartment door.

Jack returned to me, stood close with those blue, blue eyes drinking me in. He cupped my face with his hands.

"I want to be wherever you are, Sahara. I want to be *whenever* you are. Here in 1922, or anywhere in the past."

He followed the declaration with a kiss so light it seemed almost reverent against my lips.

But it roused a longing in me that I was too foolish to resist. I curled my fingers through his hair, and pulled him closer, returning the kiss with an intensity that felt as impetuous as leaping from a cliff, as audacious as leaping through time.

One warm hand still held my cheek, the other slipped around my back and drew me close enough to fit our bodies together, as he'd done under the woven coverlet in an ancient Roman villa.

"Jack." I breathed out his name, my voice husky.

He moved from kissing my lips to kissing my eyes, my cheeks, my forehead.

"Jack." Two hands pressed against his chest. Creating space between us.

He pulled away, searched my eyes, then dropped his own. "I'm sorry. Forgive me."

I brushed the hair from his eye. "There is nothing to forgive. But it's not possible. We don't belong together—"

"How can you say that? We've defied the laws of time to find each other!"

I smiled, despite the tears pooling in the corners of my eyes. " You are such a romantic."

"Because it is romantic! This—you—me—"

I touched his lips with my fingers. "You are still living in one of your folk tales, your adventure stories. We are from two different times. And I cannot be responsible for a choice like this."

He exhaled through tightened lips and looked away.

I knew him too well to believe I'd convinced him. But he was giving up for the moment, at least. Which was a good thing, since I was close to breaking.

Later, when the window was a square of black and the only sound the metal hum of the train's wheels, I lay on my cot, staring at the door connecting my room to Jack's. Willing that knob to turn.

Twice, as the night wore on, I slipped across to the door and touched the handle myself. Ready to throw my resolve under the wheels of the train.

But in the end I was strong. True to what I knew to be the right thing. The only fair thing for the man I was growing to love.

It was possible, I knew now, to open your heart and trust another person, even if you hadn't redeemed all your past mistakes or ensured your future calling.

I *could* give my heart to Jack.

But I wouldn't. For his sake.

The empty night finally gave way to the dawn, and by the time the sun rose warm across the tracks, the train found its way into the Venezia Santa Lucia railway station, on the outskirts of the famed lagoon.

Venice, City of Water.

Perhaps we could take a little time for sightseeing. For *relaxing*, as Jack was so fond of encouraging me. Not everything hinged on fulfilling one's destiny, after all. He was right. Each day could be enjoyed for its own sake.

But somewhere in this city, I would find evidence of my parents and my sister, and the time they spent here. And then I would simply take myself there, and we would be together in the past.

We stepped down the train's steps onto the platform, Jack gripping my hand in his own.

I smiled up at him. "I'm glad you're here."

He answered with a kiss, a quick brush against my lips in the comfortable way of longtime couples.

"Good. Because I'm not going anywhere."

EPILOGUE

July 2021

So another part of my story is now behind us.

Perhaps there were surprises for you. But then, you asked for the story.

I had continued to search, but now I was finding I must also let go. Release the unreliable past, yes, but even release the future which I'd only dared hope for in the quiet places of my heart.

All roads lead to Rome, they used to say. And at least for me, on a dusty one of those roads I heard a truth which was yet to be fully understood: the past cannot be repaired. It can only be redeemed. And it cannot be used to measure our worth.

And the future? It is also a worthless metric by which to measure. For when we equate our purpose and work in the world with our value, we will be crushed by a desperate need to earn it, and the sense we can never do enough.

No, I was beginning to accept that my value must come from outside myself, and even outside the illusory path of Time, which after all is only a Story being told. Accept that only the Story's author gives us meaning.

I could let go of my desperation, let it go to embrace love and even the gift of rest.

But there were still lessons to be learned. In Venice, in the Egypt of past and present, even back at the Highclere Castle of my memory.

For there is a time for everything.

A time to seek, but also a time to give up.

A time to weep, but also a time to dance.

And while there may be a time to fight and tear down, we can only embrace our true nature when we discover a way to forgive and to build.

Because there is also a time to love.

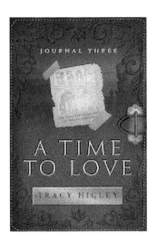

FOR A TIME TRAVELER, THE FUTURE IS NEVER GUARANTEED.

Sahara Aldridge, a young Egyptologist in 1922, is mastering the genetic surprise of time travel.

She's survived a murderous vizier in King Tut's Egypt, and taken on ancient Roman aristocrats bent on deposing Nero.

She's even managed to open her heart to the charming Jack Moretti, despite the shocking secret he's finally divulged.

But when the next clue to finding her parents lands her in an ancient Egyptian assassination attempt, Sahara's tinkering with the past just might erase her future.

Skimming across the lofty pyramids of ancient Egypt to the elegant canals of 18th century Venice, the answers to Sahara's desperate search for belonging seem only a breath away.

But an old score must be settled, and an old feud reconciled, before she can face a truth more than thirty years in the making, and a secret she was never meant to learn.

How can love be enough, when fear and hate are fierce?

Purchase *A Time to Love* at
https://tracyhigley.com/buy-love

FREE SAMPLE

Hello Friend!

I hope you'll enjoy *A Time to Weep*, and when you're done, you'll be eager to continue Sahara's adventure in *A Time to Love*.

I also wanted to give you a big, juicy excerpt of another book I think you might like—*Nightfall in the Garden of Deep Time*.

However…

One thing that always frustrates me when reading books: I'm looking at the pages of the book that are left to read, thinking there are many more chapters to come, and then the book suddenly ends and everything left is actually a big sample of another book.

Do you find that annoying, too?

So to avoid frustrating you, I'm instead giving you a LINK to the first seven chapters of my newest book. I'm hoping it'll be the next book you dive into, after you finish Sahara's adventures!

Grab it here: https://dl.bookfunnel.com/33onz156mq

Dear Reader,

Thank you for taking an adventure to ancient Rome with me! I hope you greatly enjoyed *A Time to Weep*.

You can find lots more about ancient Rome on my website, along with travel journals of my trips there.

And in case you're curious, here's more than you want to know about me…

I've been writing stories since the time I first picked up a pencil. I still have my first "real" novel—the story I began at the age of eight during a family trip to New York City.

Through my childhood I wrote short stories, plays for my friends to perform (sometimes I had to bribe them), and even started a school newspaper (OK, I was the editor, journalist and photographer since no one took that bribe to join me). Then there were the drama years of junior high, when I filled a blank journal with pages of poetry. {{*sigh.*}}

In my adult years I finally got serious about publishing fiction, and have since authored nearly twenty novels.

When I'm not writing, life is full of other adventures— running a business, spending time with my kids, and my favorite pastime: traveling the world.

I started traveling to research my novels and fell in love with experiencing other cultures. It's my greatest hope that you'll feel like you've gotten to travel to the settings of my books, through the sights, sounds, smells, colors, and textures I try to bring back from my travels and weave into my stories.

I'd love to hear your thoughts about *A Time to Weep*, or ideas you have for future books I might write. Get in touch with me at tracy@tracyhigley.com.

Now, onward to another adventure!

HOW TO HELP THE AUTHOR

I hope you enjoyed *A Time to Weep!*

If you're willing to help, I would really appreciate a review on Barnes & Noble or Amazon.

More than anything else, reviews help authors spread the word about their books.

It doesn't have to be long or eloquent – just a few lines letting people know how the book made you feel.

Thank so much!

BOOKS BY TRACY HIGLEY

The Seven Wonders Novels:
Isle of Shadows
Pyramid of Secrets
Guardian of the Flame
Garden of Madness
So Shines the Night

The Time Travel Journals of Sahara Aldridge:
A Time to Seek
A Time to Weep
A Time to Love

The Books of Babylon:
Chasing Babylon
Fallen from Babel

The Lost Cities Novels:
Petra: City in Stone
Pompeii: City on Fire

The Coming of the King Saga:
The Queen's Handmaid
The Incense Road

Standalone Books and Short Stories:
Awakening
The Ark Builder's Wife
Dressed to the Nines

Broken Pieces
Rescued: An Allegory